Ambrosia

HAMELIN BIRD

PIPER HOUSE

This book is a work of fiction. Names, characters, places and incidents are products of the author's imagination or are used fictitiously. Any resemblance to actual events or locales or persons, living or dead, is entirely coincidental.

Cover Art by Dan Liles | Dan Liles Design

Cover Design by A.A. Medina | Fabled Beast Design

Interior Formatting & Design by Fabled Beast Design | A. A Medina

© 2024 by Hamelin Bird

All rights reserved. This book or any portion thereof may not be reproduced or used in any manner whatsoever without the express written permission of the publisher except for the use of brief quotations in a book review.

ISBN: 979-8-9891980-0-9

OTHER BOOKS BY HAMELIN BIRD

DOUBLE VISION
WAYWARD SUNS
DRENCROM

PRAISE FOR HAMELIN BIRD

"Bird's creepy, nightmarish debut...keeps readers off-balance as he builds toward a satisfying conclusion. Fans of thrillers with a supernatural tinge will be pleased."
—PUBLISHERS WEEKLY, on Double Vision

"Bird's prose sets the bar high for his contemporaries in this slice-of-life tale marbled with self-destruction and ambiguous hellfire magic. Smart, deep, and honest.
Highly recommended."
—CHAD LUTZKE, author of Slow Burn on Riverside on Wayward Suns

"DRENCROM is a tightly written thrill ride that hits the gas on page one and never once lets up. Highly entertaining, with visuals that run the gamut of gruesome, psychedelic, and achingly human. Hamelin Bird is a helluva wordsmith."
—LAUREL HIGHTOWER, author of Crossroads and Below

"A gorgeously-written, gritty, sweaty, southern rock 'n roll nightmare."
—BRIAN ASMAN, author of Man, Fuck This House
on Wayward Suns

"An evocative writer, Bird's descriptive ability is jarringly effective...a well-wrought novel that fans of both hard-boiled and speculative fiction genres will enjoy."
— BLUEINK REVIEW, on Double Vision

"Bird's prose is clever, well-written, and elegiac...DOUBLE VISION features an engaging plot that touches on the supernatural, the nature of evil, and the often tenuous relationships of fathers and sons."
— THE BOOKLIFE PRIZE

AMBROSIA

Two Cocks Fighting

Two Cocks fought a Duel for the Mastery of a Dunghill. He that was worsted slunk away into a Corner, and hid himself; t'other takes his Flight up to the Top of the House, and there, with crowing and clapping of his Wings, makes Proclamation of his Victory. An Eagle made a stoop at him in the middle of his Exultation, and carry'd him away. By this Accident, the other Cock had a good riddance of his Rival; took Possession of the Province they contended for, and had all his Mistresses to himself again.

The MORAL.

A wise and a generous Enemy will make a modest Use of a Victory; for Fortune is variable.

—AESOP'S FABLES

(*L'Estrange translation*)

PART ONE

BRING
IT
ON
HOME

ONE

Cheyenne, WY

1979

SOON AFTER THEIR NUPTIALS—THERE HAD BEEN NO honeymoon—the Wards moved into a cluttered cubbyhole apartment just outside Seattle, a place they would remain for what they'd hoped to be a spell, but was actually more of a prison term. Those early days had been hard ones for Nathan and Francesca, each holding down crummy forty-a-week jobs, Francesca picking up occasional shifts at the coffee shop—and, later, a downtown deli—when she could manage. All this while both attended night classes at the community college, working toward slips of paper they one day hoped to put behind glass and hang on a wall and hope it made a better life for them.

Six years later it looked as if their gamble was finally pay-ing off. They'd moved from their apartment, renting instead a comfortable flat in a new complex across town. Sheepskins in hand, Francesca had been hired by a start-up software company out of Bellevue, while Nathan was busy preaching physics to high schoolers in nearby Meadowbrook.

Then *something* happened.

They'd quit their jobs and soon after exited Seattle, settling on a good few acres in the High Plains of Wyoming. Theirs was a simple double-story ranch house, wood-sided with a wrap-around porch, though considering the investments they'd had their fingers in they could certainly have afforded bigger, with a white picket fence out front.

Even without the fence, the Ward residence glowed as the picture of class and elegance against the late-winter sky. The house stood silent, and while on any other night the Wards would've been locked safely away inside, tonight was not like other nights and as it happened the Wards were away. And even had their neighbors been closer than a few miles down the road, they still would've been hard-pressed to notice the shadow shuffling stealthily inside.

The shadow, whose name was Drexl Samson, shook and zipped his pants, blowing a *sloow* breath of satisfaction before flushing the bowl. He'd started away when he paused suddenly, glancing to make certain the rest of his cigarette stayed down. Once upon a time he'd made the mistake of thinking little things like that didn't matter—that he could come and go as he pleased, too smooth to ever be fingered—then one night a few years back he'd gotten sloppy with his menthols. And while there'd been no official investigation by the local blue boys after finding the bodies, he'd been made to understand there were more than a few curious minds wondering at how a random cigarette butt had found its way into a house of clean-freak health nuts.

So Drexl checked the damned bowl, giving a quick flash of his mini-light—the water was clean, pure as a river—before moving down the hall, the faint smell of peppermint trailing close behind. He came into the kitchen and gulped water from the faucet, and wiping his mouth Drexl caught a reflection of himself in the window over the sink: his shining blonde hair and endless dark eyes, the sharpened ears that had always seemed a bit too large for his head. Not the prettiest face in the world—sure, he'd admit it—but it was one he'd owned for some time now, and never once had he taken it for granted.

He moved around and took a seat at the fancy bar, some sort of marble-granite deal with fruit bowls and dainty little knick-knacks, all things which seemed particularly meaningless to Drexl. Marriage shit. He'd had a family once—nice-enough wife, couple of kids—but that seemed all so far away, in another lifetime, and the idea of ever going back sent a chill straight down his soul. He shuddered, drawing one massive hand down his face before lifting his leg and letting one go. The stench rose, momentarily clouding the mint-candy smell, and Drexl kicked back in the chair and made himself at home.

On jobs like this Drexl made a habit of raiding the bookshelves of whatever house he was in, perusing whatever looked interesting. Over the past few hours since arriving he'd worked through a couple novels, a history-type book on Caesar's conquest of Gaul, a collection of O. Henry short stories. He'd then moved on to Yeats.

Strange cats, these Wards were. Real eclectic.

Drexl lifted the next book—*Tuck Everlasting*—and began to read, his curious eyes scanning the pages so quickly he appeared the victim of an epileptic fit. His eyes had always drawn attention, not just for being on the jittery side but mostly because of how damned black the things were. *You've got the devil's eyes*, a teacher had told him once, *so black you could get lost in 'em and never find your way out*. He'd hissed at her then, drawing down his tongue, just funning, but Mrs. Abigail was not the funning sort, and after school she'd led him to the woods out back the schoolhouse and given him the privilege of picking his own switch.

He scrolled the pages, mind falling away and getting lost in Winnie Foster's world, deeper and deeper until a cold finger touched suddenly on his spine and he stopped. Outside, a Chinook wind whipped riotously around the eaves, howling a lonesome note across the night; windows creaked, bowing to the pressure. Only it wasn't just the wind he was feeling here, there was something else. Something else entirely.

Drexl closed the book.

Looking on, one may have assumed the man was simply bored, restless after a long night of lounging in a stranger's home. Even Drexl himself may've assumed such a thing, way back when. But now he was older, wiser—now he *knew better*—and stood from his chair, walking to the library, returning the book to the shelf. He made a final walkthrough of the house, checking rooms, making sure everything was exactly so. *Great Satan's in the details*, he told himself. *Life's a game of inches*, he told himself, and moments later heard a buzz and felt the pager on his waist vibrate.

Drexl smiled, pleased with himself for having anticipated,

for having *felt* it before Lola so much as dialed. Perhaps, he thought, they'd forged some sort of mystic mind-meld, something to do with the Procedure. It had clearly affected their bodies, no question in that; maybe it had affected their minds as well. Some unforeseen side-effect. He didn't give one good shit either way, all he knew was that in ten minutes the Wards would come strolling through that front door and be damned if he wouldn't be ready for them.

Reaching in his pocket, he retrieved a letter written no doubt by some desk jockey with a thing for stencils but that would pass under parental scrutiny as one written by Francesca Ward herself. He'd looked it over but there wasn't much to it; the standard intimations of depression, private despair, a couple well-placed lines bordering on the paranoid. Drexl supposed it could seem cruel, to lesser minds, what he was doing here tonight. To lesser minds, the Wards were blue-eyed sparkly-toothed angels with nary a sin to their name. And for all he knew they were right—look at this house, after all, the furniture, look at that *yard*. Hell, another year and they'd probably have a rugrat running around, pulling down curtains and puking all over the place.

None of that concerned Drexl.

He did not bother himself with morals, and did not particularly care for the betterment of the human race. Far as he saw it, he was a man hired to do a job and he'd been paid well to do it. He was good at what he did—damned good, to be so bold—and the Bureau knew it. And you could bet your sweet bippy Lola Agnew knew it too, or else he wouldn't be here right now—no way, no how.

Drexl placed the letter next to a wire figurine—looked like

a gnarled coat hanger—and proceeded to the dining room, a tidy area which smelled faintly of lavender. Unlike some of the other marks he'd had the pleasure of hosting, the Wards believed heartily in the Second Amendment and were proud owners of a Mossberg 500. Presently the shotgun stood leaning against the dining room table; Drexl snatched it up now before proceeding to the foyer. Back in the Bureau's earliest days, they'd taken another approach. Played it way different. He'd read stories. But it didn't take an Einstein to realize the setup worked best when the ducks were sitting and didn't see it coming and so he'd pieced together a life of squatting in darkness, biding his time reading Hemingway or Shakespeare or the Bible.

A sudden splash of headlights swept the windows and Drexl crept forward, watching as Lola's familiar Cadillac pulled to a stop out front. Moments later the rear door swung open and the Wards climbed doggedly from the car—first Francesca, a tall goosey-looking girl with big brown hair and lanky arms, followed by Nathan, some twerp with glasses and a chest like a kindergartner. Even in darkness their faces looked ragged and worn, dug-up corpses who had yet to shed their flesh. They lumbered toward the porch, glancing occasionally to the car as it reversed and sped away, and it was all Drexl could do not to grin.

Sitting ducks?

Hell, they might as well be pulling the trigger themselves.

Nathan entered the house, pausing a moment for his wife to wander in trance-like behind him before shutting the door. He fumbled clumsily at the knob, twisting the various locks into place, and was turning to hit the lights when suddenly

Drexl sprang forward, erupting like a caged animal from the darkness.

Nathan turned, startled, his whole world spinning to life but not soon enough and Drexl unloaded, the blast nailing the boy squarely in the chest and lifting him off his feet. He crashed backwards against the wall and Drexl fired again, this one going to the gut and some of the buckshot spraying wide, tearing at wallpaper. Blood spewed, rushing out of him like water from a twisted sponge, and by the time the man-child slumped forward and sprawled motionless on the classy Karastan rug, his heart was still.

Francesca screamed, and that was her first mistake.

Any sane person would have (a) ran for their life, or (b) rushed the shit out of him, ripping the gun from his hands. She had done neither, and her second mistake was in making the first all over again as he moved in and propped the muzzle snugly beneath her chin. He watched as her face tightened, eyes meeting his and dawning with realization as she *remembered*, as she realized who he was, and though she'd not exactly been thrilled meeting him the first time, this second encounter was proving the lick of her spoon.

He reached up, giant fingers wrapping her head and dragging her down the hall to the living room. This shot was crucial, and there came a moment—fleeting as it was—when he thought this girl might just grow a pair and fight back; but the element of surprise was simply too much for her, overwhelming her ability to think and reason. Struggling to speak despite the barrel squeezing in at her jaw, she said, *"But we...we did everything...you asked..."*

Drexl gazed into her with his cold black eyes, realizing

now the fear had taken her completely, possessing and reducing her to no more than a quivering pile of flesh and bone. For some in Drexl's position, there was the temptation for such a thing to make them feel powerful, superior. But it wasn't like that for him. And though one would never guess it looking at him, it actually saddened him in a way, seeing some poor soul reduced to this, seeing them humiliated by their own base emotions. But then the weaker ones usually were...

"Not everything."

He pulled the trigger and the top of her head opened, spraying a mash of blood and brain matter up and up, gumming the walls, some of it clunking the ceiling and dropping like confetti and flitting around him in a gory rainfall. Drexl groaned and propped Francesca on the couch, lifting the girl's lanky arms and taking her hands and wrapping the gun, leaning the barrel just so beneath her ruined face and then standing back, correcting, all the while doing his best to ignore the sudden draft that had taken over the house and which he knew would forever stain its walls, because that was the way houses worked, capturing every idle thought, every emotion, harnessing and remembering them for all those who had come and gone and who no longer had any memory.

He reached down, scooping a small palm-size camera from his pocket and taking a series of snapshots showing the gruesome aftermath of the past sixty seconds. The Bureau was nothing if not thorough, and though admittedly he'd succumbed to a sick satisfaction from taking these pictures, at the end of the night it was still just business.

Always business.

He pocketed the camera and backed away, the cool rush

of the encounter moving through him, thrilling him. His hands shuddered and by a force of will he stopped them, pulling them tight at his sides. Making sure to avoid the tapestry of gore and blood spatter across the floor, Drexl slid quietly through the kitchen to the back door, slipping out, using the key the Bureau had provided to lock up after himself. By the time Lola's Cadillac appeared once more down the road, steering back toward him, the clammy feeling had left him and his heart had ceased to dance, slowing to a dry thump in his chest as he readied for the long ride home.

TWO

THE BUS STOPPED JUST OUTSIDE OF TOWN, SOME forgotten corner where one could safely view the county below but without getting so close as to actually commit to going there. Doors hissed shut as Travis stepped out and the Greyhound rolled away, slipping through a hole in the early morning fog, and for a long time he stood gazing along the road, taking in the clouds, the rain, his eyes drifting inevitably to the misty light of the streets below; Travis stared, struggling to remember those streets as they were so long ago, so dark and full of life.

He started along the road toward town, savoring the rush of clean air riding on the rain until finally the clouds broke and Travis heard only the low whistles he hadn't noticed from his lips until now—same damned tune he'd been humming since Yokosuka. He'd been lots of places since then, burned a lot of miles through a lot of states—most of them on foot—and still the tune remained, still as soft and sorrowful as when he'd first heard it back...well, back *when* exactly? And just how long *could* a song stay stuck in some poor bastard's head, anyway?

But Travis only smiled, unable to deny some gathering peace in himself.

He felt good, after all, felt *vibrant*—one hell of a lot better than he'd felt four months earlier, when he'd come here to lay his mother in the ground. Looking back, that trip seemed a thousand years in the past, a million, as shapeless and murky as the buildings rising from the patina of fog in the distance; then he came closer and the buildings took shape, one word glowing from the overhang of an old gas station up ahead: LUCKEY'S.

He stepped inside, a small bell tinkling overhead as Travis noticed an older man with a south-of-the-border tan lounging behind the counter, silky black hair pulled back in a cool-dude ponytail. The man glanced up from his magazine and, catching sight of Travis, suddenly went slack in the face, his jaw loosing to reveal a slimy puddle of chewing tobacco. Slowly, the mouth closed, kept chewing. The eyes stayed just where they were.

"Help you?"

"No thanks," he said, casually strolling the aisles. He'd spotted a spinner rack and made his way over, was turning it, eyeing the books. Romance novels, mostly. Couple spy books, some sci-fi. He found the closest thing to a creeper and took it off the shelf. Walked back to the counter and now he could make out the crackling buzz of a police scanner, of muttering voices lost in static.

"That all?" the old man asked, still with the eyes.

"That'll do." Travis yawned, adjusting the duffel on his shoulder and giving a careful glance around the store. Then he lowered his voice and said, *"That and every damned dollar in the drawer."*

The man froze, one finger dangling over the register.

"B-beg pardon?"

But Travis only stared, a spark of red fury flaring in his eyes as he reared back and readied to let loose, to slam the counter and leap like a fool and—

And then it was too much, his head dropping, a sudden grin creeping over his lips. He burst into laughter.

The old-timer blinked, life slowly draining back into his face. "*Travis?*" he asked, astonished. "Travis, is that...is that *you* in there?"

Travis extended an arm. "How's it going, Juan?"

"Get that out of my face," Juan said, waving away the hand. "You almost gave me a heart attack just now, you know that? Sick pendejo. For a second there I thought I might have to shoot you." He reached down, revealing a shiny snubnose .38 from beneath the counter, giving it a shake. "Old Betsy here, she'll knock you off your feet."

"Easy, now," Travis said, glancing outside the store windows, into the streets. "Let's not go giving anybody the wrong idea here..."

"The wrong idea—oh, and what would that be? Some long-haired screwball coming in, knockin' over a poor old man's shop?" Juan slipped away the gun and stood back, staring. "Travis, Travis, what have you done to yourself?"

"Hell, it's only a beard, Juan. Some folks even wear them year-round."

"Mi amigo, that is one beast of a beard..."

He smiled, running a hand down his face, stroking his growth. It was a beast, Juan was right about that. But after so many years with a crew cut and clean shave, the beard had been a welcome change. An outward display of some inner shift. Only now—standing here in Juan Marquez's shop, watching him jaw away at tobacco and hearing the familiar static of the police scanner—did Travis sense another shift fast on the way, that after so many years he was finally home and there was something to be made of that. On impulse, he dashed down the aisle and grabbed a bag of razors, some shaving cream, then placed them on the counter next to the paperback.

"A wise decision," Juan told him. "A nice señorita wouldn't lay hands on you with a rug like that on your face."

"A nice señorita wouldn't lay hands on me anyhow."

"That's a lie and you know it," Juan said, grinning as he took Travis's money and handed over the change. "Nice young military man like yourself...I'll bet you're beating them off with a club? Eh?"

"I'm not military, Juan. Not anymore. And not so young anymore, either."

"You, out of the service? Since when?"

So they talked. About the Navy and life overseas and about his mother, who maybe wasn't the most perfect or wholesome lady but who didn't deserve to die so young. Travis asked if there'd been any more sloshed Irishmen stopping in to chat about the spelling on the sign out front, and Juan stroked his black hair and replied no more than the usual.

Nice as it was to see Juan and fun as it was to catch up, however, Travis was anxious to get moving; he was home, yes, but his journey would not be complete until he'd made it back to Half Moon Drive, until he opened the front door and stepped inside and the empty house became his own. Until he showered in the cobwebbed stall and cooked his first meal on the old rusty stovetop.

Until he slept.

Once they'd covered the basics and branched out beyond—and once he was able to get a word in edgewise—Travis said his goodbyes and started for the door, not getting far when Juan's voice came calling after him: "Hey, Travis! Wait! How about a lottery ticket? Megaball's up to eighty million! You hear that, I said *eigh-ty million!*"

"Thanks, Juan, but I think I'll pass."

"Wait! Here, here. On the house, really." He hit some buttons, waited for the ticket to print, snatched it up. "Take it, it's yours."

Travis walked back and grabbed the ticket.

"You know what the odds on these are, right? You know you have a better chance of having your face eaten alive by piranhas than winning the lottery? You know this, correct?"

"What I *know* is that eventually somebody's gotta win. And you realize what your odds are if you don't buy a ticket? Zero, *nada*." Juan shrugged. "Can't win unless you play."

Travis studied him a moment, the man's wild, expectant eyes, full of light despite their darkness, the spreading lines of crow's-feet. Then he clicked his tongue and returned a smile, stuffing away the ticket as he turned for the door.

"You got me there, Juan. Can't argue with logic..."

§

His first year overseas, Travis had read about something called the Fibonacci sequence.

The Fibonacci sequence, he'd learned, was a fancy name for what was essentially a pattern—a never-ending series of numbers in which each number is the sum of the previous two: 0, 1, 1, 2, 3, 5, 8, 13, so on. The numbers were only the beginning, however, a jumping point for this book—*Fibonacci: Unlocking the Universe*—to delve into such head-splitting topics as sacred geometry, the fingerprint of God, and *phi*—the Golden Ratio—which is said to have figured in the construction of projects as varied as the Great Pyramids to the Parthenon.

What intrigued him most, however, was that these same numbers occurred randomly in nature, in music, even astronomy. They could be witnessed in the family tree of honeybees and heard in the works of Mozart and Beethoven. They could be counted in the fruitlets of a pineapple, the scales of a pine cone, the spirals of a sunflower. Other flowers have been known to have a Fibonacci number of petals—lilies and irises, for example, have three petals, buttercups and wild roses have five, delphiniums have eight. All Fibonaccis.

Travis remembered this now as he kept down the road, not because he was a whiz or some kind of intellectual—he wasn't—but because he'd walked two miles since Luckey's and still the song was there, stuck in his head. The dark melody repeating itself again and again until at last he heard the music in everything around him: in every breath, every heartbeat, in every step on the pavement or in the tall swinging grass, all of it building up and up—*the song was there*, as if locked into the very fabric of nature. So maybe, Travis reasoned, this was a Fibonacci tune. No, that didn't sound right. A Fibonacci ditty? Fibonacci soul rhythm...

He shook his head, whistling away as he kept down the street and his old world opened before him, becoming brand new. There was the old Leary place, quaint as ever with its classic Cape Cod charm, and the Piccolo's at the end of the lane. Through the lingering fog, he spotted the single festoon of electrical wire he and the other hood rats had utilized for target practice, using old pellet guns to peg squirrels and birds. A senseless ritual, he knew, and oftentimes he'd afterward gathered the stiffening bodies—covertly, of course—and conducted mock burials within the secrecy of his own backyard.

Finally his own house appeared and for a long time Travis stood out front, trying to remember and trying to forget. The place had changed colors over the years, he noticed, shingles loose and strewn across the yard, their harum-scarum design forming a vague sort of mandala. How much of this decay had existed four months earlier and how much had happened since, he wasn't sure; that trip existed as a blur in his mind, the only lasting image that of standing alone over his mother's grave on that gray December morning, watching as the snow flitted down and lay a blanket of ice over the only person who had ever cherished and loved him completely, even if it was an imperfect love.

Stepping inside the door, he was met by the faded stench of alcohol that had stained his mother's life for the past oh seventeen years, ever since Travis's father had left their family for the last time—this time, by way of the grave. Some weeks earlier, he'd stopped at an Internet Café outside St. Louis, making arrangements for the utilities, and after switching on some lights he searched his duffel, fishing out the paperback and bag of razors and tossing them on the kitchen table. Moving to the sink, he bent to the faucet and gulped down some water, lapping it like a dog until his belly was full and his feet carried him down the hall, where for a moment he almost didn't recognize the reflection staring back in the bathroom mirror.

It had been three days since he'd slept—a mere hiccup compared to the stretches he'd pulled in the Navy—and gazing at himself, Travis saw he had every bit the eye luggage to prove it. Over the past couple months he'd traced the very veins of this country, jagging like a heart line from LAX on across the map to the Carolina coast, sleeping in sties and waking in cheap motels, under bridges, on beaches and park benches. Part of this journey, he knew, had been a mourning for his mother, a *grieving*, though there was another, much larger part which even now he failed to comprehend. That same mysterious part that sent him searching for something in those little towns and on those long dark highways that he could only find here, always here, back where he started.

But he was home.

And for now, that's all that mattered.

§

After a quick check of the house Travis grabbed his paperback and retired down the hall, getting lost in a world a lot like his own but where the black was a bit more black and the white a bit more white and where in the end everything added up and it all made sense. Wouldn't it be nice, he thought, if the real world was as neat and tidy as the stories we created for ourselves?

But then he'd found an escape through those stories, a secret hole in the universe; reading had become as natural as breathing during his time overseas, and those first couple years he'd burned through a veritable library of books, most of them the sort of bizarre stories he'd come to love: tales from authors like Richard Matheson, Shirley Jackson, Kurt Vonnegut.

The last bit of daylight was slipping from the windows when he closed his eyes, remembering every jagged leg of the journey that had led him home, that dark melody still haunting at the edges of his thoughts.

Finally, he slept.

In the darkness he dreamed, pictures flashing like a magic lantern through his brain until finally he was twelve years old and pegging birds out on the wire. Later he collected their carcasses in a bucket, dug up a hole, and was beginning to tip the remains when he looked and suddenly the birds had *changed*, their bloodied feathers replaced now by a cache of shimmering coins, an endless river of silvers and golds clanging into the earth; Travis stared, the coins cascading like the payout of some impossible slot machine jackpot until at last he opened his eyes and now the windows were dark and he was alone.

For a long time he lay remembering the dream, playing and replaying the images until finally something jogged loose and he realized what it was: a memory of the old coin collection he'd kept as a kid. The collection was by no means extraordinary, more of a hobby his grandfather had started with a handful of Vietnamese dongs brought back from the war and that his own father had passed on to him when Travis was eight years old, each son adding a few coins of his own, though Travis had never contributed anything more than a simple Buffalo nickel. He'd cherished every piece, however—the Indian heads and wheat pennies and Canadian change—perhaps because it was the one thing of nominal value his father hadn't squandered away, and, later, because it was the only thing left of him at all.

Then one night—it was after his father had been sentenced to prison, but before he'd been stabbed to death there—Travis had decided what a foolish thing it was to have the collection displayed as it was on his dresser, in perfect view for all to see. Safes and locks were useless, dead giveaways of something valuable inside. No, he'd decided, what he needed here was some outside-the-box thinking, some subterfuge. And so, after much deliberation, he'd tucked away the collection in an old Nike box and scrawled OLD DIRTY TRASH down the side and stashed the whole mess in the attic.

Perfect.

As he'd gotten older, Travis thought less and less about the coins.

By the time he'd entered high school, he didn't care. By the time he dropped out, he'd forgotten them completely. Now he remembered, and was overcome with curiosity over what had become of the collection. Maybe still up there, he thought, still waiting for him after all these years, the dongs and wheat pennies and Kennedy half dollars—even his own Buffalo nickel.

He sat up, moving out of the room and down the hall, the springs giving a banshee cry as he lugged down the old attic door and carefully let down the ladder.

He was halfway up when he heard pounding at the front door.

BMM! BMM! BMM!

Travis froze, the eternal silence of the attic calling down

to him, beckoning him with its cold and potent finger; and for a moment he almost listened, almost scrambled up the steps and into the arms of darkness waiting at the top...until then reason reasserted itself and, slowly, he backed down the ladder. Something caught his eye through the window and he noticed the flashing blues and reds of a police cruiser parked out front.

The pounding continued, harder now.

"*Police! Open up!*"

And despite it all, he couldn't help but smile.

Welcome home indeed.

THREE

"P*OLICE! OPEN UP OR WE'RE COMING IN!*"

Travis walked over and opened the door, at which point the officer gave a startled grunt and fell back, one hand flashing to his pistol. He'd loosened the holster and gone a good ways in raising the gun when he stopped suddenly, eyes squinted as if straining to see something that was too far away. He gently replaced the pistol, closed the holster.

"Travis? Hey...that is you, ain't it?"

Travis stared at the man, not understanding, until something shone in the cop's curious brown eyes—just a flash—and it all came clicking together. He blinked, unable to hold back a smile as he appraised his old friend.

"Joe?"

The stranger smiled, a bashful glow swelling across his cheeks.

"Well, they call me Joel nowadays, just Joel," he said, and shook his head. "Damn but you 'bout scared the piss outta me. Barely recognized you with that dead cat on your face, what the hell?"

They laughed nervously, all the years silently catching up between them, all those faded memories resurrected in a moment of fleeting glory before being tucked away forever. For Travis, their shining moment had always been a drunken night back in high school when they'd gotten crazy with a can of spray paint and taken turns on the sidewall of Belangia's store, their various slogans—O.P.P., BALLER, GARGANTUAN—both meaningless and yet somehow crucial to their existence. Funny, how faded those memories seemed now.

Joel gestured to his cruiser, lights still flashing away.

"Hell, I knew you were back in town, figured I'd stop by and give you a scare. Looks like it worked the other way around though, huh?"

He stepped closer, lifting a finger to the little gold star on Joel's shirt.

"What's this, you supposed to be sheriff of this town now? That how it works—I duck out for a while and you move in, take everything over?"

Joel flashed a bitch-please expression. "You lost more than your razor over there, didn't you? I owned this town *way* before you ever left it, believe me." He turned and lifted a hand, waving casually to the motley crowd gathered in windows and on front porches, drawn to the cruiser's lights like moths to a flame. He muttered, "Evening folks, nice to see you, go ahead and wave Travis, you're star of the show..."

Travis thought of something then. "How'd you know I was

back home?"

"What do *you* think? Because I was at Luckey's half an hour ago and Juan Marquez has the biggest mouth in Pamlico. Hell, half the county probably knows by now—with the rest holding on the other line." He looked past Travis, saw the attic door hanging open down the hall. "You moving something in there? Need some help?"

"No, no, just...sorting through some things. Come on in, have a seat."

"To be honest, I'm sort of starving over here," Joel said, nodding to the cruiser. "Care to take a ride, grab a bite to eat? Ya hungry?"

§

"So what's your fancy? Anything particular? You want some drive-thru, you want Chinese? I would offer some Italian but I think"—Joel checked his watch—"yep, Alfredo's closed for the night, sorry, no Italian. What's your pick?"

Same old Joe, Travis thought. It really had been too long since they'd talked.

"Just so it's edible, Joel, it's fine with me."

"You know, I'm glad you said that, because I've had this hankerin' for some bacon *all day long*. How's about a breakfast supper? Eggs, hash browns, all that good stuff?"

Travis nodded. "Sounds...perfect."

"It's a little out of the way, but I think I know just the place."

Joel hit the gas, leveling out around seventy as Travis watched the town roll by outside his window: the eternal forests, the gaudy storefronts and shattered asphalt roads. Glancing at Joel, his body tensed behind the wheel as he guided the cruiser along, Travis felt a strange sense of camaraderie, a silly sense of pride at the dual paths their lives had taken.

"Okay, enough suspense," he said. "I've gotta know, how did this happen?"

Joel flashed a smile. "How did what happen?"

"Last I heard you were, what was it, *store* manager over at Staples. How did you become...*this*. This badass lawman?"

"Deputy sheriff, actually. And, long story short, I applied, got the job. Did more kissing ass than a chair at a piano recital. Some BLE, filled out some forms, that sort of thing. It really wasn't that hard." He looked surprised. "Actually, it was pretty damn easy."

"Well, congratulations."

Joel tipped an imaginary hat—his real one was yet to be seen—and said, "What about you? Juan tells me you're calling it quits with the Navy, I'm not so sure whether to believe that or not. Truth be told, I sort of figured you'd ride that ship to retirement."

"Yeah," he said, sort of mumbling. "So did I."

"Oh? And what made the difference?"

"You mean why'd I get out?" Travis thought about it, peering out through the windshield, out into nothingness and everything and getting lost in it all. Swept away. "Guess we all need a change sometimes..."

"Listen," Joel said, his voice lower than before. "Heard about your mom and I'm real sorry, Travis. Patti was a good woman, I don't care what anybody says."

Travis nodded, ignoring the slight chill down his neck. "Thanks, Joel."

"I'm serious. I know it's been a while since we talked, but your mother was always good to me. After I got deputy, every time she passed me in town she'd swerve at me. Almost ran me off the damn road a couple times. *Just gettin' your attention*, she'd say."

He laughed. "I don't doubt it."

"Hell, I felt like a piece of run-over shit when I missed the funeral. We'd taken the kids up north to Theresa's parents for the holidays, by the time we got back the whole mess was over and done."

"Don't worry. You didn't miss much."

"Just the same, I'm sorry I wasn't there."

Travis shut his eyes, only a moment, and saw an image of his mother, her doughy face staring at him from a too-small coffin pillow. Then his eyes opened and the image was gone, as if it never was. "I know what she was—what she became after my father died, I mean. And I don't blame people for not wanting to be around something like that. I mean, I know I didn't, shitty as that sounds. I loved her, Joel, but my mom was always her own worst enemy, sabotaging whatever shot she might have at an actual life."

His friend nodded but said nothing, the silence stretching as they burned down the highway, on and on and on. They were closing in on Reelsboro County when Travis turned and said, "So...married *and* children, huh?"

Joel lifted a hand. "Life is a sitcom."

"Like it?"

"Like what?"

"The whole family thing. You know, birthdays, barbecues, picnics..."

Joel frowned, eased out a breath. "I do, strangely enough."

"Hell freezes over," Travis muttered. "And *how* long have they been letting you carry a loaded gun?"

The small laptop beeped on the console between them and Joel tapped some keys, his eyes never inching from the road. "Three years this September," he said, tilting the wheel and speeding past a beat-up old Buick. "Can't lie, I've loved every minute. This kinda job, you know, there ain't nothing like it in the world. What about you, boss man? What's in it for you, now that you're just another dumb civilian?"

Travis considered the question, his usual fears overridden by some greater emotion, some twin to serenity that seemed to have shrouded him since arriving back in town.

For now, it was enough.

"Honestly? I have no idea. Poke around, find something that fits."

"Play it by ear, huh? Listen, you catch the fever, come September one of our deputies is transferring out. Your background and some training, you'd be a shoo-in for the job."

Travis nodded. "Thanks, Joel. I'll keep it in mind."

"*Sure* you will," he said, and spun the wheel, the cruiser bouncing into the empty lot of a bright, neon-lit restaurant. "All right," he announced. "Grab your appetite, we're here."

§

Neptune's was an old-school Eighties-themed diner that, according to Joel, had opened big a few years back but was quickly fading, and coming soon would probably close its doors for good. Stepping inside, Travis saw BIRD and JOHNSON jerseys hung from the rafters and elegantly framed photos of New Kids on the Block, of *Back to the Future* and *E.T.* and Rob

Lowe puffing his cheeks into a sax. They glanced over their menus and put in two orders for the Men At Work breakfast—three eggs, sausage, toast, your choice of grits or browns—and sipped at their mugs. Somebody dropped some coins in the jukebox, got some Eagles going. "Heartache Tonight."

"So you're back, and you have no idea what to do with yourself. How about a woman?"

Travis stirred his coffee. "Currently unattached."

"Hold on, hold on. Let me get this straight. You've been overseas for all of eight years—which, you stopped calling after the first two, just saying"—Travis opened his mouth, started to speak—"but that's for another time, we're not going there, okay, so. Moving on. You've been living overseas, been all over the world, met all *manner* of gorgeous women...and yet somehow you come home empty-handed. I don't get that. And do you wanna know *why* I don't get that? Because I've got a *wife*, Travis. I've got two *kids*, Travis. We're old as shit, the least you could do is have a *girlfriend*."

"I'm thirty-two, Joel, how is that—"

"Like I said, old as poo. This is family time, buddy, what're you gonna wait around forever? What's happening? You sick? Impotent? Are you gay, is that what this is about?"

"For the record, none of the above."

"Oh. Oh. None of the above."

Travis sipped his coffee, waited. Shook his head. "I haven't met her yet, Joel. You'll know when it happens—call me crazy, I'm sure you knew when it happened to you—and it just hasn't happened for me yet."

"Well, in case you didn't know, just 'cause you don't feel like whisking some broad down the aisle doesn't mean you can't kiss her, go on a few dates, something."

"Okay, fair enough," he said. "But I'm not rushing into anything just yet, right woman or not. I'm a solitary creature, Joel. The Navy made me that way."

"A lone wolf, huh?"

"That's right."

"That must've been the Navy then, 'cause last I remember you were pounding more tang than any of us back in high school."

"Does your wife know you talk this way?"

Joel winked. "Only if it's to her, buddy, and don't you go saying otherwise."

The teenage waitress—an ocean-eyed blonde in a cone-bra corset—walked over, setting their plates on the table.

"All right, here you go," she said. "Anything else for you guys?"

"How's about a refill, darling?" Joel asked, and the waitress scuttled away, returning moments later with a still-smoking pot of coffee.

"Let me guess," Joel said. "You're Madonna."

The waitress smiled. Posed, brushed back her hair. "How'd ya figure?"

"Oh, I don't know, took a wild guess. Now how about him?" He nodded to Travis. "Who does he look like? Go ahead, say it."

The waitress looked at Travis, scrunching up her face. "*Hmm.*"

"Go ahead, don't be shy. Who is he?"

"I honestly have...*no* idea." She giggled, tossed up a hand. "David Beckham with a beard?"

Joel scoffed. "You kidding? This man is a dead ringer for Ted Kaczynski."

"Pretty funny," Travis said, "coming from Buford T. Justice here."

But the waitress only smiled, her bright blue eyes dancing back and forth. She said, "Who's Ted Kaczynski?"

Joel chewed his food. Chewed and chewed and chewed.

"He's no one," he said. "Never mind. Thank you for the coffee."

"Oh, don't pay him any mind," Travis told her. "I don't know who Ted What's-his-face is either. Joel just has this thing, he has to feel smarter than everybody. Ain't that right, Joel?"

Joel stared, still chewing, his eyes as cold and glassy as those of a stuffed trophy mule.

"No, it's okay," the waitress said, still with that ginger smile. "It's my fault, really. I'm *soo* bad with celebrities." She asked if they needed anything else, smiled awkwardly, and strolled away. Travis glanced up and Joel was staring at him, still chewing away.

"Ted What's-his-face?" Joel shook his head. "You shouldn't have lied."

"You were embarrassing her."

"Maybe she *should* be embarrassed, did you ever think of that? Don't they teach American History anymore? Guy is one of the most sadistic homegrown terrorists of the modern era and he's forgotten like a bad dream. This is scary, Travis. Really, I'm scared. If a nation does not know its own history, it is destined to repeat it." Joel held up a finger, made it tremble. "There are babies—*babies*, Travis, *infants*—right now over in China, who know more about the Revolutionary War than most high school *graduates* in this country. Probably speak better English, too. A grim situation, my friend. Grim. And who the hell is David Beckman?"

Travis just stared, grinning despite himself.

"What? Why are you smiling? What did I say?"

"Nothing," he told him. "Nothing at all."

§

They talked awhile about Pamlico, which had grown nicely since Travis left, though not nearly enough to change its essentially pastoral character. After a quick recap of the town they'd started in on Memory Lane and the fates of a couple people who lived there, fallen friends and enemies and exes cast along the wayside of life. This took a bit longer and left Travis feeling hollow inside, a person who had lost something without being aware of what he'd lost.

They finished their meal and, despite her ignorance of domestic terrorists, left Eighties Madonna a generous tip—an easy enough thing to do, considering their bill had come to all of two dollars and change. "Pigman special," Joel explained, giving a wink. "Perks of the job." Joel asked if there was anything he needed in town, and remembering his empty fridge at the house Travis asked if there wasn't somewhere they could stop, maybe grab a few groceries. Joel flashed a funny smile and said sure thing, old buddy.

Twenty minutes later they climbed out of the cruiser and, looking around, Travis felt the smallest shiver down his back. He stared, eyeing the brightly-lit box of an old-time supermarket, familiar somehow. Then it all clicked as he glanced down the road and could make out the pale effigy of Benjamin Franklin looming out front the high school, one hand still raised in a dignified gesture of courage.

"Same as you remember?"

Travis made a face. "Even worse."

Joel laughed, clapping him on the back. "C'mon, gotta show you something."

He led Travis along the pavement and around the side of the supermarket, down to where the big oaks reached out and covered the sky. He whipped out a flashlight, clicking it on.

"Look at that. Still there, ain't that beautiful?"

Stepping closer, Travis noticed the remains of three messages, their colorful curvy letters faded but still legible across the tarnished brick wall.

| O.P.P. | BALLER | GARGANTUAN |

"Well, it's good to know we left a lasting mark," he said. "We're dead and gone, these words will still be here, confusing generations to come."

Joel stared at the wall, adjusting the light to take it all in. "What the hell does *gargantuan* mean anyway? I never got that."

"Means big."

"No, I *know* that, I *know* it means big. But why the hell'd you tag a wall with it for? What does it *stand* for?"

"It doesn't stand for anything."

"Then why'd you write it?"

"Because," he said, "that's the point."

"Writing it is the point?"

"No, that it's meaningless. It's meant to be *ironic*."

Joel blinked, staring at the graffiti. "I think I have a headache."

Finally they turned and started inside, Joel heading over to chat with the cashier while Travis grabbed the basics—bread, lunch meat, cheese. Toothbrush, toothpaste, deodorant. He'd quit soda a few years back, but he grabbed a jug of whole milk and a couple bottles of red wine. And, last of all, a paperback from one of the shelves near the checkout.

They'd just stepped outside when they heard the shouting.

Across the parking lot Travis saw a tall man bouncing outside of a pickup, shaking his fist and swearing. The driver flicked a cigarette—maybe it was a cigar—sending it bouncing off the big man's forehead, then jumped out the truck and took an empty swing of his own. They stood dancing like two boxers outside the pickup, bobbing and weaving.

"*Hey!*" Joel called. "*Hey, you two! Cut it out!*"

He walked over and spoke to them softly, using his arms to paint a pleasant picture of the two of them going their separate ways, going back home, whatever. And maybe it was being back in town after so long and with Franklin High so close but, seeing Joel in action, Travis couldn't help but imagine him as young Joe Collier, just a teenager again, all costumed up in his daddy's clothes and playing Big Mr. Law.

Only that was a mistake.

This wasn't show-and-tell, and the gun on Joel's hip was no snap-cap toy. It was a Glock that fired real bullets and caused real damage and that could easily knock the life from a person's body. This was the real world, Travis knew that, and was not foolish enough to forget it.

When he looked next the men had caught the message, muttering as they climbed into their respective vehicles and peeled out of the lot. Hopefully, Travis thought, not headed down the road to finish out that dance. Joel strolled over, shaking his head and laughing.

"See a squad car parked *right* here, they're gonna try and pick a brawl. How's that for intelligence?" He laughed again and stood gazing down the street, his eyes peering into the shadows and searching behind every bush. "I'll tell ya, Travis, there is no shortage of knuckleheads in this world..."

§

His mind drifted as he put away the groceries, thinking how good it had been seeing Joel, catching up. Now that he was home, he needed people in his life—needed *friends*—and Joel was a nice one to have, warts and all.

He was turning from the fridge when Travis's eyes fell on the old attic door still pulled low down the hall. For a long time he studied the darkness at the top, thinking how tired he was and how much easier it would be to go up in the morning and take a look around—it was near midnight, after all. No sense going and stirring around so late, no sense at all...

Moments later he was at the top of the ladder, the bottled heat of the attic falling around him as he switched on a light and then promptly set to work, picking through strewn crates of Christmas lights and moth-eaten clothes and forgotten toys. He found the shoebox tucked away in cobwebs beneath an old piano bench, OLD DIRTY TRASH faded along one side.

He hoisted the box with both hands, the cardboard turned brittle beneath his fingers. But mostly he was thinking how damned *heavy* the thing was, how foreign it felt in his arms. He hauled it out to the light and lowered it gently, almost reverently to the floor, then snatched back the top and peered inside and...

And a glittering mound of coins stared up at him.

Not his collection from childhood but something else, the shining coins piled high and nearly spilling out of the box. Without him knowing it, the Fibonacci tune had returned, thrumming in his mind, an image of something clearing in Travis's thoughts—not just an image, he realized, but a *memory*. A faraway vision of an endless sea, and undulating waters beneath a golden dawn. The shuddering roar of a Navy ship, and then another sound, echoing from the deepest depths of the ocean and filling his worn-thin soul—

He blinked and the image was gone, vanished again into the darkest shadows of his mind, and Travis found himself once more in the smothering heat of the attic, peering at an impossible pile of change.

He grabbed the box and heaved it over, coins spilling in a steady tide across the attic's wooden floor. Already he'd spotted a few gems: No Cents Liberty Heads and Bicentennials and 1943 steel cents. And there were Buffalo nickels and Susie B's and Mercury dimes and...

And none of these were here before.

He stared, peering harder now across the hillock of coins and realizing that no, that wasn't exactly true. That some of these *were* here before—not many, but a few...

So how did these other coins get in the box, smart guy?

Hm.

No answer.

He glanced the surrounding darkness, startled at the notion he wasn't so alone in this attic as he'd once believed. He called aloud—*hello?*—feeling suddenly foolish, like he'd just woken from a dream.

But there was no one there, and somehow this only made things worse.

He reached down, snatching up a coin—an 1864 two-cent piece. He gave it a quick study—Small Motto variety, well-preserved—and though the tender seemed legit he registered a funny feeling with the piece in his hand—little aftershocks of the dizziness he'd felt earlier, perhaps.

He dropped the coin, backed away.

Whatever this was, whatever was happening now, he didn't like it—scared him shitless, truth be told—and so he did the only thing there was left to do: he lumbered to his feet, careful to avoid the rafters, and slowly, slowly retreated toward the ladder, never turning his back on the gathered riches at the center of the attic.

The coins glimmered back at him, a thousand teeth smiling up from the darkness.

FOUR

OURS LATER HE LAY IN BED, STRUGGLING FOR SLEEP but unable to find it.

Despite all that had happened over the past eighteen hours, again and again his thoughts turned to the attic, to whatever strange thing had happened to him there. To the fact that, just maybe, he'd reached out like a blind man through the darkness, and his fingers had brushed on the impossible.

Assuming, that was, his mother—or some charitable neighbor, perhaps—hadn't come along and added their own anonymous bits to the box.

But Travis knew better.

And knowing it made him uneasy, as if he were somehow losing control. He'd witnessed a fleeting glimpse of the inexplicable and now felt pale and somehow hollow, not like himself. *It was nothing*, he thought, *just some silly stroke of luck*. Except, no, that wasn't right either: luck was beating the rain or a straight flush—what he'd experienced was *more* than luck, it was...

What?

The question hung before him, dangling like a curse. Swinging back and forth and back.

And the winning answer, of course, was that he had no clue what it was—or *how* it was—or *what* it meant...

But it had happened.

Finally, he slept.

And as night sank into early morning Travis's dreams were filled with the dark melody that had followed him home, a distant voice rising lone and sorrowful from the depths, the most beautiful thing he'd ever heard, sweeping through him in a mournful dirge that beat on and on and on...

FIVE

San Diego, CA

1986

DEBRA AUERBACH SLIPPED FIRST ONE BARE FOOT, then another out of the car—she'd tossed her heels six hours earlier, once the chafing had given way to blisters—and hoisted herself from the Cadillac's roomy backseat. It was a movement she'd performed hundreds of times before, thousands, though never under these circumstances.

No, never like this.

And though she'd long since moved on from that phase of her life, Debra did not bemoan all the sweat-soaked hours she'd spent getting plowed in backseats and hotel rooms, did not lay awake nights puzzling over how she'd ever been so naïve as to get swindled by a profession that chewed up girls like gum and spat them back out into the world, broken and used up and, more often than she'd like to admit, with a bitching case of rigor mortis.

Some people—what her friend Sissy Beauregard called "those of the tall-nose sort"—may judge her for the decisions she'd made in life—and that was their prerogative. Rode hard and put up wet, they'd say. A doe-eyed, streetwalking, woman of the night, they'd say—and again, they had every right in the world. But then they hadn't seen her options. Couldn't have known her dirt-poor past, about hand-me-downs and the cruelty of middle school imaginations. Or about her stepfather, who when she was fourteen had started welcoming himself into her room, a midnight ritual that continued for three years until one night she'd jammed a number two pencil clear through his testicles and her mother had raised hell and tossed her out.

Stripping her clothes for cash had come naturally after that.

She'd started in the dollar-bill heaven of strip clubs and then went to hooking and stayed at that a while, gathering a list of high-end clients, climbing the tedious whore social ladder to escort until at last a better idea had presented itself. Same concept, different payout. Some called it gold-digging, and that was okay. But really it wasn't anything like people thought, wasn't like that Eagles song. Hands as cold as ice she could suffer; it was life in a cardboard box that gave Debra Auerbach the jeebies. And a choice between sweaty backseats and giving it up to some delusional golden oldie who smothered her with diamonds until death did them part? A choice between baths in a porcelain fountain or a sopping gutter trough?

Well, that was no choice at all.

Sometimes she saw the regular people in the world, the people who flipped their noses and crossed the street, and Debra couldn't help but laugh. Scrunch their faces all they wanted, she knew how the world worked. She knew the hard facts no one liked talking about, much less staring in the face. That hard work doesn't necessarily pay off, for one. That blood and sweat are always second fiddle to pleasure, and as long as you can provide that much for some old toad willing to dish out the comfort, life was peachy keen with sunny skies ahead. And when the sweet geezer *actually croaked?* Actually dropped dead and left her everything but the fillings in his teeth? Shucks, he'd just as well left her the Taj Mahal.

And just when she'd thought life's true surprises had run dry, Debra Auerbach witnessed the impossible. A true miracle, beyond anything she'd ever known to exist. In the way of miracles, it had changed her in some profound way she did not understand and was in no position to put into words. But leave that to the poets, she thought; she felt no need to elaborate on that which she couldn't comprehend, nor to explain her sudden decision to leave Mr. Robert Burroughs—ninety-six years young, with a heart of gold and bank account of steel—and strike out on her own, broken and penniless.

She'd had the *episode* two months later (the term "vision" frightened her to no end, though that's precisely what it had been—a literal open-eyes vision, showing what appeared to be a working-parts diagram of a device she could never have imagined in a million years). With trembly arms, Debra had scribbled a blueprint of what she saw—an innovative design for windshield wipers, as it turns out—and eight months later obtained a patent. A year after that she'd went national. Even now, all this time later, she couldn't *quite* believe all that had happened, in the same way she supposed those who'd seen ghosts or been abducted by aliens couldn't believe it, though considering the last few hours she had no choice but to believe.

Hell, if that wasn't proof she didn't know what was.

Debra watched as the Cadillac fled into the night, noticing the first creep of sunrise off to the east. Had it really only been one night? Was that all? When she looked next the car was gone and Debra continued to the door, slipping in her key and walking inside and through the darkened foyer to the kitchen. For once, it felt good to be alone, in her own place.

It felt good to be *home*.

She went upstairs, meaning to brush her teeth but instead crawling into bed. A parade of images swam against the darkness, cascading up and down and all around; pictures of things she'd scarcely have believed had she not witnessed them hours earlier with her own two eyes. One of those pictures was of the thing she'd first glimpsed all those years before. A *siren*, they'd called it. Only this time the creature's face was different, no longer joyful and serene but twisted into a startling rictus of fear, betrayal outlined in its—in *her*—terrible black eyes.

Never in her wildest dreams had Debra imagined a second glimpse of those eyes, and remembering them now her mind was filled with music, with the melody she'd first heard all those years ago, the song she'd been given. She opened her mouth, the first syllables creeping forth—*fah-sha-lu*—when her mind flashed instead to the woman who had served as her glorified tour guide for the night. To Lola Agnew—*the Bitch*, as Debra thought of her—with her cold dry hands and funny sweet smell. Just thinking of her Debra got a creeped-out feeling, like bugs crawling all over, and abruptly sat up, knowing now without a doubt that sleep was out of the question.

She moved to the bathroom, deciding a nice warm bath was probably the best thing to clear her mind and wash away the stress. Funny how often over the past frantic hours she'd wished for nothing more than sleep—*real* sleep, not the kind from a needle—had *craved* it—yet even now it proved elusive.

Yes, a nice warm bath would do her well.

Debra opened the faucet and stripped down, tossing her clothes in a pile in the corner. Then the tub was full and the first fingers of morning had come creeping through the window, blowing its soft breath onto the glass.

A new day, she thought. *A new day, so make this one count...*

She slipped into the tub, groaning at the magical all-over warmth of the water. It wasn't long when her eyes drifted shut and her mind turned again to the plane, to the island—the *Lodge*, Agnew had called it—to the graceful monsters which had made all miracles possible. But was it real?

Had she really experienced everything she thought she had?

Yes, she decided. It was real.

It was real and as she lay there in the water Debra had the overpowering urge to tell the world what she'd seen. They had a right to know. No one, not George Washington himself, had any business keeping such wondrous creations a secret. Her heart raced as she decided that yes, she would be the one to tell them, to grab up a bullhorn and let the world know. There were a couple of bullhorns she had in mind, but Samantha

Bowles was the best, had done a story on Debra's rags-to-riches turnaround a few years back when Sammy was still at the *Post*. Debra would call her as soon as she got out of the tub. She would tell her story, starting seven years ago with that night on the beach—how often she'd thought of that night—straight up to being dropped off only an hour before. *I'll hold nothing back*, she thought, *because the world deserves nothing less*. She would explain all that she'd seen and heard, give detailed descriptions, she would name names and...

Something stopped her then.

What it was, she didn't know.

Debra hesitated, and was about to shrug it away when it happened again—faintly, oh so faintly—and this time she knew what it was.

Peppermint.

It was the smell of *peppermint*.

She stopped, trying to remember why this smell seemed so familiar.

And then it came.

Agnew.

Of course, that funny sweet smell, she'd stunk of it. But...

But before Agnew there'd been someone else, she knew there had. Who was it?

Who?

As she struggled for an answer, a ray of morning light pierced the window and arced across the tile, settling on what she'd assumed to be a shadow around the corner. Only then the shadow moved, sliding impossibly from the wall and stepping into the light and when she realized it was him her first instinct was to demand what was he doing here, how he'd gotten into her house. Before she could open her mouth, Debra realized she knew the answer: that he'd never left, that he'd been here all along, waiting...

Waiting...but why?

§

Drexl approached the tub, watching as the Auerbach woman struggled to put two and two together. Then it came—he could almost hear those puzzle pieces snapping into place—and she opened her mouth to scream.

But he didn't hear the scream, only the steady hum of the hairdryer grinding to life in his hand. Then that hum rose to a roar and he stepped closer, staring with still-water eyes while the woman splashed and scrambled and then he tossed the hairdryer into the tub. Tossing it at her feet so the juice had plenty of room to grow, gaining strength as it worked its way up. A standard hairdryer could serve quite a jolt, no doubt about it, and after the hour or so he'd spent tweaking this one the blast should be mighty indeed.

A single spark the color of the sun dashed across the water, spreading its fingers over Debra Auerbach's chest. The flesh there went black, like magic, and now the water was sloshing as Debra commenced to dance, her sweet Gibson-girl figure going taut as a wire, veins yanked tight and glistening blue-purple as the current warped cap-a-pie, rattling every bone as it went. Her pretty green eyes popped in her head, bulging out and out like a pair of bejeweled eggs until one of them—the left—at last breached the socket and went slip-sliding down her cheek.

Drexl watched, not enjoying himself exactly but not hating

the experience. He was neither hot nor cold. Life, he'd learned, was an education, and no facet of existence was immune to that education. Joy had a learning with it, and sadness had a different sort of learning. Envy, rage, lust, all just colors on a spectrum of light. He watched as her skin became dark, every hair standing on end. The secret was soaking up the most from every opportunity, not going out of one's way to make yourself miserable but not chiding the sour times when they came. Sometimes you were full, other times empty. Holy hell, and now the broad was *smoking*. Man, she was cookin'. He couldn't imagine she could hold up like that much longer, the stress was too much; her spine would snap.

Then a sudden fizzing as the water fell off from boiling and Debra Auerbach slumped low in the tub. Drexl moved to the tiny window—looked like a porthole—and peered out, watching as the sun crept full of bounty over the horizon, calling out the birds to sing and the wind to whip its way toward destiny. He took a deep breath, hoping to catch some of that dewy morning freshness, but all he got for his trouble was a nose full of burnt air.

The sweet and the bitter, yes indeed...

He saw yesterday's paper on the sink and picked it up, read the headline. DISASTER IN THE SKIES! SEVEN DEAD AFTER SHUTTLE EXPLOSION. He skimmed the story, learning how classrooms all across the nation had been huddled around TVs as the doomed Challenger made liftoff and, moments later, burst into a bright ball of fire, killing everyone on board. All that carnage, Drexl thought, all that death witnessed by such innocent eyes, by such young and impressionable minds. Earth would never be enough, no sir, and leave it to us to find some fatal flaw in shooting humans into outer space.

It was enough to keep you up at night.

He returned the paper to its place, had started to turn away when something caught his eye. He leaned in close to the mirror, brushing a hand through his sleek blonde hair, combing back and forth and fishing out a single strand of gray. Drexl stared a moment, brows knit in wonder, before pinching his fingers and plucking it out. He went to drop it to the checked-tile floor, then cursed himself—*sloppy sloppy*—and stuffed the strand in his pocket.

After snapping his pictures he walked downstairs, letting himself quietly out the back door. The sun wasn't so bright here, shaded by massive redwoods, and Drexl strolled casually through the backyard to the next street over.

He lowered himself to the curb, watching night come into morning as he scooped a clunky Motorola from his belt and dialed and a moment later sat puffing his menthol and staring at the sky, spying out the bloody aftermath of dawn as it crept through the trees. He smiled, enjoying himself, soaking up the sauce of life. They were all just rag and bone men, after all, every man, woman, and child: rag and bone men, peddling their wares wherever they may roam.

SIX

TRAVIS STAYED BUSY THOSE FIRST FEW WEEKS—repairs mostly, cleaning the house, replacing furniture with things that didn't have ghosts or some sad story to tell. He installed a new hot water heater and bought all new drapes, went crazy with it. Even got around to shaving, what a splendid mess that was.

But more than anything he thought of that night in the attic and the coins still scattered down the hall. Their presence teased him, many nights Travis staying up late poring over the collection without knowing why, sifting them as one might sift a stash of stolen Rembrandts: thrilled by their existence but not quite sure what to *do* with the damned things.

Then one day it was too much and he'd contacted a dealer just outside Bethesda, a kindly woman who'd offered just shy of six grand for the entire collection; but Travis had demurred, instead selling it piecemeal and using the cash for whatever project he busied himself with that week; the first had been buying the Mitchell's old Toyota two doors down.

Joel became a regular presence in his life, and soon the Collier family was having Travis over twice a week. Probably they felt sorry for him, all alone out there in his dead mother's house, but Travis didn't mind. He wasn't above pity. Especially considering how taken he was with Joel's daughters—twins, one more sly than the next.

Theresa's buttermilk biscuits didn't hurt either.

"You've got a great family," he told Joel one night after dinner. They were lounging on the deck, sipping beers and watching as the girls spun circles inside.

Joel shrugged. "Eh, they're okay."

"Must be a good feeling."

"What's that?"

"Having something that's...*yours*. People to love and care about—and who love you right back, just for being you."

Joel smirked. "Saying you want a taste of family life?"

But he'd only scoffed, rattling off the usual items—finances, responsibility, the lady problem—before Joel cut him off and said, "Mark my words, buddy. One day she'll come and soon you'll have the damn Brady Bunch running around. And you know what? You'll love every minute."

"How about I start with a dog? Just a puppy, a front-porch hound, something?"

Shake of the head. "Nope, 'fraid not. It's straight to the Brady Bunch for you."

Still, Travis had other things to think about.

During his Navy years he'd put aside a decent savings,

enough to get by on for a couple years if he played his cards right. His cross-country tour had nipped at that plenty, and fixing up the old house had nipped plenty more. He had zero idea what he wanted to do with himself and yet remained oddly aloof from the fact, bedazzled by the curious peace he'd felt since moving home. He'd worked hard, after all, had put in his time—eight years, never to be returned—and so figured he'd earned a little vacation. Some downtime to clear his thoughts, maybe find some direction in life. In the meantime, he drank cold beers with Joel and watched the game and hung around the house, watching stand-up and reading from his mother's shelf of old horror stories.

Then something happened, and all that changed.

He'd discovered the ticket in early September, tucked away in a pair of muddied jeans on their way to the washer. He'd meant to throw on some laundry before heading over to Joel's for dinner but now only stared, turning the slip—along with a crumpled receipt from Luckey's, dated May sixth—in his hands. He peered closer, reading the numbers printed in a neat little line: **02 28 32 49 50 29**

Can't win unless you play

He thought back, remembering that first foggy morning back in town, Juan pushing the slip into his hand. And staring now at the Megaball ticket he felt suddenly dizzy—not unlike, he thought, that night in the attic—and when the dizziness had passed he walked over, snatching a handful of Susie Bs from the remains of his collection down the hall.

Then he grabbed his keys and walked out the door.

§

He cruised the streets calmly, asking himself a thousand times what he was doing, a thousand times receiving no answer. The old Toyota still carried an odd waxy aroma the Mitchell's had warned him about and that reminded Travis of crayons, but he wasn't thinking about the smell. He was thinking he'd never considered himself a greedy man but then neither was he a dumb one, and on the off chance Lady Fortune was so resolved as to shine on him, well, he was more than inclined to lend a hand.

Finally he saw the station up ahead, an island of lights and concrete and painted-green pumps. He parked and climbed from the truck, and had taken his first steps inside the store when he noticed Juan missing from his stool behind the counter, replaced instead by a younger-looking boy with a nice shock of styled blond hair.

"I help you, man?"

"Is Juan around?"

The boy appeared confused. "Oh, you mean Mr. Marquez? Yeah, uh, no, he ain't here. You wanna leave a message or...?"

Travis shook his head, feeling somehow unnatural here in the store without the low, conspiratorial glee of Juan's laughter. "It's not important."

He handed over the ticket, the boy holding it to the scanner and a moment later the scanner beeped and the boy returned the slip, unimpressed.

"It's a stinker, dude," he said, wiping a little something from his eye. Then he waved absently at a gnat and asked, "You, uh, wanna ticket for tonight's drawing?"

"Yes," Travis told him. "Yes, I do." And as an afterthought: "Make it five."

"Got it, dude. Big spender here. Quick picks?"

"Excuse me?"

"Random numbers or you wanna choose?"

Travis considered. "Random."

"You want Mega Play or regular?"

"What's the difference?"

He cocked his head, as if reciting a well-known poem. "Mega Play increases your non-jackpot winnings, so if you only get a few numbers your prize money gets multiplied. Hit the jackpot, Mega Play means shit."

"How much extra?"

"Dollar."

Travis shrugged. Playing the lotto had never been his thing. "Mega Play it is."

He dropped ten Susie Bs on the counter and for a moment the boy only stared, uncomprehending. He picked one up, turning it in his fingers. "No offense, dude, but are these like... *legal tender?*"

"They're legal," Travis said. "Trust me."

§

Dinner was as expected, a southern banquet of Carolina rub BBQ and made-from-scratch biscuits and Theresa's famous Hot as Hell hickory beans. Travis did his best to act normal, because everything *was* normal, though of course nothing was normal and hadn't been for weeks, maybe longer. At quarter to nine he said his goodbyes, saddled the Toyota, and followed his headlights home.

Hours later he sat in the living room, the long slip listing his five tickets centered on the table before him. Next to this sat a half-empty bowl of buttered popcorn, a glass of milk. One cigar. He gazed at the television, waiting until at last he heard the first trills of corny music, saw the cheap set and baskets of turning balls. A well-dressed man with a funny-looking tie and skinny microphone stood grinning into the camera.

"All right, ladies and gentleman! Here they are, your winning Megaball numbers for the night! Let's get started!"

He watched as the first of the bubbling balls spun rattling to its slot, followed by a second, a third. He tensed, eyes dancing from ticket to screen, ticket to screen, until at last the final ball dropped and the man with the microphone belted a final number. Travis eyed the ticket, and when he looked next the man was gone and the local anchorwoman had breaking news, something about a high-speed chase over in Canonsburg.

Travis finished his milk.

§

Juan was back the next day, perched again on the same wobbly stool he'd been perched on for the last fifteen years and that Travis had noticed empty the day before. Also returned were the familiar murmurs of the police scanner, warbling away as he walked over and handed Juan the ticket.

"Lotto numbers, eh?" Juan offered a sly smile and said, "Whatsa matter, Travis, thought you didn't believe in all that. Was a waste of money, you said, remember? That you'd have better luck—what was it?—getting your face gnawed off by piranhas?"

"I know what I said."

"Oh?" Juan lifted the tickets. "So what's with these, wise guy?"

Travis shrugged. "Can't win unless you play."

"If truer words have been spoken, darling, then I haven't heard them. Let's see what we're cooking with here..." Juan leaned forward, holding the ticket to the scanner, Travis watching as the old man's eyes suddenly bulged in their sockets, a grin turning at the corners of his mouth. "Well, suck me sideways," he said. "What'd I tell ya? Easy as pie, huh, isn't that what I said? Looks like you just won yourself eighty bucks, hombre." He punched some buttons and the register clanged open and he reached inside, handed over the cash. "Must be your lucky day, eh?"

Travis stared at the bills, a part of him wanting to laugh at the absurdity of it all, an even larger part wanting to cry. Later he imagined that for one fleeting moment he'd been tempted to take the money and walk out, to shuck the whole crazy notion of cosmic luck and magic lotteries and go home and fiddle some more with his coins.

But Travis knew better—don't ask him how, but he did—and instead he only stared, feeling toyed with suddenly, feeling teased. It wasn't a feeling he liked. He glanced up, saw Juan frowning at him with tired puppy-dog eyes. The bills dangled between them.

"Well, you want the money or don't you? Go ahead, won't bite."

Travis waited, considering the question.

"Keep it," he said. "Give me tickets for the next drawing, as much as eighty dollars will buy."

"All eighty?"

"Every cent."

Juan nodded, an inspired gleam stealing into his eyes.

"Hell yes, son," he said. "Go big or go home, that's the

spirit." He tapped at the register. "You want quick picks?"

§

He waited.

Waited for the music to come shrilling from the television, for the man with the skinny microphone and Venus-colored ties to come grinning into his home. On the table, his tickets—forty of them printed on eight slips across the polished surface. A bowl of untouched popcorn, glass of untouched milk. And next to this: a yellow legal pad and pen resting neatly on top.

Occasionally Travis caught flashes of himself as if from above, floating and staring down at this arrangement, and couldn't help but wonder what sort of ominous commentary this was on his state of mind. Was this insanity? he wondered. Was it only a matter of time now before he went out and bought a couple hundred cats, put some rusty lawn mowers out front, started fooling around with homemade explosives? Left lollipops out for the kids?

Then the music, the cheap-looking set.

A basket of balls spinning, spinning, spinning.

"All right, America! Get ready! Here they are, tonight's winning Megaball numbers! Good luck to everyone!"

The balls bubbled and danced and dropped, Travis jotting the numbers one by one into his pad until—faintly—he heard the music, lonesome notes faraway and familiar and teasing beneath the television and—

Travis ignored it, pushed it away.

And that's when he jotted the final number into the pad.

He looked at what he'd written, staring as the numbers

donned an odd sort of significance, as if he were staring at the signature of God:

08   13   21   34   55   03

He reached down, lifting the first of the tickets and dragging a slow finger down the numbers, again and again until finally the music returned only different this time—*purer* somehow—and then everything went black and when he opened his eyes the room was smoky and his hands trembled like maracas.

He looked down, a half-smoked cigar burning in the tray. TV chattering on about wars and murder and robberies and then he stood and hurried down the hall, bursting like a man on fire into the bathroom.

He toppled clumsily over the toilet, groaning like death, head hung low as the sudden rush of vomit exploded out of him, pouring forth in a red-hot wave that burned even after it was gone and that left Travis sweaty and gasping for air on the tiled bathroom floor. He was still lying there sometime later when he closed his eyes and fell into a deep and dreamless sleep...

SEVEN

TARA REILLY BREATHED DEEP, IMPLORING HERSELF TO *take it easy, stay calm,* fingers dancing along the wheel of her battered old Mazda and beating a silent prayer to the gods. Nothing better than Raleigh gridlock, she thought, nothing better than wasting a few precious hours of her life; she was young, after all. She could take it.

Suddenly the heat was too much and she cracked a window, noticing as she did a pair of younger-looking guys—college kids, probably, both tanned, both good-looking—in a cherry Corvette the next lane over. Her stomach sank when she noticed them staring in her direction, beaming foolish school-boy grins from the safety of their over-priced sunglasses; now the grins grew wider as they offered a pair of little waves.

Tara flashed a smile from behind her own pair of overpriced sunnies before jangling a few fingers and looking away. She'd learned early it was best not to feed the bears and, based on her reflection in the rearview, these two here were on the south side of starving. When Tara left the house that morning, she'd looked—for lack of a better word—immaculate: her hair a flawless rain of silk, her make-up a work of art, clothes stylish and sassy-fun but casual enough for lunch with the gals.

That had been hours ago, however, and now she was hot, she was sweaty, her hair was an aftermath, and if she felt any more bloated she might try popping the buttons of her pants. Which made the idea of these handsome bozos in the next car fawning over her even more ridiculous, absurd. Was the male species really that depraved? Were they really *that* bad off?

Traffic inched forward and, passing the cherry Corvette, Tara glimpsed the boys inside, grinning like clowns, and then playfully puffed her lips and blew a kiss.

Later, studs...

She kept down the road, her trusty Mazda chugging along as she thought back on her long afternoon, about how glad she was for it to be over. She'd spent the day with old college friends, girls who for four magical years she'd leaned on and bickered with and loved. Their little tribe had broken more laws than Al Capone during their stint at Chapel Hill, indulging the sort of wild, careless mischief they'd still be dreaming of—and having nightmares about—well into their sixties.

The afternoon had started well enough, the four of them meeting at the Crabtree Valley Mall and indulging a spurt of shopping before lunch at P.F. Chang's. Oh how they'd laughed, doing girl-talk and trucking out old times and chattering away like monkeys as they traded stares, forming silent judgments on the women they'd become and were in the process of becoming.

But then they'd headed back to Laura's for some drinks, where they were joined by Laura's boyfriend...and Marybeth's husband...and, a little later, fresh from the office, Tessa's new fiancé, Rodrigo. Then for a couple hours Tara had listened patiently as if she had any interest whatsoever in traditional vs. contemporary wedding décor or the complexities of kick-ass wedding vows (not dripping sweet, but intimate enough for eternity).

Now—despite the traffic, despite the horny gawkers—Tara was grateful to be on the road. One more stop and she could spin this hood and head back home, and the closer she came to her destination the higher her blood pressure rose, her body humming and growing sticky-slimy with sweat.

The music blared, her fingers tapped.

After another twenty minutes of Raleigh gridlock, Tara parked the car.

She snatched her purse and reached inside, revealing a small rectangular card. RED WHITE & BLUE CASH the card said. TOP PRIZE $25,000! Her eyes floated to the grid of numbers, zeroing in on the slot marked $12,000 and then tipping to the vague fireworks symbol—it looked like hieroglyphics—which indicated a winner. Staring at this, Tara felt a sudden swell of hope, the first bit of it she'd felt in a long time.

In the worst moments of that afternoon she'd been tempted to blab her little secret, to shout it from the rooftops and steal the show if only for a little while. Twelve thousand dollars from a two-buck scratch-off, after all, was notable news indeed.

But then her grandmother had taught Tara a couple of things in life, and one of them was to never go talking about free money. In addition to this nugget of wisdom, Granny Reilly had espoused a general suspicion of the human race and in Tara's experience this, too, had never steered her wrong.

She climbed from the car and, turning south, spotted the Lottery Claim Center at the end of the lot, faded brick against a perfect blue sky. It was moments later, wrangling her hair into a careless side pony, that a sudden breeze came along and toppled her purse from the hood, spilling an instant mess of make-up and receipts and...

Tara's heart did a quick somersault as she spotted the winning scratch-off—*her* winning scratch-off—fluttering along the pavement.

Please, she begged, inching closer. *Please-no-no-no*

The card shivered once, twice, and then was gone, lifting like magic and flip-fluttering away on the breeze.

Tara lunged forward, giving chase as the ticket turned tricks through the air, skittering like a thing on a string across the asphalt and over into a small park set back off the lot. She was still crossing the pavement in that direction when she heard the squawk of bad brakes and froze in time to see an old work van slam to a stop, honk its horn, speed away.

When the van had passed Tara sprinted over, searching the grounds, finding nothing. She glanced around, the sun cutting her eyes despite the overpriced sunnies, and saw a mother spoon-feeding a baby in a stroller, a landscaper pulling weeds, a homeless man asleep in the shade. Minutes later her fear had turned to panic and still she searched, nails turned black with dirt as she dug under bushes and beneath wooden benches.

But it was no use, and she knew it.

The ticket was gone.

Mother nature, fate, destiny—call it what you will, but *something* had come along and served her a ripe bitch-slap to the face and now the scratch-off was lost—gone with the wind *ha-ha*—and she was out a cool twelve grand. Sad, yes, but also true. And though she hated, absolutely despised herself for doing it, Tara sniffled once, attempted to put a lid on it, and promptly burst into tears, burying herself in the safe, sweaty darkness of her palms.

"Excuse me? Hey, you okay down there?"

Dropping her hands, Tara glanced up and her first thought was simply that he was beautiful. Dusty brown hair, piercing blue eyes, the sort of five o'clock shadow she'd loved on a man since she was seventeen. He smiled and Tara was instantly self-conscious, wiping at her tear-soaked face.

"No, I'm fine, just..."

"Hurt? Need an ambulance?"

"*Noo*," Tara moaned, laughing, embarrassed, "I don't need an ambulance."

The man offered an easygoing smile, scratched at a perfect shock of silky brown hair and said, "Well, not trying to be nosy or anything but I, uh...think this might belong to you."

He raised a small card in one hand, crumpled, a little dirty.

Tara stared, not understanding; then it all came clicking together and she leapt to her feet, squealing laughter as she gripped the stranger in an awkward bear-hug embrace. He gave a laugh and scuttled back, handing over the scratch-off as she pulled away and stood staring at the card.

Tara glanced up and now the tears had returned, were threatening to spill over.

"*How did you...?*"

But the man only laughed and said, "It's no problem, really." He aimed a finger across the lot. "I saw what happened, couldn't help myself, honestly. Took me a little longer than I expected to find the thing, but..."

She looked at him, noticing the small scraps of paper on his shoulder, little blue ones and pink ones. Like tissue paper. "Where did you find it?"

He gestured to an area at the far corner of the park—farther than even she had searched. Farther than she'd thought to. "Patch of chickweed."

Of course, she thought, *the landscaper*.

Only up close, in a nice-fitting polo tucked into even better-fitting slacks, he was dressed nothing at all like a landscaper.

Not any landscaper *she'd* ever seen, anyway.

"Thank you," she said, meaning it.

Again he shrugged it away—*no biggie,* that shrug said, *happens all the time*—and nodded toward the Claim Center. "Better get in there before they close up shop," he told her. "I'm parked that way, I'd be happy to walk you?"

Tara smiled and said that would be fine.

They started over, the faded brick of the Claim Center looming in the distance. Only it wasn't the Claim Center Tara was thinking about. She was thinking how miserably sweaty she was, how ruined her make-up must look. She wasn't a vain person, but then neither did she get some thrill rocking the strung-out scarecrow look. They'd not walked far when he turned to her and said, "So I take it that ticket was pretty important to you, huh?"

"Just a little, yeah. What gave it away?"

He smiled, scratched at his head. "Call it a hunch."

"Call it what you want," she said, "but I work too damn hard to see that kind of cash pissed away in the wind."

He gave her an appraising look. "Let me guess...*truck driver*?"

"I'm a *nurse*, smartass."

"A nurse, of course. Should've known."

"Oh? And why's that?"

He thought about it. "You just have that look about you, is all."

"Which look is that?"

"Oh, you know...kind eyes, good heart, that sort of thing."

Tara felt herself blush. Had she the stones to tell him what she was really thinking, she would've said *You're full of shit, mister*. Tempting as this was, she only smiled politely and said in her most neutral voice, "I see."

"Do you work here in Raleigh or..."

"Greenville, actually."

"Pitt Memorial?" he asked, and when she nodded he grimaced and gave off a whistle. "Busy place."

"Fourth largest hospital in the state, so yeah, we stay on our feet. I mean, the best part of my day is *eating lunch* and half the time I don't even get to do that." She glanced at him casually. "Do you live in Greenville?"

"Me? No, no. Been through a time or two, though." A funny sort of light shone in his eyes. "You know, Ray Bradbury said if the world ended tomorrow all we'd need to rebuild were libraries and hospitals. One to care for the people's bodies and restore health, the other for the mind, to salvage a blueprint of society."

Tara felt something hot burst inside, sweeping over her in waves. She liked the sensation—or thought she did—and yet sensed a sudden apprehension, a warning flare of danger she'd encountered more than once after so many years in the dating game. She sensed herself squirming, didn't know what to do with her hands; instinctively they clenched, fingers digging into her palms.

When she looked next, a parade of well-dressed souls had moved out of the Claim Center, some lugging cameras as they shuffled down the broad concrete steps, a few of them looking over and waving. Seeing them, the man lifted a hand and returned the wave, baring a smile that in Tara's eyes could only be described as *forced*.

"Friends of yours?" As they watched, the herd moved toward a crowd of channel news vans, a few dropping into sedans.

He nodded. "Something like that."

A moment later they reached the parking lot, stopping at a pickup that was nice enough without being flashy, a couple dents and dings but otherwise in good condition. He climbed inside and started the engine, cranked down the window. On his neck, she spotted more of the colored tissue paper she'd noticed earlier.

"Thanks again for your help."

"Don't mention it," he told her. "That's just my way, lending a helping hand to damsels in distress, wherever they may be found."

"Still, I feel bad." An idea occurred to her then. "So how about a reward? How about fifty bucks and we'll call it—"

But he waved it away. "Keep your money. I appreciate the gesture, really, but my cup runneth over as it is."

"Wow, turning down fifty bucks. I didn't know that existed anymore."

"Guess there's a little wonder left in the world after all, huh?" He gave her a wink, popped the truck into gear. "Now what're you standing around for, get in there and cash that puppy." For a moment their eyes met, neither one looking away. "You take care of yourself."

Tara smiled shyly and offered a clumsy wave before continuing up the steps of the Claim Center. She was almost to the top when she looked back, noticed the truck motoring out of the lot and around the little park, off toward the Beltline. Watching him go, it occurred to her that, though she'd told him plenty about herself, he'd offered next to nothing concerning his own life: where he called home, what he did for a living. His marital status.

And then it hit her: *he was married.*

Seems everyone else in Raleigh was hitched or else on the fast-track to it—particularly folks she knew—and so why not? Sure, pretty wife, couple of kids. He was speeding home to them now, exhausted after a long day of carefree living and easy smiles and a little innocent flirting with the girl at the Claim Center to cap off the day.

Married, she thought. *Of course.*

Tara stared at the ticket, still not believing, still running blind fingers along the shape of her reality, then turned and hurried the rest of the way up the steps. By the time she arrived home to her little apartment it would be dark and, not for the first time that day, she wondered what it might be like to have someone waiting for her when she got there.

§

Travis gunned his pickup onto the Raleigh Beltline, unaware of the small whistles working like birdsong from his lips. In addition to the perpetual smell of Crayola crayons, the pickup boasted one other extra-special feature in its radio, which had never worked and was about as useless as a brick jammed into the dashboard. The silence had bothered him at first—seemed *unnatural*, somehow—but eventually Travis had come to appreciate this time alone with his thoughts; today he was particularly grateful, eager to unwind as he settled in for the long drive home and images from the past few hours floated in his mind.

He'd arrived at the Claim Center slightly before one p.m. He was only the seventh Megaball jackpot winner in the history of the Carolina Lottery and they'd certainly made a scene of it, cameras flashing and recording his every move, confetti flying. There was a nice young woman dressed in some sort of colorful dumpling outfit, just sort of laughing and wiggling around. Reporters from the local stations were there, and they'd asked him the usual questions.

How often do you play the lottery?

When did you find out you'd won?

And the million-dollar question: *What do you plan on doing with your winnings?*

Travis tried shooting it as straight as possible, with amendments here and there when it came to that. There was no mention of any coin collection, for example, just as there was no mention of the fact that this was every bit of his third time playing the lotto. He'd went a little crazy, he told them, had gambled hard. He'd gotten lucky. Shit happens.

He'd hoped to avoid such a circus altogether and claim the ticket anonymously, though the nice folks at the Lottery Headquarters had made it clear—in vaguely legal terms—there wasn't much of a snowball's chance in hell of *that* happening. And so he'd rolled with it and played nice and gave big smiles and at the end they'd presented him with an Acme-sized check for thirty million (he'd taken the lump sum, and so would be lucky indeed to see half of that).

As if affirming its existence, Travis glanced to the check propped snugly behind the seat. He noticed more of the blue-pink confetti resting like dandruff on his shoulders, brushed it off. Slowly, surely, his thoughts turned to the girl he'd met after leaving the Big Show. Nice enough girl, sweet. Smart. Real easy on the eyes, too. Not too often you catch all those things in one girl, but there she was. A guilty grin crossed his face as Travis remembered the stolen glances, the surreptitious stares.

Careful now, he warned. *If I didn't know better, I'd say you were smitten.*

Travis started to object, to shoot down that kind of thinking before it got started, only...

Only he couldn't.

Or wouldn't, it didn't matter which.

So all right, he'd liked her. Liked their jive, the easy way they'd talked. And, for the briefest of moments, that funny feeling of having wings, a momentary free fall in the otherwise fixed wheel of his existence. He'd never felt that way with anyone before, not that he could remember, and definitely not with anyone who smiled the way this girl had smiled.

Then it hit him.

This girl.

He didn't even know her name. Hell, here he was going on about some stranger and he didn't even know her name. He was crackers after all.

Still, crackers or not, talking to her had been the best part of his day. Which was saying a lot, considering he'd been handed an oversized check for thirty million dollars.

But had the feeling been reciprocated? Had she shown even the slightest interest beyond simple gratefulness for a winning scratch-off returned from the dead? Had she *dug* him?

Travis wasn't so sure and it occurred to him that it probably didn't matter, that she more than likely had a significant other anyway, some artsy-fartsy intellectual-type who played piano for homeless people.

Nice girls like that, they go fast.

Joel was waiting for him when he got back home. Off-duty this time, crouched on the front porch steps with a cold sixer of Bud at his heels. He walked over, lifting a beer from the pack and handing it over.

"So? How'd it go?"

"It went." Travis cracked open his beer, took a swig. "Now all I have to do is duck and cover, wait for this whole thing to blow over."

Joel was the only person he'd confided in about the ticket. Of course, as a stipulation (spelled *request*) of the Carolina Lottery, he'd done an interview with the local paper, forty minutes on a Thursday afternoon, with the story set to run tomorrow morning. Soon all of Pamlico County would know about his nifty little windfall.

"*Duck* and *cover*." Joel shook his head, perturbed. "One hell of a way for a man to live."

They stood awhile on the front steps, polishing off their beers as they stared at a thousand and one stars twinkling overhead. Travis reported on his wild afternoon at the Claim Center: about being filmed for posterity and doused with confetti, and the wiggling girl in the dumpling outfit. He went to the truck and lugged out the oversized check, making fun with it, running around the yard and brandishing it like a pro wrestler with a ringside chair.

"Thirty million," Joel said, giving a whistle. "That's quite a nest egg, my friend. Who needs a 401(k) with that hairy ape in your bank account? What's that look like after taxes?"

"Take-home, quoted figure was in the neighborhood of thirteen million."

"Oh, you poor thing."

Travis shrugged. "It's basically like I never won."

"Yeah, yeah. Must be another of nature's cruel jokes, huh? First those girlish good looks, now this. Y'know, you could be a regular Hugh Hefner if you'd pull your nose out of all those books you're all the time reading, actually got out a little. Speaking of, when you gettin' a new place?"

Travis gulped more of his beer, wiped his mouth.

"What's wrong with this one?"

Joel blinked. "You're shittin' me."

"What, now I gotta go out and buy a new place? I mean,

this house is paid off. I grew up in this house. Why move out?"

At this Joel tottered backwards, a man struck blind.

"Why? *Why?* Because you owe it to your *mother* to move out of this roach crypt. She won the lottery, you think she'd hung around waiting for the floors to fall in? No, she'd have moved out, she'd have built the biggest damn house on the block, and she'd have loved every minute of doing it." A grave expression came over his face. "Travis, I will *kidnap* and *murder* you if you don't get out of this heap."

"I don't know, Joel. This place has...sentimental value."

"*Sent*imental *value?*"

"I'm serious."

"No, no. Something's off with you. You're acting weird."

Travis stared at the ground, shaking his head. "I don't know what you're talking about."

"Wait a minute, wait." A sudden light in his eyes. "You met somebody."

"No."

Joel giggled, wagging a finger back and forth. "You *did*. You actually met somebody, I can't believe it. Congratulations, looks like that lotto's already working its magic. Was it the dumpling chick?"

"What? Joel, no."

"What's her name?"

He wanted to laugh, couldn't. "That's actually kind of a... sore subject."

"Well, is there anything you *can* tell me about this mystery chick?"

"Such as?"

"Such as, where'd you meet her, numb nuts?"

So he shared what happened outside the Claim Center: about watching from his pickup as the scratch-off was taken by the wind, about meeting his so-called mystery chick, chatting. Joel listened with near rapt amusement, a kid at a drive-in movie.

"She pretty?"

"Yeah, she was pretty, Joel. Which means she's probably somebody's girlfriend—hell, probably she's *married*."

"Get that vibe?"

Travis considered. "Not exactly, no. But who knows? Maybe she was just being nice. Maybe she was just happy I found her ticket. Doesn't matter. I've got enough on my plate without worrying about some girl I met once in my life."

Joel looked at him, a slow grin creeping into his face. "You're so full of doodoo it's coming out your mouth."

Travis swallowed the last of his beer and said nothing.

§

His company gone for the night, Travis showered and had some salmon leftover from the night before. He ate alone in the kitchen, his oversized check propped like a surfboard against the old refrigerator, a copy of *'Salem's Lot* spread on the table before him. The house hummed and creaked around him as Travis munched his food, finished, and sat for another hour combing the streets of a bloodsucker-infested New England town.

Afterwards he staggered down the hall, collapsing into bed, warm beneath his covers but not quite able to roll over and shut his eyes. As the image of pale-faced vampires scratching balefully at bedroom windows faded from his mind, the reality of his situation hit him all over again—and again, he felt utterly overwhelmed. As Chuck Sanders at the Carolina Lottery had told him that afternoon: there is no owner's manual for winning the lottery. And that much was true; the history of the lotto was littered with tragic tales of some lucky duck's swift descent from top of the world to bottom of the barrel to, at last, an efficient dismantling of everything once held dear: cash comes in, sanity goes out.

Most of all, though, he worried the winnings would make him even more alone than he already was. As a child, he remembered his mother warning him about what she called the "deceitfulness of riches" and, though he'd always listened out of respect (and with a bored-to-death expression on his face), he now found himself recalling their conversations with renewed interest.

Not surprisingly, there wasn't much to recall.

Not that it mattered. He wasn't a child anymore, and he didn't need his mother to outline the basics of human nature any more than he needed her to take his temperature or brush his teeth at night. He realized that money had a way of changing things—relationships, attitudes, even tastes—and he wanted no part of it. The delicate sneaky-snake allure of power, of prestige, of hobnobbing in glamour-filled sandcastles in the sky—it was a slippery slope indeed, and Travis had no plans to brave it.

He would live well, yes, and help others, sure, but one thing was clear from the outset: there would be no private planes, no collection of classic cars in a storehouse in the Midwest. He would purchase no orangutans, nor bathe with his own harem of dugongs. Stay simple, he thought, that's the key.

Which left only one unresolved issue in Travis's mind.

Lying in the darkness of his childhood room, he stared at the ceiling and asked himself the one question money could never answer: what did he *really* want from this life? When cash was no issue and he had all the time in the world, what was the *one thing* that would fulfill him as nothing else could?

His immediate thought was simple: finding love. No dollar-sign amount could ever compare with that. Of course—barring a cupid's arrow—neither was this something he could force. Which left only one thing. The only thing that in his mind and limited scope could lend true meaning and purpose to his life.

He wanted to write a novel.

EIGHT

Lowell, MA

2010

JUDGING FROM THE VARIOUS POSTERS ALONG THE walls of his Chelmsford Street apartment, Craig Donovan might well have been some Hollywood expatriate softly crying out for home. Encased behind glass and with frames much too ornate for such transient fare, the films represented were blaring testimonies of technology run amok. Action flicks mostly, the majority of them the sort of muscle-bound machismo Drexl Samson enjoyed himself. Of course, his passions ran more in the way of Bruce Willis and King Ahnuld than that of the spandex crowd displayed here: mutants and space rangers and debonair rich men with toys.

Call him crazy, but he preferred his heroes minus the

tights and codpiece free.

He strolled to the bedroom, seizing from a shelf the foot-tall model of a creature who looked neither alive nor completely dead. Long scowl of teeth, ropes of drool slavering from a ridiculously unhinged jaw. Slimy serpentine tongue. VENOM said the plate on the weighted base.

Drexl returned the model to the shelf and let out a breath.

He'd been meticulous this time. Apartments were always tricky, with no shortage of eyes or ears to spoil the fun. But then Drexl knew that what you lost in privacy, you gained many times over in both anonymity and apathy. In sewers like this mum was the word and the ones who lived well were the ones who kept their noses to themselves and didn't go around inserting them where they didn't belong. That would work in his favor.

Of course, Drexl knew something none of these nice neighbors were aware of, which was that—despite his slovenly appearance—Craig Donovan was actually doing all right for himself, was a nationally-recognized *Magic* champion and reigning badass of the Horde. He was awkward socially and often ridiculed, and he had close to three million dollars stashed away in a bank account soon to be made void—honest money, rightfully his, though he would likely be shy to explain how that had come to be.

Worst part of it was, after nine hours of sitting around Donovan's apartment, gobbling nachos and chicken wings and reading his massive collection of hero comics, Drexl had actually started to, well...*like* the kid.

Part of it was pity. Sure, he admitted it.

And while this wasn't the first time he'd felt such emotion

toward a mark, neither was such emotion very common, not anymore. But this was more than pity. Kiss his ass, but he actually *cared* about the little twerp. As a young man Drexl knew what it was like to be counted out, ridiculed. To want nothing more than to go and lock yourself away in a world of your own making, or else live in those others had created. As an agent of the Bureau this tendency had served him well, giving him precisely the sort of cold-blooded detachment the intelligence community required.

What troubled him most was the knowledge that for Craig Donovan this was, unfortunately, the end of the line. There would be no denouement to his life, and certainly no next chapter, and that saddened Drexl in a way he did not understand.

He went to Craig's small bed and climbed on top. Crawled beneath the covers. Snuggling. Earlier he'd come across the boy's Iron Man getup in the closet and slipped inside, posing in the mirror and imagining he was a superhero from some other galaxy. Only an hour later, paging through the comics, did he learn that Tony Stark was very much human. Even so, standing there with his large thighs stretching the fabric and his face sweating inside the helmet, Drexl couldn't help but wonder if he wasn't getting bored with the job. Now here he was getting cozy under the damned Ninja Turtle covers, and he found himself wondering it all over again.

He'd almost drifted off when he opened his eyes, sat up.

He took a deep breath, waiting, and moments later when his phone buzzed, Drexl grinned and answered the call.

"How long?"

"Twenty minutes." Her voice, so smoky, so sexy this hour

of morning. "And Drexl?"

"Yes?"

"Drexl?"

Drexl lowered the phone. Looked around the room—at the posters, at the collection of comic books and anime and Transformers still mint in their packages. Last of all he looked to the trophies, each gleaming like the golden shields of Valhalla. He put the phone to his ear.

"I'm here, Lola."

"*Focus.*"

The phone went cold.

Drexl pulled himself from the covers and sat on the edge of the bed. He noticed more comics on the floor and picked up a Marvel *Two-in-One* from back in '77, Spidey hoisted high over Thanos's head.

When Lola first phoned him with the assignment, Drexl would've sworn it next to impossible to so much as comprehend what these comics *meant*, much less admire them. All he knew of such fare he'd learned from Freddy Glass, but old Freddy was dumb as a bag of snot and oftentimes drooled, and somehow as far as comics went Drexl had never caught the bug, never really *got it*.

Craig Donovan had helped him *get it*, and for that he loved the boy.

Drexl dropped the comic, standing to his feet. Fifteen minutes later when the key came rattling at the lock, he was waiting at the small dinette set in the alcove off the kitchen. He listened as Craig entered and shut the door, slipping out of his jacket and turning the locks over heavy breathing. A light came on, the squeak of a swivel chair. The whir of a computer booting up.

Drexl let out a breath. Was the kid really doing this? He'd wanted to give him more credit than that. But then the expectations of the twenty-first century, he admitted, were well beyond his scope of understanding. He sat waiting in the alcove darkness until at last he sensed the touch of Lola's lips on his ear, smelled the cool rush of peppermint breath as she whispered her singular warning:

Focus.

Drexl rose silently to his feet, sweeping around the corner to find Craig perched at his computer. Closer still, and now the image of a tattooed couple appeared on the screen, a biker chick going reverse-cowgirl on some grease stud. Craig stared at the image, absorbed, a pair of moaning headphones slipped crookedly over his ears.

Drexl let out a breath all over again.

He reached over and tapped the boy's shoulder and Craig Donovan leapt out of his seat, headphones flipping from his ears as he twisted to the floor.

"Get up," Drexl said. "On your feet."

The boy gaped back in horror, mouth jawing mechanically as he did a quick crab-walk away from Drexl, away from the computer. "What—what are you doing?" He couldn't get the words out fast enough. "The fuck, man, haven't you heard of *knocking?*"

"Craig, get on your feet. Come on. Playtime's over."

Drexl reached over, seizing the computer mouse and stopping the biker-girl's moans with a click.

"What the hell, man—what are you *doing* here, huh?" Craig stood and began pacing in the kitchen, trying to catch hold of himself. "Agent Agnew said that was it, said I was *done*. She told me it was *over*."

Drexl gestured to the dinette table. "Craig, sit down."

"No." Still pacing, back and forth. Like his head would explode. "And where's your partner, huh? Mr. Needles? He hiding out in the clothes hamper or something? Should I stay out of the closets?"

"Couldn't stick around. Said he had to go and see a man about a mule. Craig?"

Craig looked at him.

"*Sit down.*"

And this time Craig listened and stopped pacing and, slowly by slowly, picked his way to the alcove.

"So what is this?" he huffed, settling into a chair. "I mean, I did my part, I sang the fucking song, you got what you wanted. So what the hell?"

Drexl walked over, took a seat. Spread his long too-thick fingers across the table, struggling with how to proceed. For the first time, he thought his hands—webbed and cracked by this ugly New England weather—actually looked old. Ancient, almost.

He said, "Craig, I'm here to kill you."

A look of sheer astonishment swept over Craig Donovan's eyes. He blinked, shook his head. "Wait...*what?*"

"It's true."

He seemed at a loss for words. "*Kill* me? *How?*"

"Well, I was gonna...come up on you from behind there." He reached down, revealing the narrow rope that for the last few hours had been burning a hole in his pocket. "Use this line here to make it look like you accidentally offed yourself."

He gestured to the computer, the screen blaring a close-up of some unknown orifice. To Drexl, it looked like something you'd find on the floor of a meat factory. "You know, strung yourself up. Autoerotic asphyxiation."

Craig stared at him, an almost pained expression dawning over his face. "How dare you."

Drexl shrugged. "My apologies." He slipped away the rope and said, "Watching strangers screw for the fun of it. My, I'd call that a hop, skip and a jump from a normal relationship, but hey, that's okay. Whatever floats your boat."

"Wait, wait, lemme get this straight. You come here, whisk me away for a little magical mystery tour and then bring me back to—to—what? *Murder* me?"

"If that's the way you want to put it. Yes."

"But now you're not."

Drexl stared at the boy, his black eyes full of some mystery beyond comprehending. After what seemed a very long time he reached inside his jacket, revealing a short club-looking stone with a sharp rounded top and placing it on the table between them. "I've been carrying this for a while now," he said. "As a reminder, I guess you'd say. A *remembrance of former times*."

Craig stared at the smooth green rock, taken by it's simple but crude insinuation of brutality. "What is it?"

"It's a weapon, Craig. A *mere*, the most revered of all Maori weapons. To the Maori, the mere is a symbol of authority, *chieftainship*. Done proper, it could take a craftsman forty, fifty years to whip one of these bad boys up. Some were made from wood, or bone, but the best—the *mere pounamu*—were made of nephrite jade. Tougher, harder. Less likely to fracture." Drexl hefted the object, gave it an adoring stare. "And this...this is one of the best. Check that flawless greenstone. Perfect jade, see the way it shines?" He turned it in the light, back and forth. "See that? That glow?"

As Craig watched, a distant gaze crept over Drexl's face, his dark eyes shown purple in the weapon's bright emerald glare. He smiled, as if remembering a favorite childhood memory. "Some believe the mere holds a kind of...kind of life-force, a *mana* all to itself. Something that grows, gets stronger down generations. Personally I think it's bullshit, that's just me. But I've worked with all sorts of weapons over the years—and the mere? The mere is my favorite. Legend has it, you know what you're doing and with a slight flick of the wrist, you can rend a skull easy as pie. Split it wide open."

Craig swallowed. "Have you ever..."

Drexl pulled a smoke and lit it. Blew clouds across the table.

"Once," he said. "Was playing around, caught this guy just right. Damn! Was like the bastard's whole *head* just came apart and everything came spilling out—blood, brains, everything. I remember the room got cooler when it happened. Like I'd opened up something in him and let all that cold air out."

The boy appeared depressed. "Thanks for that."

"But like I said, the mere was the most revered of the Maori weapons—hell, even *losing* the old rock was a sign of bad luck. But listen, did you know, a Maori chief would rather be killed by his own mere than give his life to another weapon? A less honorable weapon?"

Craig nodded slowly, not understanding. "And you're telling me this because..."

Drexl stared at him. "Craig, I like you. You remind me a bit of myself, and well..." He waved it away. "Listen, son, after tonight, it's done. No more. I've been ordered to exterminate you and I intend to do just that, and there's nothing you can do to change it. I'm sorry."

Craig tried to stand, couldn't make it. He said, "You're out there, man. I mean it, you're over the fucking *moon*..."

"You can't change it but there is something you can do, which is take the high road, Craig. You can *choose* your own exit, do it on your own terms. Same as any true warrior would do." He leaned forward, as if imparting some great secret. "*You can use your own mere.*"

"*Use my own*...shit, man, I don't even know what that *means*..."

Drexl removed a small box from his shirt pocket, placing it on the table.

Leaning close, Craig Donovan saw that it was a box of razorblades. Big bastards, too.

He gave the boy a long hard stare and said, "The things you've seen, everything that's happened tonight...did you really think we'd let it end there? Some random nobody strolling around with that type of sensitive material knocking around upstairs?" Drexl stubbed his cigarette into a makeshift tray, tucked it away. He tittered, brushing a hand toward nothing at all. "Hell, the whole story'd wind up in one of these damned comic books one day."

"So you have to—what? Wipe me out? And for what exactly? *National security?*"

Drexl said nothing. Just stared back with those endless black eyes, his pupils swirling, waiting for Craig to at long last consider his options, open his fucking eyes, and accept the inevitable. Not the easiest thing in the world to do, sure, especially for a kid right out of diapers, but then it was a sad fact of life that tragedy never made appointments, and more often than not the shit blossomed right under our noses. Besides, beyond the boy's Peter Pan exterior, Drexl sensed a certain quiet strength in Craig Donovan. He hoped his instincts proved him right.

Craig stood to his feet. "I'm calling the cops."

He started for the kitchen, more in disbelief than any sense of urgency, and Drexl rattled out a breath and curtly swooped in, his two massive hands collapsing over the young man's neck. A simple twist, side-step and thrust, and Craig went sprawling to the bruised linoleum floor.

"I thought better of you than that," Drexl said. "Have you no shame?"

"*Shame!*" the boy screamed. His face crinkled, boiling over with rage and incredulity and fear. "I don't wanna die a *virgin*, how's that for *shame?* I've got my whole life ahead of me you *stupid fucking moron!*"

He was getting loud now. Too loud. He kept on and Drexl would have to shut that down.

"Nobody wants to die, son," he said, his voice nice and soft, what Drexl thought of as his baby-talk voice. "But there comes a time when it happens, no matter how much we fight for it not to. What you don't seem to understand is that *this is your time*. There is no more life for you. That's over, it's done. Come on, stand up."

Drexl reached down, helping him to his feet and over to the chair. Sat him down and plopped the box of blades on the table before him. Craig dropped his head and began to weep, weeping as Drexl had seen men weep so many, many times before.

"No, no," he said. "No, now. None of that. No tears. No sorrow. Head held high as you rise to meet your fate."

"*Pleeease,*" Craig sobbed, "*please noo...I'll do anything...*"

"Focus, Craig. Do the honorable thing. Don't succumb to the lesser emotion of fear." He reached over, lifting the box and removing one of the blades, holding it out. "Go on," he said. "Take it."

Reluctantly, the boy reached out with one shaking hand and took the blade.

"You are going on a journey," Drexl told him. "An escape into the unknown. Soon the last sacred ounce of life will seep from your body and in that moment, in the twinkling of an eye, you will know answers to questions that have plagued mankind since the beginning of time." He gave a magical flourish of his fingers. "Existence will be bared and you will be one with its secrets. And look at yourself. What are you doing? Bawling like a baby."

"*I'm not...*" Still with the sobs. "*...not ready...*"

"Every minute of every day, we're ready. A great chief once said, *there is no death, only a change of worlds*. Do it, Craig. Make the change."

"And if I don't?"

Drexl hesitated. The darkness flared in his eyes, the oily blackness of it consuming his face. He said, "*You will.*"

Craig looked away, the boy's face now blushed and ruined with tears. Moving slowly, he reached forward and carefully picked up the razorblade from where he'd dropped it on the table. He was still holding it, the massive blade catching the light and spinning reflections, when he looked up and said, "I've written down everything. Recorded it all, ever since the beginning. Somebody'll find it."

"I know you did, on your laptop. File name *Lucky Stars*. I deleted it."

"So you're a hacker now."

"I wear many hats."

"I also saved it online. Cloud-based. It's out there."

Drexl exhaled. He was losing patience. "Now you're just lying."

Craig was making some sort of noise. Something between a growl and a whine and a heart-attack wheeze. He wiped his face as the tears poured down, sobbing, struggling to somehow pull himself together. Only there was no pulling himself together, not by a long shot, and if the boy didn't know it before then he damn sure knew it now. Drexl could see that, and knew that soon Craig Donovan would give up, would accept his fate and be shed of this mortal coil. And for the briefest of moments Drexl sensed a strange emotion welling up inside, swirling up and down and all around. Then he realized what it was.

Envy.

He put a hand on Craig's shoulder. "It's time."

The boy puffed out his chest, trying to be brave but not knowing how. Taken by some notion, he jerked the razorblade to his wrist, applied its edge to tender flesh. He was breathing harder now, panting almost. *In and oouuut, in and oouuut.* Sobbing despite himself, he pressed down hard on the blade and the first rose of blood burped from his skin.

"Cut down," Drexl instructed. "Never across. You'll bleed faster that way, sever more wires."

Craig was shaking now.

Trying to concentrate, steel himself. He was a big boy, that look said, and he was going to prove it. He huffed and puffed and made a face and then he opened his mouth and vomited onto the floor, the stink of it filling the small alcove and bringing water to Drexl's eyes.

Drexl cursed and moved around the table, watching as Craig wiped his mouth and groaned and leaned back in his chair.

"*I can't do it,*" he said, bubbling. "*I can't—*"

Drexl snatched the razorblade and buried it in the boy's wrist.

A dark gout of blood gushed into the air, splashing Drexl's face and seeping into his eyes, slipping down his cheek. He tugged at the blade, jagging a crude line from wrist to elbow until at last the boy found his voice and screamed and Drexl stuffed two fat fingers into the boy's mouth, probing into the soft flesh of the mandible. Holding a person like that was akin to having them on a leash, and as Craig writhed and squirmed Drexl drove harder on the blade, getting into it now, pressing down, putting his weight into it. Blood jetted and sluiced, pooling across the table.

Moments later a glassy distance fell over the kid's eyes as, slowly by slowly, his mania was replaced by a creeping lethargy. This was it, Drexl knew, the tipping point, that crucial moment in the great balance of existence when death became greater than life.

He did not waste a moment; lifting the blade, Drexl moved

quickly to Craig's other arm and dug in, not so much slicing as sawing his way down. Ripping, rending, tearing. As he did so, Craig suddenly lifted his head, looked Drexl Samson in the eye...and *laughed*. A softly soothing giggle that didn't seem quite right coming from his mouth. No sooner had it come than the laughter faded, the boy's eyes sinking away to ice.

His body slumped.

Drexl stood, watching as consciousness slipped away and blood pooled across the table, dripping to the floor. Arterial, by the looks of it, which meant he'd dug wide and death would come sooner rather than later. Already the kid's body was rolling through the various stages of cardiac arrhythmia, severe hypovolemia, shock. Circulatory collapse would come next, followed by cardiac arrest.

Abandoning the blade inside the boy's arm, Drexl stepped around the vomit and ran a brief hand through Craig's curly red hair. He should've known better than to offer a finer way, a higher path, to offer any sort of honor in death. The living were interested only in life: had he expected anything different? Had he expected young Craig Donovan to somehow see through the veil of fear and into the perfect beauty that lay on the other side, the perfect beauty of being forgotten by the universe? Of embracing oblivion and forfeiting the knowledge of oneself? Of forgetting *to be?*

He backed away, watching as the blood rolled like warm jelly across the table. The puddle had slid within inches of his mere when Drexl snatched it up, tucking the smooth clubstone back inside his jacket and then reaching around, revealing a single piece of paper with Craig Donovan's signature at the bottom. As his mentor Roland Garrett had taught him, the first rule of killing was to always have a backup plan, an insurance policy, and damn if that two-cent worth hadn't come in handy tonight. *Parting is such sweet sorrow*, he thought, and walked to the small bedroom and unfolded the paper and dropped it on the bed. Removed a camera and snapped a picture of the letter on the Ninja Turtles bedspread.

Snapped another, another.

He stood staring through the lens of the camera, staring at the bed, struck by the fact that Craig Donovan would never sleep there again. Then it was too much and he pulled away, dropping the camera from his eye and walking out of the room. He made his way down the hall and was approaching the alcove when he felt it, like a potent cloud around the table. Somehow he'd grown accustomed to this sensation—it was hard not to, in his line of work —but he'd never gotten comfortable with it. *Death*. The sudden subtle absence of life and warmth. That odd chill in the air that only happens as emptiness settles over the human soul. Truth was, if he thought about it enough, that damn chill kind of spooked him...

Time to move.

He clicked away with the camera, capturing images of a deathly pale Craig Donovan with his arms ravaged open and head slumped down over the table, hair greased with blood. He'd almost finished with the pictures when the silence was too much and he walked over, unplugging the headphones from the speakers and clicking at the mouse, filling the walls with the loud cacophony of intercourse. Two people coming together in the greatest union mankind had yet to offer. Someday that union would be usurped by another, Drexl thought, which was the literal meeting of two or more souls into one.

How it would happen or when he didn't know, though he believed it had something to do with death and with death's presence in the vast reaches of space. In those zones the scientific mind had not thought to explore but that the mystical had failed to exploit. A vast wilderness untouched by love or pain. An emptiness waiting to be filled.

A paradise...

He'd started for the door when he stopped suddenly, eyes catching on another of those silly Club America jackets which had recently become so popular with the Lodge boys. Why Our Fearless Leaders had decided on such a fashionable blessing as a gussied-up sport coat, he'd never know.

But then neither did he much care.

He slipped it from the hook by the door, folding it over his arm, as he had folded all the others like it, and minutes later when the endless moans had faded and the room fell silent once more, Drexl Samson was no longer there.

NINE

N THE WEEKS FOLLOWING HIS AFTERNOON AT THE Claim Center, Travis noticed a curious rise in the number of guests he had over to the house.

Old friends dropping by to welcome him home, though he'd been home for months, asking about the Navy and life overseas and how the hell he'd been. Former gal pals knocking at his door with shy smiles and tight outfits and, more often than not, some sort of offer: dinner, lunch, a movie sometime. He'd even had a few strangers come knocking, though if you believed the way they told it they were actually distant cousins, kindergarten pals, or "friends" of his mother's.

Those usually got a door in the face.

The others he entertained with a patient sort of skepticism, waiting to see who mentioned the lottery and who didn't. Those who didn't he invited into the kitchen, where the giant novelty check still sat propped against the fridge. THIRTY MILLION DOLLARS, right there in big bold capitals. Even then some simply averted their eyes, as if that side of the house didn't exist, chattering on about *how long* it had been and *how nice* it was to have him back home.

Entertaining enough at first, this revolving-door routine quickly grew tiresome and, for the first time, Travis found himself considering Joel's advice about a new place. As it was, he sat smack dab in the middle of a rough-hewn block in Pinedale with every resident of Pamlico County itching for some excuse to stop over and chat. And the house, though full of tasty memories of growing up, was—let's face it—*el dumpo*.

Travis thought a new homestead would come in handy in one other way, as well—that is, as a getaway for the spirit. A haven to seclude himself while he got in touch with his inner swango. The desire to become a novelist—to find "the truth inside the lie" as one writer put it—came as no surprise to Travis, despite the fact his greatest claim to literary fame was the single word GARGANTUAN painted neon pretty on a brick wall.

He'd considered what kind of story he wanted to write, and though nothing had stuck it felt good to sift the kernels of ideas, squeezing them like supple fruit to see which was ripe. Whatever his decision, he was determined not to rush himself. Unlike professional authors who pounded the keys for a living, this was not a job for Travis, wasn't about making money or even being published; this was a *search* for something—laughable, but true—a search for whatever truth he had buried deep inside himself. *I write to discover what I know*, said Flannery O'Connor, and Travis couldn't agree more. He wanted to pull out that fossil of meaning and examine it, prod and study it, and if it so happened someone out there wanted to publish the results, then great.

Even better.

In the meantime he occupied himself in other ways: built a patio table and two benches to go with it, learned some new recipes. He was contemplating an addiction to those snazzy Sudoku puzzles when a better idea presented itself. Since he was a child, Travis had always dreamed of having a pet he could call his own, a loyal friend that followed wherever he went and who came running when he got off the bus; his mother hadn't shared his dream, however, and neither had the United States Navy.

Now none of those people mattered.

And though he'd dropped in on a couple different shelters before finding the right match, as far as Travis was concerned it had been well worth the wait. Gage was a Boykin Spaniel with long frizzy ears and swishy brown hair like a rock star from ages past. They'd met and played for ten minutes in the shelter's backyard, though it took only two of those for Travis to make up his mind; he'd driven home with the Boykin perched in the Crayola-flavored cab, head slung out the window or else nested quaintly on his leg.

From then on they'd taken up like old friends, Gage greeting him every morning with a series of sneezes and sloppy kisses, nuzzling his hands as Travis picked through a book or, later, tapped away at his laptop. They'd picked up jogging that fall, sometimes around the block but usually in parts more remote, someplace he and Gage—and Joel, occasionally—could escape the madness of it all, pretend it never was.

Of all escapes their favorite was the woods outside Silver

Hill, winding trails that offered a good nature walk with the occasional scenic view. He'd trained Gage to sit and roll over up there, and to play dead, and there was a lake farther back where they played fetch in the water. As the sturdy-looking woman at the shelter had informed him, Boykins are active dogs and need constant exercise—and, as far as Gage went, Travis intended to give it to him.

Today they'd come not only to bask in the weather—highs in the eighties, a luxury this late in the fall—but also in hopes of squeezing in one last run before the official death of summertime. Together they braved the wilderness, the golden warmth of the sun spilling through the pines as Travis turned his calves to fire and gunned it full throttle, pushing faster, Gage either rushing ahead or bounding up not far behind. They were drawing near the end of their latest sprint when the trail opened and Travis saw the lake just ahead, its smooth surface a near-perfect reflection of the world above.

Following a quick round of fetch in the water, a sopping-wet Gage went sniffing through the brush as Travis took a seat on the bank. He reached down in his pocket and retrieved the coin he'd put there that morning, as well as every morning before that. A Morgan silver dollar—the only remaining piece of his collection, though he wasn't sure why he'd held on to that one, exactly, or kept any for himself at all. *A memento*, he supposed.

A memento of a miracle...

Only it had actually turned out to be more of a first fruits.

He held up the coin, measuring it against the sun. The coin blotting and then unblotting the light, an eclipse on-demand. Moments later he climbed to his feet and, flipping the coin as he went, started along the bank, heading south and hopefully out of the worst of the afternoon's heat. He wasn't feeling right suddenly and wondered if the sun had anything to do with it, if the heat was getting to him. Glimpsing Gage farther down the bank, Travis turned and saw the brooding, almost feral gleam in the young dog's eyes; he walked over, brushing a tender hand over his head.

"Gage? Okay, buddy?"

But Gage wasn't okay, and Travis was beginning to think that neither was he. Thought that maybe he should pop a squat, cool his heels awhile. That last leg of their run had been a long one—brutal, actually—and now his head felt like a microwave, like he was cooking his own brain inside. That sounded crazy, he knew it did, but that's how it felt: like a microwave cooking away at his brain. He worried he might be coming down with something, getting a migraine. A tumor maybe, some big sweaty bastard right behind his eye.

Though normally discomfited by the thought of pulsing tumors in his head, today Travis only grinned, giving over to it now and letting the feeling carry him, a soft euphoria made all the stronger as the first familiar notes of that dark melody came haunting through the pines; his mouth parted, the words flowing smooth as silk from his lips—*nyeh-katuh-nayuh-fa-elstro-laecopa*—a nonsense phrase that meant more to him than he could reasonably explain. The birds cheeped and twittered, and were one with the song; trees bobbed, dancing to the movement. His voice a lonesome call over the water as the song poured out of him: a meditation. A private incantation to the sky. He thought of his dead mother, of his father who seemed even more dead. He thought of the life he'd been handed and the world he lived it in. He thought about problems that had no solutions, and some things that mattered and many that didn't. Reckless notions whirring and tumbling until finally it was as if some magical white glove reached in and turned down the volume of his own head, silencing the clutter, and in the vacuum that followed something was broken in himself—some shy and vulnerable part shattered to fragments and Travis knew he'd reached that other place, that mental free-fly zone where one questioned the basics and where the center could not hold. For an endless moment he stood wondering what might happen next—*needing* to know it, needing it to hurry up and fucking *happen* or he'd bust open inside…

It came from across the lake, the house appearing there like a ghost-manor along the pines at the other side. He stared, mesmerized at the house's existence—a big colonial-style, double-storied with a fancy balcony jutting out up top—even more mesmerized by the girl skip-dancing toward him now along the eastern shore. Sixish, big brown eyes and coffee-colored hair done up in ribbons…although somewhat *out of place*, Travis thought, way back here alone in these woods.

Only then the girl wasn't alone as a second figure appeared up the bank, Travis's heart racing as he realized who it was, as he stared into her face and was lost in those deep almond eyes. The ribbon-haired girl ran to her, the two of them sharing laughter and drinking freely of their joy as the woman snatched her up and gave a twirl, spinning round and round.

He watched it all with an obscene wonder, allowing the smallest of grins but knowing he was as alone on this far-away lake as he'd been half an hour before, no matter what fantasies his eyes described. The woman—that is, the girl whose name he still didn't know—pulled her daughter close, swaying gently, and following her gaze he noticed a shadow limping now across the elegant lake house balcony. Then that shadow took form and became flesh and Travis saw two bright eyes and the dark shading of a beard fitted mask-like over the bottom half of his face and...

And realized it was him.

Travis gazed on this gossamer image of himself—older maybe, a little thicker in the gut and with a world-weary stare, but *him*—heart bouncing like a gone-wild bull at the center of his chest. He shut his eyes, opened them; his doppelganger stared into nothing and sipped coffee from an oversized mug. And in the reaches of his mind Travis still heard the music, that distant dark melody running a loop through his soul.

He'd started closer through the trees when the woman turned, glancing back as if hearing him for the first time, her eyes glinting in the noonday sun. In a moment that existed outside of time, their stares met and he was swallowed whole, lost irrevocably in her eyes—and his knees suddenly buckled, pitching him forward in an awkward collapse. His forehead thwacked the earth, slamming hard against the twisted root of a nearby oak and—

And then only pain, a sudden crackling bolt that chilled his bones and covered him in darkness. Sometime later—how long, he couldn't be sure—the darkness broke and Travis opened his eyes on the chasm of a perfect starlit night, Gage trotting over and lapping a warm, too-heavy tongue across his face.

He sat up, one hand clutching his aching head as he fought back the frenzied notion of finding and talking to her, of saying all the things he'd been too chickenshit to say before. But it was no use and he knew it, because they were gone: the big house, the skipping girl in ribbons…and *him*, that shadowy version of himself.

Gone.

Vanished back into the thin air from whence they'd come.

He sat thinking of all he'd seen that wasn't there—of a memory conjured by things that never did exist—and muttered a silent heavenward prayer, hoping beyond hope there was some sanity left in himself after all.

Moments later he stood to his feet, eyes catching on the sudden reflection of his Morgan silver dollar lost among the leaves. He remembered the music then, remembered the *song*—and just what *was* that he'd heard out of his mouth anyway? Latin? No, not Latin. But old. Don't ask him how he knew that, because he didn't; he *felt* it, the way one feels love or the eyes of an unwelcome stranger.

Travis bent and scooped up the coin, his mind sure of only one thing as he led Gage away from the lake and toward the waiting darkness of the trees.

Those aren't exactly the type of lyrics you pick up on Top 40…

§

Walking into Luckey's an hour later, Travis found Juan completely in his element: hunched over the counter, jawing away at some chewing gum as he sat deciphering the static of the police scanner.

He started to speak and was waved quiet, Juan turning the scanner louder. Travis heard some exchanges, couldn't make out much. After a moment, Juan cut the volume and looked up. His eyes bulged.

"What happened to *you?*"

Travis froze, suddenly not sure of himself. Then he remembered and smiled, touching a gentle finger to his forehead. "Oh...right, the, uh. Little bump on the head. Wasn't much to it, I'll live." He nodded to the scanner. "What's the latest hit?"

"Meth bust," Juan muttered. "Big one, out towards Vandermere. I ask you, when will this county clean itself up and stop it with these drugs? It's terrible, just terrible." He wiped a hand down his face, as if wiping clear his mind. "What can I help you with, amigo? Besides an extra-large band-aid for that lump on your noggin."

"A piece of real estate, actually," he said. "I mean, hypothetically."

"Oh? And what piece would you have in mind, hypothetically?"

"Who owns the property down the old DeWitt Road?"

"Ah, the DeWitt Road." Juan nodded, stroking his fuzzy chin as if he'd realized some great truth about life. "Out past the landfill?"

"That's the one."

"That's a long road. Lotta land. Some folks go hiking up there, I hear."

"You don't say."

"Hmm, let me think. I believe that's...that's Dietz property. Sure it is. Gordon Dietz. Real big-wig lives out to Oriental. Why you wanna know that for?"

"You think Gordon Dietz is in the selling mood?"

"For you? I mean, considering who you *are* now? What sort of *capital* you can get ahold of?" Juan worked away at his gum, his chubby face scrunched up like a sponge being wrung dry. After a moment he said, "Yes. May cost you an arm and a leg, but yes."

An arm and a leg, Travis thought.

After what he'd witnessed, that almost seemed cheap.

TEN

HE WOKE UP EARLY.

Showered, dressed, put down some breakfast for Gage and was ready to go. He'd need something for himself, he thought, but then Travis supposed there would be plenty to eat where he was going. He even skipped his usual cup of morning coffee, and presently had never felt more awake in his life.

Gage galloped over as he started out.

"Stay, stay," Travis told him. "Gotta sit this one out, buddy."

Gage pleaded adoringly through sad yellow eyes and then, getting the point, gave a plaintive yip before shuffling back to his bowl. A moment later Travis stepped out, was still turning the lock on the door when he heard a sudden voice from behind.

"Hiya, Mr. Barnes."

Turning, Travis was surprised to see Mr. Thorgerson, his old high school gym teacher, standing like a statue just off the porch. His mustache, always so thick and black, was just as thick but now the color of snow. He wore windbreaker pants and a plain white tee, armpits a pale-yellow shade, and should Travis ever have thought of Jim Thorgerson during his time overseas—he hadn't—he would have pictured him in duds a lot like these.

"Remember me?" he asked. He was sweating terribly. "Mr. Thorgerson, remember? Kids used to call me Mr. Whiskers? I had you one year, must've been back, oh when was it? Fifteen years ago? Sixteen?"

Travis locked the door, offering a smile as he walked down the steps to shake his hand. "How are you, Mr. Thorgerson?"

"Me? Oh fine, just fine. How about you? You doing all right, uh? I heard you were back in town and I thought, well, I thought that—"

"Sorry, Mr. Thorgerson, but I'm afraid I was just heading out for the day."

"Heading out? Oh, you were leaving. Oh, of course. Well, maybe we can catch up another time then?"

Travis placed a friendly hand on Mr. Thorgerson's shoulder. Despite failing him for Team Sports—which he'd deserved, no doubt—Mr. Thorgerson had always been good to Travis, always encouraging him to put his body to work for him, scholarships, that sort of thing. He'd demurred at the time, but looking back Travis realized the man really had been trying to help.

"Are you sure there's nothing I can do for you *now*?" he

asked. "Nothing I can help you with?"

"Well..."

"C'mon, Mr. Thorgerson. What's on your mind?"

"It's just that, well, my wife and I are having our twentieth anniversary next month, and, well, I was hoping I could do something a little extra special for her." He looked down at his feet, booted the grass. "Twenty years, you know...that's a lot of pressure."

Travis squeezed his shoulder. "I guess you're right, Mr. Thorgerson. It sure is." He fished out his wallet, reached inside. Drew a stack of bills and stuffed them in Mr. Thorgerson's hand. "Here. This should help out. Make sure you do something real nice for her, Mr. Thorgerson. Something extra special, all right?"

Mr. Thorgerson blushed, looking away at the sky, the clouds, wiping his eyes. He mumbled a quick thank you before shuffling off like a ghost, vanishing into a faded hatchback just down the street. Travis stared after the vehicle as it rolled away, not quite understanding what had just happened, but glad for it.

Twenty years *is* a lot of pressure, after all.

§

It was quarter to twelve on a Wednesday afternoon and Pitt Memorial Hospital had been haunted by another morning of calamity. A big rig with a haul of corn had been T-boned and nearly toppled by a second rig over on Mead Street, while a botched holdup the night before had resulted in three bloody deaths with a likely fourth to follow. Otherwise all over Pitt County people were falling down stairs or getting hit by buses or blowing body valves and soon enough they would all end up here, a never-ending postal system that dealt in flesh and bone instead of stamps and envelopes.

Despite these things Tara's morning had been fairly harmless, all of it blurring together as she made her usual Wednesday rounds. She'd managed to avoid the worst of the new day's catastrophes—they were mercifully overstaffed—instead whiling away most of her morning at the bed of one Mr. Lyle Getty. He was an old man, fat-bellied with a big wrinkly face. Admitted for a shaky heart that had finally gone poof. And though he was no charmer—Mr. Getty's idea of being kind was letting you know the bedpan was full—there *was* some oddly endearing quality to him which Tara could not resist; unbelievably, she'd actually sort of come to *like* the old crank. To pity his utter love for his daughter, unrequited all these years. To sympathize with his own inability to communicate with her, to win her back by any device, all because of an affair on her mother that he'd regretted a thousand times before and would give anything to unlive. Alas, it could never be so...

Still, it was nice spending time with the old fart, crab pot that he was, and Tara was still feeling the buzz of their time together when she pushed through the cafeteria doors and took her place in line. She'd had four bites of an apple that morning for breakfast, and working slowly past the food Tara pleaded with herself to *do the right thing*, to buckle down and play it safe with a good old-fashioned fruit cup or grilled chicken fill-in-the-blank, no matter how tempting that other food looked behind the glass.

Moments later she was handed a plate brimming with pork chops, ham-seasoned green beans, mashed taters topped with a thick brown syrup.

Well, she thought, *I'm gonna feel like shit.*

She turned and glanced over the tables, hoping to find that one magical seat off to itself. Someplace she could be alone for once and gorge down her meal in relative peace, all in ten minutes or less. Her focus settled on a cozy booth near the doors—a perfect table, she thought, save for the fact of some bookworm with a half-finished plate of...was that *spaghetti and tater tots?* She walked closer, eyes dipping to the spooky lettering across the book's cover: *Something Wicked This Way Comes.*

Only then the cover shifted and she saw his face and Tara stopped cold in her tracks. And though there was no name to put with that face, this wasn't the first time it had crossed her mind; far from it. A woman doesn't easily forget eyes that blue, nor lips that perfect, and more than once Tara had wondered what it might be like to kiss them. She'd wondered it a lot, actually, and staring at him now she wondered if she wasn't slipping into some long lost dream.

Sensing her gaze the man looked up, their eyes locking the way it happens in those cheesy *meant-to-be* flicks, the ones where beautiful people fell victim to kismet and played dress-up for the world. Instantly she wished she'd had a moment to gather herself, do her get-pretty-in-two-seconds-flat routine. She wished she'd washed her hair the night before. But if wishes were wings then pigs would fly and now she was helpless, the two of them staring for what seemed an eternity before Tara started anxiously forward. Coming closer, the man lowered his book and grinned.

"Well-well," he said. "If it's not Little Miss Lottery."

"My hero," she sang. "What happened? Dropping by for

your weekly enema?"

He laughed. "No, no. That was yesterday, believe it or not." Raising the book, he said, "Just catching up on a little reading, is all."

Tara glanced over the cafeteria, at tired nurses in bright blue scrubs and sad mopey faces and old souls waiting to die. "Don't they have parks for that sort of thing?"

He shrugged, his smile faltering. "I...well, I like hospitals."

"Excuse me?"

"No, it's true. I enjoy the...atmosphere."

Tara had noticed an oversized bandage on the left side of his forehead. Flesh-tone, but obvious. She pointed to it now and said, "What's this? Walk into a tree?"

She'd only been joking but he looked at her funny then, blue eyes dancing, and was about to say more when an old couple moved between them and out the doors, their faces cast down. When they were gone he looked at her, smiling his perfect smile as he nodded to the empty seat across the table.

"Well? Wanna sit down?"

So she did.

PART TWO

WATCHERS

ELEVEN

THE FIRST RAYS OF DAWN BURNED BRIGHT THROUGH the windows as Travis slipped out of bed and into his robe and crept to the door, turning for a moment to stare at his wife lost among the covers. It had never occurred to him how strange an act it was watching someone sleep: a deeply maternal gesture that, no matter how sweet, smacked vaguely of perversion. But then perversion suited him just fine this morning, and for a while longer he stood savoring the moment before going downstairs and putting on some coffee. He opened the back door and Gage shot like a bottle rocket into the yard, leaping and bounding and free among the pines.

Before long they were settled in their usual places on the patio, Travis poking around on his laptop and sipping a good Columbian blend from a mug the size of a soup bowl. Despite the birds or occasional snapping branch, Gage had taken a passive-aggressive approach to the local fauna; so far this morning had been a passive one, the Boykin sprawled beneath the shade of the mosaic table he and Tara had bought at an art boutique in Miami. Somehow, Travis never thought the table looked as good here in his own backyard as it had down in sunny Florida.

As it happened, Gage liked it just fine.

Travis spent the morning same as he had every other over the past four months, poring over edits of what would soon become his debut novel. Earlier that spring, after months of early mornings and a few late nights as well, Travis had put the finishing touches on his first manuscript, a supernatural suspense story. Following some helpful suggestions courtesy of a couple publishing blogs, he'd sent out queries and, miraculously, was signed to a literary agency out of New York. Three weeks later, *Dawn's Early Light* sold to Mizner House, a small but prestigious publisher the reputation of which was enough to give Travis chills, and later that night he and Tara had made martinis and ran naked through the house, two shameless children without sense enough to know better. A tentative release date was set for the following spring as Travis began working with an editor, a fantastic and disturbingly intelligent woman by the name of Diane Skaggs, to make the story the very best that it could be.

He'd been at it a couple of hours when he glanced at his watch and felt an instant swell of relief—almost quarter of nine. Tara hadn't been sleeping much lately and he was glad that, of all mornings, she was getting that much-needed rest today. And though the trip had come up last minute—and

Tara had indicated she'd rather put a hot needle through her eye than spend another weekend keeping time with Tessa Velazquez—Travis knew deep down it was a good thing. That it was just another diversion—more than the occasional shifts at the hospital, than all the hobby crafts and decorating—one more welcome distraction to take her mind off things, if only for a while.

For that, he was grateful.

He stood from the table, hiking down to the lake with Gage close at his side. A slight chill clung to the air but still it felt good to stroll the banks, the rich smell of the trees starting the blood in his veins as Travis skipped stones and watched the fog dancing in waves over the water. He'd passed beneath the gloomy boughs of an old pecan tree when his phone buzzed in his pocket.

"Hello?"

"Heya, buddy. Still on for tonight?"

"What's the matter? Scared already?"

Joel laughed. "All that lovin' has made you soft in the head, my friend."

"Prove it. Six o'clock."

"I'll bring the peanuts, you bring the beer. Gotta go, buddy."

Travis smiled and pocketed the phone, and glancing up moments later noticed Tara tossing down a wave from their balcony, a spill of her brown hair flashing briefly in the sun. Slowly his gaze expanded to the imposing figure of the house itself, measuring it against the one he'd seen once before in these same woods, finding the fit true. Only in that version of things there existed a certain doe-eyed girl, a skipping, laughing, spinning child who wore red ribbons and made that world an altogether more charming place to live.

But that world was an ethereal one, subjective at best—a realm of whispers and clues and endless prognostications—and in this world, where he lived, Travis was happy enough in having the woman of his dreams and the job of his life and the fulfilment that only living one day at a time could provide. He'd have to be, after all.

What choice was there?

§

Tara watched while Travis picked his way slowly back toward the house, Gage following behind and bouncing like a pinball through the autumn bursts of the trees. Staring, she was reminded again of how thankful she was for the living postcard that greeted her every morning, and the man willing to spend the rest of his days existing with her inside of it. Bypassing her fears, she'd come to accept this place as home and the future as it lay before them, and Travis as the one she would go through it with.

He was caring, handsome, intelligent—everything she'd ever wanted in a man. And though not many would believe her, it certainly wasn't about the money, which had actually freaked her out a little at first; it was everything, from their passion for Chinese takeout and love of Zeppelin and 80's slasher flicks to the fact that both were essentially alone in this world. Her own parents had been killed in a car crash when she was four; not the sort of highway pile-up that makes the news but only a slippery road on a bad curve at too late an hour of night. Asleep in the backseat at the time, Tara had no memory of the accident—fate's best offer of a silver lining—and were it not for the saving grace of her grandparents, she would've inevitably become the latest unwitting addition to the foster care system, a threat which loomed dark in the back of her mind throughout adolescence.

Travis's story was a little different but ended essentially the same, and from this common bond of solitude and loneliness they'd built a life together, a damned fine one—and had hoped to build more.

She stopped herself then, that old depression sweeping back as she walked inside and started up the shower. Afterwards she toweled off and went downstairs and coming into the kitchen found Travis scrambling eggs at the stove, a glass of pulp-free poured and waiting in her place at the kitchen table. The smell of warm toast filled the air.

"Almost ready," he called. "Go ahead, have a seat. Eggs coming up."

Tara settled herself at the table and soon they were chatting over a meal of fresh-cut apples, eggs, turkey-bacon and toast. Still, as nice a gesture as the breakfast was, considering the weekend ahead of her it seemed more bittersweet than anything.

Travis chewed away, dipping his toast liberally in the bowl of molasses he'd poured. He wiped his mouth and said, "So where's Rodrigo off to this week?"

"St. Lucia, I think? Or maybe it's St. Louis." Tara thought about it, gave up. "Doesn't matter, Tessa gets the names wrong half the time anyway. That's really repulsive, by the way, what you're doing there with the molasses."

"Sweet sorghum, actually, and it never tasted so sweet.

You gals going out?"

"Please, don't even say it."

"What? Bad juju?"

Tara picked off some bacon and tossed it to Gage. "Raleigh, on Friday night? With judge Tessa Lynch presiding? I'd rather go apple bobbing with Dr. Kevorkian."

"You mean judge Tessa *Velazquez?*"

"A rose by any other name," she said, getting up and pouring a second glass of juice, topping Travis's off. "I trust the two of you can behave yourselves till I get back?"

Travis glanced to Gage. "I suppose we could do that, eh, boy?"

"No hookers, no heroin? No soiling the sheets?"

Travis lifted his scout fingers: "Just a man and his dog."

"How about it, Gage? You gonna look after the old man, make sure he doesn't crap up the bed?"

Gage sat on his haunches and began to dig.

Travis grinned from across the table, a dark smear of sorghum gooped across his teeth. "I think that's a yes."

§

Later Travis packed up her bags and walked out to the car, pulling Tara close and breathing in the sweet rush of her hair.

"Another weekend in the city, no big deal," he told her. "Relax a little, have some fun. And please, no putting your eyes out. I kinda like them, you know."

"Hey, I look at it like charity work," she said. "Without an adult around, who knows, Tessa might set fire to the place. Rodrigo could be a widower-in-waiting."

He stood watching the sun glinting in her eyes, and though

they were as deep and vibrant as ever he sensed the usual sadness about his wife this morning. That long grey emotion that seemed to hang over her lately but that he'd first sensed so many months ago, not long after they'd started trying.

He considered bringing it up, thought better.

"It's Friday the thirteenth, you know."

She smiled. "I noticed. Better lock up tight."

"Nothing to be afraid of here," he told her. He scowled, eyes turned to flint as he put on his best Walter White: "*I AM the one who knocks.*"

"Mm, you know it gives me a boner when you do Heisenberg."

Travis squeezed her ass and then they kissed and she told him goodbye and that she loved him and she'd be home sometime Monday afternoon, sooner if she could. She scratched Gage's head and gave him a smooch and then she was gone, Travis watching as the bright Mini Cooper pulled away, vanishing among the colorful sprawl of the trees.

§

An hour later he sat at his desk, working over the remainder of that day's words and trying not to think about that last look he'd seen in her eyes—just a flash, enough to know it was there. You didn't live with a person without picking up a thing or two, and whatever that last look might've been, whatever it might've meant, it broke his heart and made everything—all of it, the whole idea of a family—seem so fragile, so ready to collapse right over their heads.

The decision had not come as easily as he'd expected.

Bringing a child into this world was a big decision, after all—the biggest, some might say—and while obviously there'd be undeniable joy in raising such a creature, there was also great burden. The world was a dangerous place, after all, with bad things happening every day. And who was he, who had inherited his own share of an evil heart, to bring a child into such piss-poor times as these? And besides this Travis knew that, faced with a cruel world, he would be tempted to take his child and sequester him or her away, safe and protected from the tragedies of modern living. Mozart during nights, PBS during the day, NPR when the child was old enough. Home-schooling would be in order, potential friends vetted, no Internet.

Grand result? After ten years the child would be afraid of their own shadow.

In time, however—and after reading several books Tara placed strategically around the house—Travis accepted that such fears were common for couples considering parenthood. He searched himself and discovered that to go through life with Tara and not have a child by her would be only half an existence, not really an existence at all. Lying asleep one night, he'd dreamed the two of them climbing a tall jagged-edge cliff, though really the cliff was one of time, of years. He'd dreamed them reaching forty, forty-five, fifty, and then turning, looking back, viewing the great chasm of darkness below. A chasm separating them from the family on the other side, the family they'd never had and never were, the family he'd given up and surrendered to the years once and for all. The image was chilling, and in that moment his decision was made. Over breakfast the next morning he'd told Tara what he'd seen, and that afternoon they'd promptly set about getting pregnant. They renewed their efforts that evening, and again later that night.

That was seven months ago and now, in a time when other couples would be throwing baby showers and buying overpriced cribs, they were making doctors' appointments and wondering which of them might have the faulty plumbing. The first of Travis's appointments was scheduled the following week, when Dr. Gaines would run his tests and wave his wand and, for a nominal fee, tell them what the hell was going on.

He stood and walked to one of the photos ranged along the antique sideboard, the two of them on their honeymoon in the Bahamas. Tara puffing out her tongue and doing a goofy pose in her bathing suit, Travis trying his best to outdo her. At the time she'd said it was her favorite place on earth, that she'd never seen anywhere so beautiful and were it possible she'd live there forever and would never complain.

The next showed him and Tara among a crowd of strangers in an ocean of colorful balloons, everyone smiling and laughing. He'd been the millionth customer in a store up near High Point, won some swag, five hundred cash. Great as that moment had been, however, it was only one in a blur of good times, and looking back Travis realized it had been the best year of his life. Not because of the lottery, or the novel, but because of Tara Reilly, who had joined her dreams with his own and brought some kind of magic to his life; who had completed him in a way he'd never imagined another person could.

He stared at the pictures, struggling for some semblance of the joy they'd had before all this, back when their love was pure and simple and carefree. That joy seemed so distant now, a forgotten pleasure, and Travis was still chasing it down when he glanced out the window and noticed the sun burning low through the pines. Joel would be here soon, he thought, returning the picture to the shelf before heading downstairs and out the front door.

He drove through Silver Hill and off toward Bayboro, taking the twisted stretch of blacktop known officially as Phillips Road but that most in Pamlico simply called Big Curve Road. He bought some fresh veggies from a stand on Beaufort Street, and stopped at Belangia's for some steak cuts and beer for later that night. He was just out the door when his phone rang, Tara letting him know she'd made it to Raleigh. He asked about the weather and Tara said, "Fine here. What about you?"

"Well..." Travis stared at the sky, which had bruised considerably over the last hour and now loomed an ominous gray at the horizon. "Might get that thunderstorm they've been talking about."

"Aw, poor Gage. Give my baby kisses."

He thought again of that last sad look in her eyes.

"Listen, I was thinking when you get back we could start looking online for that equipment you'll need for the darkroom. Maybe get started cleaning out the basement, get things prepped for when you're ready to set up."

"Sure, that would be great. We'll start as soon as I get home."

He smiled at that, more on the inside than out. "It's a date."

Travis hung up and started for his truck, not getting far when something occurred to him and he turned, heading around the side of the store. He stepped over a few broken bottles before arriving at the twisted oaks at the back of the lot, staring at the place where fifteen years and a lifetime ago he and Joel had transcribed the universe with a single can of spray paint.

If he'd been expecting progeny, however, he was sorely disappointed: their poignant slogans were gone, painted over by a half-decent mural showing what looked to be a fiery phoenix rising from the ashes.

Travis let out a breath.

"*Fuckin' kids*," he said, and started back for the truck.

§

Tara tossed aside her cell, concentrating on the road ahead as she bore west along the great sprawl of I-40. She drove another twenty minutes before spotting the first signs for the airport, a part of her wondering if she was actually doing this—and another, more reckless part wanting nothing more than to be on the plane already, to be settled on a beach with some fruity drink that came with an umbrella and watching the waves crash blue and white against the sand.

Her trip had gone smoothly so far, including the small detour she'd made to Early Grace Cemetery in Galveston where she'd left no flowers and said no prayers but for a little while visited with those who had meant so much to her in life. Here rested the remains of her parents, as well as those of an aunt and uncle whom she'd never met and, coupled beneath the boughs of an old cherry blossom, her Granny and Grandpa Reilly. And if it was under this tree where Tara spent most of her time, she supposed it was only a testament to the sweet-souled woman who had inherited her with aplomb and become the best second mother a person could hope for. Her grandfather, a quiet, sober-eyed man who occasionally smoked a pipe, had passed only weeks before her sweet sixteen, and yet despite this loss her granny had remained strong, lasting until

Tara finished college before being bedded by the pneumonia that at last pressed the final gasping breath from her eighty-year-old body.

Afterward she'd placed a quick call to Tessa, checking in with her and Rodrigo's big plans for the weekend—a Kenny Chesney concert down in Myrtle Beach. The conversation took longer than expected, though for once Tara found herself glad to hear every happy detail of their pregame; as ditzy as she could be, Tara supposed Tessa Velazquez was the last good friend she had left, and in an imperfect world that must count for something.

Now she threaded her way along the patchwork of lanes that led past the airport, the first feelings of betrayal bubbling up—*what had taken so long?*—as she parked and lugged out her bags and started toward the shuttle stop. On the way she was greeted by a bushy-browed gentleman carting a lemonade stand with an American flag at the corner, who asked if she wanted to buy a drink to support the troops. So she handed over a buck and said you're welcome and, sipping patriotically at her cup, kept across the lot.

Minutes later the shuttle arrived and Tara climbed onboard, returning the smile of a rheumy-eyed driver and settling into an empty seat near the back. Then—just like that—the small bus shuddered to life and sped away, the guilt growing stronger now and gnawing quietly away in the pit of her stomach as they rolled toward the airport and whatever destiny lay beyond.

Tara closed her eyes and saw waves.

TWELVE

JUAN MARQUEZ BY NO MEANS CONSIDERED HIMSELF a superstitious man, but then neither did he discount the impossible in his interpretation of the universe. Fate was a little too broad a concept for him to embrace—too much bad shit had happened for him to believe that—but that forces outside himself existed that he didn't quite understand, that much he could give traction to. Outside the storm clouds were already raging, a vast darkness moving in from the south, and although Juan had kept his eyes on it all afternoon, waiting for the bottom to fall out, so far he'd been kept in anticipation.

He was in the midst of counting down the register when a man in a bathrobe walked in to pay for the couple gallons he'd pumped at #4. Juan reached over, lowering the volume—just marginally—of the police scanner to his left and telling the man he'd be with him in one second, at which point the man blew a breath and rubbed at his belly, then blew another breath and said, "*C'mon, old man! I got cold stuff in the car!*"

Juan finished, put back the till, rang him up, handed over the change.

He was almost out the door when the man muttered something under his breath—"*see if ah ever stop by this shit-dump little store again*"—and then the bell jingled and the next customer stepped into line, the slender woman sending instant chills down Juan's neck. Something in her face, the way it looked. Pale, sort of pinched. She stepped closer and his nostrils flared with the stench of her, a sweet candy smell—only something about it turned his stomach and made him want to puke. What the hell was it?

"Can I help you?"

She stared, her eyes green and bright but somehow distant, as if lost in her skull. "Is this where it happened?" she asked. "The Megaball, I mean? The winning ticket?"

And for some reason Juan had the sudden urge to keep his filthy mouth shut. To excuse himself suddenly, make up some whoppers, anything. Only he couldn't think with the woman staring at him like that, drilling him with her eyes; a feeling of helplessness swept over him.

"That's right," he said. *Damn you, Juan.* "Right here at Luckey's."

"The man who bought it...Barnes, I think his name was." She smiled vaguely. "Do you know him?"

Juan could feel her eyes. "Sure, I know Travis." *Double-damned!*

"And what kind of person would you say he is?"

"Travis, well, I dunno, he's a good guy...him 'n his wife, they..." Then, reasserting himself: "Miss? Is there something I can do for you? Something I can *help* you with?"

An uneasy feeling then, a slow-moving darkness he tried to ignore but without success. The woman tried another smile, and somehow this was worse than her stare. "I apologize, I was only curious. There's usually a sign on the window. *Winning-Megaball-Sold-Here*, that sort of thing?"

In fact Juan had taken the poster down only last month; damn thing had blocked his view to the pumps, along with most of the sunlight.

"No, nothing like that, I'm afraid," he called, watching as she strolled down the aisles, strolled back. Went to the fridges and grabbed a bottle of water from inside. Juan punched at the register, and handing over her money their fingers brushed and to Juan the broad's flesh was icy cold. Again that sweet smell—like peppermint—and he quickly gave over the change, trying but not able to conceal the slight tremble in his hands.

"Oh—and one lottery ticket, please. Quick pick is fine."

Juan printed and handed over the ticket, his trembling hand going wide and snagging the penny tray and sending coins spilling across the counter. The woman offered her best polite smile, pale skin stretched sickeningly across her birdish skull.

"Easy there, Juan. Stress is a toxin; it's bad for the body. Too much of it, you'll kill yourself. Almost like a poison, wouldn't you say? Like a *cancer*..."

Juan felt his face burning, felt sweat creeping down into his eyes. He opened his mouth and for a moment it hung there like an open shelf until, finally, Juan found the words he'd been looking for.

"Get the hell out of my store."

But already she'd snatched up her ticket, the little silver bell jangling softly as she marched from the counter and out the door. When she was gone Juan sat for a moment rubbing at his eyes, the scanner warbling on and on until finally he stood and walked to the window, the pumps a stark silhouette against the formless gray of the clouds. He scrubbed his eyes and looked again across the empty lot, but it was no use.

The woman was gone.

THIRTEEN

JOEL ARRIVED LATER THAT EVENING, TRAVIS WALKING out to meet him as his old friend shuffled up the front steps. He stood a moment appreciating the scenery off the porch, majestically arcadian despite the bank of darkened clouds looming over the lake.

"You know, this view, it never gets old," he said. "Way out here in the middle of nowhere, you could do anything you wanted. Me personally, I'd probably never wear a stitch of clothing again. Stock up on beef jerky, watch some HBO. That's just me."

Travis slapped him on the back. "That's why I like you, Joel. You think big."

Contrary to Tara's suggestions, there was no shitting of the sheets nor nary a hooker as the two settled down for an evening of feigned bachelorhood. They drank and smoked cigars, tossing cards across the table like two old pros though neither of them had much to offer in the way of two-player card games. They played their requisite best-of-three pool matches—Travis lost the first and no more—and, when the clock struck nine, ate good cuts of Porterhouse and a conservative grilled chicken salad smothered in buttermilk ranch.

Afterwards they sat drinking the last of their beers and caught up on reruns of *Seinfeld*.

"What d'ya think? Think I should get a new belt buckle?" Joel indicated his buckle, a grand silver oval with the silhouette of a sheriff's star dead center.

Travis told him he thought a man's belt buckle was his own business.

Joel considered this solemnly. "How's the babymaking?"

"Dr. Gaines is awaiting my penis next week." Travis gulped his beer and said, "In other news, Tara's decided on turning the basement into a dark room."

"Hey, well that's kind of cool, right? I didn't know Tara was a photographer."

Just then lightning flashed outside the windows, and in its glare Travis remembered their first date at the new house, when things were first getting serious and they'd walked out to the pier and, later, made out in the rain. It was a good date; it was also the night he knew beyond a doubt he would gladly spend the rest of his life with her. Travis shut his eyes, all of those memories as alive as the flash of lightning and the thunder rolling outside, and when he opened them again the room was dark and his beer was empty.

"Yeah," he said. "Neither did she."

§

It was just after ten when Joel checked his watch and stood to his feet.

"Getting late, partner. Time to roll."

"Work tomorrow?"

"Bright and early," Joel told him. "But listen—how about you come over for dinner tomorrow night? Theresa wouldn't mind, be like old times. She'll whip ya up some of that pecan pie, you put in a request. Want me to pass it along?"

He liked the sound of that. "Sure thing, Joel."

Joel gave him a wink. "You bring the peanuts this time, big boy."

He watched from the porch as the old cruiser rattled to life and motored away, Joel giving a quick flash of the roof lights as he vanished down the darkness of the DeWitt Road. He took Gage for a quick stroll around the yard—he'd always been skittish of storms, and Travis figured now would be a good time to make sure those sheets didn't get soiled after all—before moving back inside to the kitchen, picking at leftovers.

For a long time afterward he sat in the cool darkness of the living room, eyes closed as he listened to the rumbles of far-off thunder.

And that's when he heard the knocking.

Travis pulled himself up and stumbled to the door, opened it and for a moment stood staring at the pair of figures on the other side: the first an older-looking man, big with dark eyes and silvered hair past his shoulders; the other had a lantern jaw that made him resemble Jay Leno.

"Mr. Barnes?" the first asked, simian eyes gleaming in the darkness. And though his voice was low and tone marginally polite, there was something Travis didn't like in those eyes, something he'd seen a few times in other men before that he'd not liked then either.

"Can I help you gentlemen?"

The first man stepped closer now, affecting a cordial tone: "Your wife...Tara? She home by any chance?"

Travis glanced down, noticing a slight bulge beneath the shorter man's jacket; then the man turned and Travis caught a glimpse of a small but deadly-looking nine-millimeter.

"She's, uh...out of town, actually," he said, his body registering the first dizzy waves of adrenaline, registering *fear*; not the ordinary kind but that of a trapped animal. Which is a very practical, very useful kind of fear—the kind that will keep a person alive when they would otherwise be dead.

The men nodded politely, glancing past him into the house, down the hall. Leno leaned forward, offering Travis another generous eyeful of the nine-millimeter.

"Come on, fellas," he said, those last few beers doing wonders at keeping his voice even. "Somebody wanna tell me what this is all about?"

The tall man only smiled and took another step.

"That's why we're here, Mr. Barnes. To take you to somebody who can." Then he looked around and said, "Anybody else in the house?"

Leno stepped forward, his eyes like flint.

"How about you just come with us, buddy? How about that?"

Only before he could answer Leno lunged forward, one hand grabbing Travis roughly, the other stabbing something sharp into his arm and—

Travis hit him, his fist connecting in an automatic reflex that sent the man stumbling back. He looked down and noticed an odd sort of syringe half-dangling from his arm; he took it carefully between his fingers and slipped it out, tossed it across the floor.

"*Easy now,*" said the tall one, arms raised. "*Easy, Travis...*"

He was quick with it, driving home a deep gut-punch that pushed air—it smelled like peppermint—from the big man's mouth, his massive frame pitching forward and Travis meeting his face with a hard swinging kick that sent the man sprawling out the door.

Leno glared at him, the Hitler-mustache of blood beneath his nose unable to mask a feral scowl that softened to a grin as he dipped one hand inside his jacket, revealing a stun gun, giving it a spark.

Travis turned, eyes skittering over the array of Iznik vases on a shelf to his left; he snatched one up and gave it a toss, the vase forming a brief hollow note as it struck the man's forehead and then fell shattering to the floor. The man grinned all the harder, making it mean something, giving another sharp crackle of the stun gun as he started forward and then stopped suddenly at the sight of the dog barrelling down the stairwell to their right.

"Gage! *Heel!*"

But it was too late, the dog's bright yellow eyes brimming with fire as he leapt forward, performing a brief levitation as he sailed over and then went to work: burying his teeth deep into the bastard's ankles, up his thighs, and then—striking gold—the mushy clump of his genitals.

There was a long, high-pitched squeal as the man pried himself loose and fell struggling to the door, Gage keeping the momentum and springing after him, snarling and growling and biting...

"*Handle it!*" his partner called, lumbering now to his feet.

"*I'm trying—damn mutt won't—*"

Travis saw it before it happened, the slow knowledge of it transforming Leno's face into a darkened leer; before Travis could stop him, the man buried the stun gun deep into the dog's dark curls and gave it a blast. Gage yelped, a propulsive spurt of blood spilling from his nose as he fell mewling to the floor and, when the worst of the convulsions had fallen off, leapt to his feet and then out the door.

"*Son-of-a-bitch!*"

The man leered back at him, giving another spark of the stun gun. "Come and get it, sonny..."

But Travis didn't come and get it.

Instead he took all his rage, all that bright-burning fury and stuffed it deep inside, fighting back a sudden wave of nausea as he turned and fled down the hall. Down, down in a twisting jag and then doubling back for the study, a cool breeze sweeping past his face as he slipped silently out the door onto the patio. He'd started around the house when something caught his eye on the mosaic table, one of the bulb-shaped kerosene candles Tara had bought for cookouts that summer.

Travis hefted the candle in one hand, kerosene glimmering darkly through the pale-colored glass. He gave a quick study of the area, had almost given up when he spotted the grill lighter on a garden stool near the door; he snatched it up, falling back into the darkness of the yard beyond the patio.

He fired up the wick, waiting, waiting until the two men ran scrambling from inside and then he leaned back and took aim, pitching the bulb in a wild flickering arc across the sky; the first figure saw it and hurled his massive frame out of the way, his partner not so lucky and glancing up as the candle came shattering in a bright explosion of fire over his head.

A sudden shriek split the night.

Travis watched, aware now not only of a certain dizzy feeling in his head but a sour burning sensation at the back of his throat, growing hotter with every breath.

He moved stealthily, sprinting away from the house and into the trees, and was still pushing through the darkness of the forest when the hulking form of a helicopter appeared grounded in the clearing up ahead; he stopped, staring as the rotors spun soundlessly against a black thundering sky.

Only then that image faltered, nausea sweeping down like a hurricane that brought him swiftly to his knees. The darkness throbbed around him, swelling at the corners of his vision until finally he heard voices and the last of his strength slipped away.

And then he felt nothing at all.

FOURTEEN

HE AWOKE TO A HEADACHE, HIS FIRST THOUGHTS NOT of fear but rather a momentary rush of confusion, the feeling of waking in a stranger's bed and not knowing how you got there. Only at the bitter taste in the back of his throat did the memories return, Travis opening his eyes to find himself in a space that was not very big, oddly cylindrical in shape but with small tables and lamps spread here and there. Dotted along the walls were occasional shades pulled down over what Travis assumed to be porthole windows.

As he watched, one of the shadows detached itself and leaned forward.

Another lamp switched on and now he saw a woman, her slim figure nestled behind a small table fixed from the wall. In contrast to her all-over black suit—it looked like a one-piece— the woman's complexion appeared coarse and milky, a china doll after a long night out.

"The headache will pass," she said, grabbing up a folder and riffling some papers. "One of the side effects of the sedative you were given—a very mild one, I assure you. Just relax."

Travis leaned forward, almost toppling from the seat. When he spoke, his tongue felt like sandpaper: "What...what is all this? And who the hell are *you?*"

The woman tossed something, sent it flying over and landing in the seat next to his own, and for a moment Travis held her gaze, feeling nervous suddenly and not knowing why. He reached over, hands trembling slightly as he raised the small leather case and flipped it back, though by this time Travis thought he had a fair idea of what was inside.

He wasn't disappointed.

During his years in the biz, Travis had seen plenty of government shields: DEA, FBI, CIA. None had looked like this—a silver badge showing a trident thrust upward from a dome, the twin serpents of a caduceus coiling upward through the prongs. UNITED STATES OF AMERICA looped overhead, ID numbers down below.

"You gave my boys quite the workout tonight, Mr. Barnes," she told him, her voice thin and cold but inherently self-assured. "Poor William, as I understand he'll be in need of a new face before it's all said and done." She raised a penciled-in eyebrow. "A Molotov cocktail?"

He tossed back the shield, glad to be rid of it.

"Get bent, lady. That badge, that's supposed to make everything kosher now? What, you expect me to walk over and shake your hand, say, gee, thanks for the needle in the arm?" He laughed, reveling in it, the absurdity of it all. "Aren't you supposed to, I dunno, get some sort of *permission* for that kinda thing first? You know, read me my rights, that sort of thing?"

"Under normal circumstances, yes," she told him. "Absolutely. Jurisprudence has shown the dazzling light of wisdom and we believe in that light, in the letter and in the spirit of it. That having been said, there are certain situations where the Bureau has been given special jurisdiction—"

"Jurisdiction to what? *Body snatch* people?"

"No one has been *body snatched*, Mr. Barnes. Merely *detained*, same as if you'd been hauled into the local precinct. Only this precinct flies seventy thousand feet above the earth, rides faster than you'd believe, and as it happens was expensive enough to make even Elon Musk skip a heartbeat."

Travis glanced around the room, its curving walls, its funky lighting and hidden porthole windows. Then, remembering, he said: "I saw a helicopter…"

"Just a connecting flight, I'm afraid. I apologize for the late hour, Mr. Barnes, but we're on a tight schedule here tonight. The mission to take down Bin Laden was a decade in the works and yet was carried out in a matter of hours, and *he* was the world's most wanted man. This is far more important than even that, and we have been given full reign of the government's resources to make sure the job gets done. In the end, I think you'll agree it was necessary."

More important than Bin Laden?

Suddenly he thought of the men, the sharp crackle of the stun gun and—

"Gage," he said, all the fuzzy details coming into focus. "They—"

"Your dog is fine, Mr. Barnes. He's been taken care of and will be awaiting you as soon you get back to the house." Her face broke into what might've been the beginnings of a smile. "His tail going a mile a minute, I'm sure..."

Travis stared, for the first time sensing something otherworldly about the woman, as if she were hoarding some secret not meant for mere mortals. It was something in her skin, he thought, in the way it looked—not just the paleness, severe as that was, but in the subtle way her flesh seemed to be cracking, splitting at the seams, falling apart. She was attractive enough, he supposed, in the perfect contours of her face and the tender slope of her neck; but there was the presence of something else overwhelming whatever beauty she might have owned. Her green eyes didn't shine but glimmered sickly in the darkness, her black-clad frame hanging in sharp angles over the chair; she seemed more ghoulish than anything.

"Mind telling me what this is all about?"

In lieu of an answer she reached over, grabbing up another folder from the table.

"In 1951 an FBI agent knocked on the door of an editor of a certain science fiction magazine," she said. "Recently the editor had published a story that had caught their eye and the agent was wondering if he might ask him a few questions about it. As it turns out, apparently one of the features in that week's issue involved some...*specifics* of a certain top-secret project the government had going at the time—the hydrogen bomb, if I remember correctly. Needless to say, that little work of fiction definitely raised some eyebrows at the Pentagon."

He chuckled, couldn't help it. "They kidnap him too?"

"No reason," she told him. "As it happens it was all one

big misunderstanding, the story a coincidence, and shortly thereafter the agent departed and was never heard from again. Now as I understand you were in the service"—she glanced to a page—"the Navy for eight years? Served with the Seventh Fleet out of Yokosuka, with travels to India, the Persian Gulf, down to Australia. Been a little of everywhere, it seems." She smiled then, a pleasantry that in the half-darkness seemed somehow obscene. "Tonight is a very special night for you, Travis, whether you realize it or not. You'll be given the chance to serve your nation in a way few others have. We all have a common goal in this, and as long as you keep that in mind I believe we can work together well. I hope you take a similar view."

Travis stared at her, half not understanding what the hell she was talking about, half not wanting too. The thought crossed his mind that she was nutty, a psychotic of some sort, but no, no, despite the coolness there was an intelligence in her eyes, a half-lidded fire Travis interpreted as belonging to someone who knew what they were doing and who—just maybe—had done it many times before.

But done what exactly?

He groaned, the pounding in his head feeling worse all of a sudden.

"Listen, I realize you're just salary, ma'am, but at this point I'm going to have to ask you to cut the bullshit and give me some answers. You call this tin rig a precinct, then book me. If not, I'd rather be getting on home."

But she only gave another smile, peering back at him with those endless green eyes.

"Very well, Travis. As you wish."

§

Her name, she told him, was Lola Agnew, and she was an agent of the Bureau of Non-Traditional Weapons Defense. Travis had never heard of it and told her so, and she said there was no reason he should have. "We work for a government only four percent of which are even aware of our existence," she informed him, the gleam in her eye telling of either pride or else some erratic notion of patriotism. Travis went for the obvious question and asked what the heck was a *non-traditional weapon*, and Agnew answered with a lengthy discussion of research into what she called *fringe physics*, a field of study that—as the name implied—was far from mainstream, but that they'd succeeded in developing into a science like any other: from ESP and transglobal mental spy techniques, to biogenetics, to an ongoing study regarding the Indigo Children and their eastern counterpart, the so-called child psychics of China.

Among other things they'd played a pivotal role in Project ARTICHOKE—later MK-ULTRA—had consulted with several agencies on the Looking Glass and Stargate Projects and in the advancement of remote viewing, as well as spearheading the Starling Initiative—their flagship program, and the one for which she was on duty tonight. Their work, she told him, was of the utmost importance, not only to national security but to national prosperity, and with his cooperation—

Travis stopped her there.

"Whoa, slow down...listen, I don't mean any harm but I'm done with the military. I'm married now, left all that behind. And besides, I've got nothing to offer."

The woman stood and walked over, dropping a slip of

something into his lap. He looked at it, saw it was a lottery ticket. Turned it over and saw that it was *his* lottery ticket, his illegible signature jotted along the back. When he looked up, she was back in her seat.

"In August of last year that single piece of paper changed your life. Not the biggest lottery by Megaball standards—quite small, in fact—but plenty enough for a simple man to make a life on." Her eyes sparkled. "But what if I told you it was no accident? That your winning was all affected by some greater force? That it was...*dictated*, by some outer will?"

"I don't believe I follow."

She didn't say a word. Just stared at him with those cold green eyes, and staring back suddenly Travis caught the faintest hint of flavor in the air. Sharp and sweet, like peppermint. After a moment Agnew reached over, lifting a small binder from the next seat, removing a folder from inside.

She lifted a page, cleared her throat, and began to read:

"Peering closer I caught a shimmer of light over the waves, a dazzling sheen of flesh unknown to human hands, and beheld that which at first—consumed by a worldly mind—I did not, could not believe. And not believing I was engulfed, an otherworldly dread plunging deep to my soul as I laid full eyes on her and, seeing, had no choice in believing: perhaps five feet from her dangled curls to the tip of her slender tail, with a sloping forehead and the face—undeniable—of a woman, but with a simian mouth and the small, delicate teeth of a carp. Despite the glare of two jeweled-over eyes, pale in their ascent, her features remained sharp, her various bumps and hollows crudely carved, almost brutish, and beholding them I

was ridden by a terror too great for words. Finally the trance was complete: the great fish rose gallantly over the waves, her voice giving way to a song like that of a skylark, like a flute fingered by an angel and blown by the source of the four winds, and it was then I knew I was going to die. Knew it intimately, the way one knows a familiar lover or the path of our sun across the heavens. In that moment I warmly accepted death for all it meant and for all the joys and sorrow it held. But more than death—I accepted life. Accepted life and relished it just as warmly, as a depraved man relishes even the slightest scent of reason."

Travis remembered the words, remembered the creepy-crawly feeling up his spine as they tunneled out of his soul and onto the screen. In his story, it was the experience of this creature which frightens the man Gershwin to the point of questioning his own existence, forcing him to embark on an urgent cross-country adventure to discover the nature of his true spirit. What Gershwin didn't know was that he was being followed by a race of mind-welders who had decided to use his brain as their temporary warehouse for wayward souls.

"You describe it so well, like I can almost hear it." She raised the page in one hand, fixing him with a firm gaze of her green gimlet eyes. "So let me ask you, Travis...is there anything you'd like to tell me about hydrogen bombs?"

He leaned forward, not speaking but only staring silently at the woman and wondering what she was after when suddenly the entire cabin began to shake, shuddering wildly and bouncing them in their seats. The nausea returned, pushing him back in his seat, and when he looked next the thinnest of smiles had crested over the woman's ghost-pale face.

"Good," she called, her voice raised over the turbulence. "We've arrived."

FIFTEEN

SHE LED HIM OFF THE PLANE ONTO A DESERTED tropical runway where, moments later, they were joined by two men in similar dark suits—the first a petite soul with perfectly-combed hair and unassuming eyes, the second dark-skinned and beaming a slightly mischievous smile. Agnew turned to them and said, "Travis, I'd like you to meet my secretary, Bruce Cowan, and this is Bailey Wyck, my ground and air man."

They shook hands, Travis shooting the second man a funny look that wasn't reciprocated as the man leaned forward and offered a dead fish handshake. In the silence that followed he heard the soft crashing of waves over a beach not far away, and staring beyond the earthen runway saw a reflection of moonlight over distant waters, of stars twinkling down like diamonds on a velvet shroud. A scattered jungle of palms flanked them on either side, their fronds rustling gently as a slow breeze swept across the night.

"Anybody wanna tell me what this place is?"

But Agnew said nothing, only casting another of her cryptic smiles as she started away, leading them along an ascending cobblestoned path through the palms. Minutes later they arrived at what appeared to be a classic Malibu beach house fitted with a flair for the gothic: towering white pillars reaching to the sky and gargoyles leering from perches, but also sprawling umbrellas and front porch rockers and, looming from an upstairs terrace, a great and glimmering telescope pointed to the stars.

Travis stared at the fortress, his head still swimming from whatever kick they'd slipped into his veins. Judging from the series of security cameras he'd noticed along the cobblestoned path, whatever mystery this place held was very important indeed, and knowing this Travis's head ached all the harder. Agnew climbed the steps and approached the set of double doors out front, an ancient tree with its twisted boughs hewn intricately into the wood.

"Welcome to the Lodge," she announced. "Before going further, let it be made clear that this is a top-secret installation. Anything you see is considered classified information, and we'd prefer it to stay that way. Considering your past, I believe you can respect that."

Travis gave the house another stare. "Well, you've got my attention at least. What've you got in there, anyway—Jimmy Hoffa or Jurassic Park?"

Agnew laughed, not finding it funny, then swung open the doors and stepped inside; a moment later she vanished through the vestibule and into the play of shadows beyond, Bruce Cowan following close behind. The other dark-suited man turned to Travis and whistled.

"Woman knows what she wants," he said, chuckling, "and brother, she don't ask directions to get it."

Travis turned and looked at the man, fortyish with salt-and-pepper hair and a burgeoning beer gut. "You ever forgive them?"

"Who's that?"

"Your parents, for that name. *Bailey Wyck?*"

The man shrugged, ran a hand down his belly. "Well, it ain't Sue, so at least there's that." He spurted more laughter, then leaned close and said, "Truth is, the name's sort of a... an *alias*. You know, a fake. Join up with this outfit, man, you get named straight-off. Either they *give* it to you or you pick one yourself, but either damn way you're getting one, some security thing they got goin'. I just got a sense of humor about it, is all." He reached out a hand. "Real name's Bill Jordan. I'm from Omaha."

Travis shook it, nice and firm. "Aliases? Isn't that a little... *excessive?*"

"Protocol." Bailey shrugged and ushered Travis inside, shutting the heavy doors after them. "Hey, at least they didn't give us numbers."

"*Gentlemen, please keep the pace!*"

Agnew.

Bill Jordan from Omaha shrugged. "Duty calls, brother."

Agnew was waiting inside, escorting them through a dizzying maze of rooms that appeared to have come from another century entirely: ornate furniture with cabriole legs, classical flowing drapes, odd-glowing lamps with squat Victorian shades. Moving through these and down another corridor, Travis noticed a pair of French doors flung wide to his left, opening onto a grand moonlit balcony. At the center of the balcony sat a lonesome figure in a wheelchair, eyes poring over the emerald jungle below, and staring at him Travis sensed the smallest stirrings of memory, something familiar about the man ghosting in his mind. Catching up to Agnew moments later, he said: "Excuse me, but that man back there on the balcony...who was that?"

"Don't worry, the polio's gone," she called, not stopping. "But Frankie's an old dog; he prefers the familiarity of the wheelchair." She glanced back, shaking her head in a go-figure expression. "Roosevelt's always had a thing for the balcony."

He wasn't sure what to make of that and so said nothing as they continued down the hall, soon arriving at a second pair of solid oak doors. Agnew balled up a fist and pounded the door—once, twice, three times—and then the door opened and Travis found himself gazing into a crooked smile he'd seen plenty of times before—only this time not in the pages of some high school history book or television screen.

For a moment he stared, not believing his eyes.

"It's nice to have another Navy man in the house," the man said, reaching out and taking his hand, shaking it profusely. He welcomed Travis inside and said make yourself at home, then leaned close and whispered: "Nowhere *near* as nice as Bohemian Grove, believe me, but it'll do..."

"Thank you," Travis managed, the punch of nausea hitting him all over again.

The man grinned wildly, choked a laugh, and then wandered over to Bailey. As they talked, Travis edged closer to Agnew and whispered, "Was that who I think it was?"

"You mean Tricky Dick? You wouldn't believe the trouble we had getting him in here, let me tell you. The boys had to vote three times just to get a consensus."

The next minutes were a blur; more dream than reality, more grand hallucination than dream. Ushered around the elegant ballroom, Travis was introduced to people whose faces he'd known only in pictures since the time of his youth: Harry Truman clapped him on the back and said welcome aboard, LBJ offering a stern handshake and friendly, all-knowing smile.

All around bottles were opened and glasses poured, Travis staring with wonder as the men laughed and swooned and chatted away. Several, he noticed, were still in pajamas, plaids, slippers and robes; others stood dressed to the nines in tuxes and pinstripe suits; a mournful Beethoven sonata played softly beneath the noise. Hung over the fireplace he noticed a photo of the former leaders of the free world playing poker, cigars clamped in their mouths: Truman was giving Herbert Hoover bunny ears; Eisenhower flashed a strained grin, while Bill Clinton leaned back in a pair of dark sunglasses. To Travis, they looked like the pair he'd worn while jamming that sax on Arsenio Hall.

No sooner had he thought this than the man himself appeared, waltzing through the door wearing Bermuda shorts and a shirt straight off the back of some extra from *Blue Hawaii*.

"Mr. President?" Travis blurted.

The room grew deathly quiet, the creaking of necks nearly

audible as every head save Agnew turned to face him. Travis blushed and looked away, clearing his throat.

He turned to Clinton and said, "I, uh…I thought you were still…"

Agnew stepped forward.

"Following Bureau protocol," she told him, "when we first approached Bill with our arrangement following his tenure, he insisted on joining the Lodge immediately."

"But—I saw him on TV just last week, he was giving an interview, he—"

"A body double," Agnew explained. "Bill still writes his own speeches, of course, but once electing to undergo the Procedure no one is allowed to leave the island. Normally a death notice makes the headlines and the usual service put into motion, but in this case, following a family meeting, a rare exception was made. We searched long and hard for that double—the infamous Clinton Twin—before finally finding our man."

"Listen," Bill said, a genuine smile on his face, "I'm having the time of my life out here, I really am. These old bags have stories you wouldn't *believe*." He slapped Travis a good one across the back, his excitement contagious. "Listen, we're having a luau here tomorrow night—should be prepping the pig in a few hours? Can Travis come back for the luau?"

Agnew smiled indulgently. "I'm afraid we'll have to take a rain check on that, Mr. President; we have quite the journey ahead of us, as you well know. Country first."

Clinton gave an aw-shucks grin and fingered Travis's shoulder. "How about this one, doesn't she crack the whip? Don't you just love that?" He said, "Lola, how long have you been with us now? How many years has it been?"

"I believe I've lost count, sir," Agnew said, flashing another smile and shepherding Travis along with her hands. "As I said, we have a schedule to keep here, boys, I'm sure you all remember something about schedules. Our Mr. Barnes is in dire need of answers and I was hoping you gentlemen would enlighten him."

"It would be our pleasure," a voice rang from the back, and turning Travis saw a dark-haired man with mingled wisps of white rising from a chair, flashing a smile so pretty it could crack fine china. He walked over, beaming confidently as he extended an arm.

"Nice to finally meet you, son."

"Uh, you too," Travis said. "Pleasure's all mine, sir."

"I'm sure you're standing there, asking how is it you're talking to me right now? Asking yourself, I thought that old man was worm food? Well, I'll tell you, Travis. We'll all tell you. But let me start by saying that, simply put, the real answer is *you*—that this is all possible because of everyday hard-working Americans just like yourself. Because other brave men and women stepped up to the plate and assisted us here in this project which is like no other in American history—or, for that matter, all of history itself."

Travis swept the room, eyes dancing curiously over the famous grinning faces, the glistening chandeliers. "I don't understand, I mean...what is all this?"

Reagan smiled, that trademark twinkle flashing in his eye.

"Come right this way, and we'll tell you all about it..."

SIXTEEN

DREXL WAS LAUGHING.

He was angry—pissed all to hell—and he *couldn't stop laughing*. First on the outside and then, getting hold of himself, even louder on the inside. He tossed the last of the shrapnel into the bag, remembering again the image of the little lantern shattering over Will Styron's head, the flames crawling up his face, the screams. *Those screams!* Then it was too much and Drexl broke up, chuckling all over again as he snatched up the bag and started inside.

Still, shitty as their pick-up of the Barnes kid had gone, Drexl hadn't needed a crystal ball to see this one coming. Fact of the matter was he should've taken the fire to Styron himself, that thickhead flubbing the dose the way he had. As it was, Styron had no business in the field with him in the first place—within the Bureau, Drexl was recognized as something of a lone wolf; he did solitary work and it suited him well—but at the very least they could've paired him with a professional.

But, no, no.

Instead they'd saddled him with Dumbass M.D. and now he had one hell of a mess to clean up and—just to make things interesting—a wounded family pet on the run. And who the hell ever heard of stun-gunning a dog anyway? He'd been at this job a long time, and during his tenure performed the impossible both backwards and forwards: had crashed helicopters, blown up cars, and beaten men to death with his bare hands. He'd tortured people: from bamboo shoots to waterboarding, you name it. He'd blasted veins with syringes of air and drowned people in sinks and twice he'd lopped off heads with an axe.

But what he'd never done—he'd *never* tasered a mutt, and he'd *never* flubbed a dose, and he'd never—*not once*—went and got his face turned into a blowtorch. Just as his hair had silvered from gold, a crown for the ages, so he hadn't always been the best—it had been an uphill battle—but far as Drexl was concerned, somewhere over the last few years he'd finally attained perfection: he was a precise man, cold, methodical, but crazy where it counts. Like most people, the events of 9/11 had cut him deep, reawakening some passion for the job that he'd lost over the years. At last he saw the need for *real* heroes, the down-to-earth kind, and thought he might be cut from that cloth. That he had what it took. And he'd be damned if some bargain-bin bozo was going to come along and sully his reputation as *the best*.

Yet that's exactly what was happening, fresh before his eyes, and dropping the bag at the door Drexl wondered again at how much longer he could stand it. Lola wanted to go casting pearls before swine, then fine, that was her business. But that sort of thing cuts both ways, always had, and so *Styron* could be the one to answer for the mess Drexl was cleaning up now—not him, not by a long shot. And at the end of the night if this house of cards ended up all over the floor, well, he could answer for that too.

The stench of burnt hair ran deep as he entered the hall and caught sight of Styron leaning at a bathroom mirror, picking gristle from his singed eyebrows and fire-licked face; Drexl slapped him on the back as he passed.

"Lookin' a little extra crispy ain't ya there, Willy Boy?"

"Egghhh fuck you man! Look at this—shit—I'll never get laid again—"

Drexl kept walking, ignoring Styron's chirps as he whistled down the hall and through the rooms on that side of the house. The place was big, no doubt about it, and following procedure Drexl sifted the rooms waving his scanner and searching for frequencies—security trips, nanny-busters, all the usual party-crashers that might come back to bite. Mostly he noticed the pictures, many of them still-lifes and artsy-fartsy paintings but with photos of the Barneses spread here and there. Grand Canyon, Machu Picchu, Niagara Falls, they'd hit all the hot spots. He saw a photo of the dog that had taken part of Styron's leg—and hopefully one of his balls—a Boykin, what some folks called a *swamp poodle*. Another showed the happy couple surrounded in a supermarket, balloons galore. Probably some Jackass of the Year award.

He'd made it up the stairs when he came to a room with a crib and plain-but-pleasant wallpaper, pale yellow with the whited silhouettes of horses and elephants on the march. No rugrat, though, a fact Drexl made double-sure of as he walked over and ran two fingers down the crib's soft linen bedding.

No baby...so why the fucking crib?

Then again, maybe it was Barnes's. Maybe that's how he rolled. He was an eccentric millionaire, after all. And a writer to boot? Doesn't get much wackier than that. Only thing missing here was his mother's dried-out corpse in an attic, a predilection for taxidermy, yessir, that would seal the deal...

He moved to the next room, bypassing the old Henkel Harris four-poster and heading straight for the balcony doors, watching as the storm went on raging over the lake below. For a moment he stared, lost in the darkness, until finally the little hairs came rising at the back of his neck, softly tickling, and following their lead he looked closer and noticed the headlights, two high beams pushing slowly through the trees.

Drexl tensed, his flesh pulled tight as a snare drum around his tired bones, a wave of purest hell flushing down his face. As if by magic, he broke into an instant cold sweat, the walls spinning around him—

But no, no.

He'd been around too long—had seen too damned much—and watching the steady advance of the high beams Drexl took in a breath, heaved it out. He shut his eyes, his massive hands clenching into fists, and when he opened them next the fear had faded. The walls ceased spinning, his former cold sweat replaced by that ancient fire rising like an old good friend in his belly while Drexl watched the car's slow but inevitable approach toward the house...

§

Juan pushed through the rain, cursing himself as he steered his old Subaru down the bumpy darkness of the DeWitt Road. Cursing himself for having come here at all, for being so paranoid and—yes, okay, he'd admit it—just a little crazy after his strange encounter earlier that night.

But then why *not* feel crazy?

It was Friday the thirteenth, after all, and only twenty minutes earlier he'd been safe and warm at the store, looking forward to a big pot of veggie stew back at the house and a long night in front of the tube. They were showing a Bond marathon on Turner Classics and he didn't want to miss it.

Only something hadn't sat right about that woman, not by a long shot, and after locking up he'd stepped into the rain and an unbidden image of her had risen in his mind. The way she'd stared at him with those cold dead eyes, the questions. And what had she said? Had she really said *the C-word?* He remembered she'd been asking after Travis and that got him wondering what business a woman like that might have with Travis Barnes, and by the time he'd cranked his engine and started home, Juan was drawing blanks.

He'd made it a few miles when he had the silly compulsion to go and tell Travis about that strange woman with the funny smell and white skin and those cold sifting eyes. *Warn* him, maybe, though of what Juan wasn't sure. Now here he was, the darkness of the old DeWitt Road closing around him as he drove against the rain, bumping along until finally the endless forest opened before him and Barnes Manor loomed in the distance.

Juan pulled to a stop at the side of the house, squinting past the rain and noticing lights on in several of the downstairs windows. For a moment he sat motionless behind the wheel, thinking of the woman and wondering all over again just what in hell he thought he was doing here.

Not having an answer, Juan Marquez took a deep breath and then climbed out into the rain, running tippy-toes around to the front of the house. He was following the old stone path to the porch when he glanced up and the lights had faded now from the windows, the house grown suddenly dark.

Everybody tucked in for the night.

Juan spurted hollow laughter, amused at his buffoonery and the image of himself standing here all alone in the rain when he should've been kicked back at the house with Pussy Galore, all because of some flounder-eyed biddy with a staring problem. *Juan, mi amigo, as the saying goes, check yourself before you wreck your—*

His eyes caught on something at his feet.

Juan bent low, ignoring the pain through his body and scooping it up, peering closer as the rain splashed around him. In a sudden flash of lightning through the trees, he saw it was some kind of collar, a single golden tag gleaming in the darkness: **GAGE**

He searched the night, staring past the pouring rain and over the solid blackness of the lake. Then back to the house, a ghostly finger touching cold on his neck as the front door opened and a figure stepped out; the porch light switched on, throwing shadows down the man's tall sloping forehead and wild rodeo eyes, past his long gray hair—almost as long as Juan's own.

He raised his hand in a beckoning motion.

"*In here!*" he called, his voice hoarse over the rain. "*Inside, *come on!"*

But Juan didn't want to do that.

He didn't want to do that at all.

He glanced back to where he'd parked, imagining the .38 under the seat, wishing for it now, for the sturdy weight of it in his hand. But wishes were second only to assumptions as total wastes of time and now his hands were empty save for the collar and when the man walked down, slipping his massive fingers across his shoulder, Juan felt a tingle down his crooked old spine.

"What's your name, friend?"

"Where's Travis?" Holding it together, staying strong. "What's going on?"

But the man only laughed, tightening his grip. *"You first, hombre."*

There was a slam from inside the house, someone yelling.

"What the hell have you done?" Juan demanded, struggling away from his grasp. "I swear if you've laid a hand on that girl—"

Pain exploded like fireworks at the back of his neck, where the man had slid his fingers and was now clamping down back there, doing something with his nerves. He dropped to one knee and then the other before the man let up and brought him to his feet.

"How about we settle this inside? Whaddya say, tough guy?"

SEVENTEEN

"COME RIGHT THIS WAY, AND WE'LL TALK TURKEY..."

Reagan turned, leading Travis away from the ballroom to a smaller, sparsely lit area arrayed with a glass-topped conference table. In one corner stood a marble chess set, black and white pieces frozen in play across the board; in another he saw a somber portrait of John F. Kennedy, its swirling oils lit by the flame of a solitary candle. Standing at a coffee station not far from this Travis noticed another familiar figure, only this one dressed in a ridiculous blue-purple onesie, an elf-like beanie cap dangling from his head.

"You'll have to excuse Dwight," murmured Reagan. "He's not much of a night owl."

"*Night?* Much longer and it will be sunrise," Eisenhower grumped, his fifty-plus weight gain showing in the ruby chubbiness of his cheeks. He stirred his coffee and said, "I don't understand—why on earth would *anyone* be up at such an hour as this?"

Reagan offered an apologetic smile and gestured to the table, asking Travis to have a seat. He did, and not long after was joined by Clinton, Gerald Ford, others, all of them chatting away. Agnew stood sentinel at the back of the room.

Finally, Reagan waved for quiet and began to speak.

"Travis, what you are witnessing here tonight is the culmination of a long, strange series of events. Happenstance and luck played a part; so did meticulous studies, hard work, and, yes, perhaps a little of that daredevil spirit we Americans have been known to get from time to time. But really it all started a long time ago with a Dutchman by the name of Johannes Visser, and a certain nautical journal from the eighteenth century. Visser's account was far from thorough, and his descriptions nowhere near as good as yours, even before translation...but he painted a pretty convincing picture of what he saw—and everything that happened after. Or at least, what he *perceived* to have happened." Reagan leaned forward, a knowing gleam in his eyes. "But based on our discoveries...I'd say he was right on the money."

Travis turned to face Agnew, noticing for the first time the constellation of red-eye lights around the room—more of the cameras he'd noticed earlier. "You mean—my novel? The *nymph?*"

Agnew appeared amused. "Is that what you call it, Mr. Barnes? A nymph?"

He stared at her, crazy bitch that she was.

"What else would it be?"

Before she could answer Reagan reached over, flipping a

switch on the wall to his right. As he did so, the room began to change, the wall at his back opening to reveal the cool glow of a massive floor-to-ceiling aquarium.

As Travis looked on, the soothing blue ambience of the tank filled the room, a sudden apprehension taking hold of him as he realized this glow wasn't solely that of the tank but also of the (*monster*) swimming *inside* the tank—a phosphorescent flash of scales, the jumbled mass of her body twisting to a forked caudal fin as thin and wispy as twin rags of tulle.

Her movements slowed, the breaths grown shallow in his chest when Travis noticed two gargantuan hands hung limply from her speckled, skeletal arms. Her face remained veiled, clouded in the water by a stalk of wild honey-colored hair, parting just enough now to reveal a pair of piercing opaque eyes, a cat-fish snout—and then, at last, like a secret long-forgotten by the earth, the bulging mound of a wither-lipped mouth. In a motion too quick for human eyes, she again took flight, lunging effortlessly through the water.

Reagan gestured grandly to the glass, the big reveal of a magician doing his trick.

"We call them sirens, Travis. Our top-secret boys in Washington have been well aware of their existence since—well, since the earliest days of the First Word War, I believe. Before that they'd been mentioned for hundreds of years, not just by drunks and mythology but by sensible men, of their right minds. Explorers, mostly. Most know them by another name, of course, but then mermaids are pretty little ladies who sit all day running combs through their hair and falling in love. A *siren*, on the other hand...is another creature entirely. Mermaids are myth; but sirens, Travis, they are the truth inside the lie. In 1493, Christopher Columbus reported seeing three just off the Haitian coast. A hundred years later, Henry Hudson logged the coordinates where he observed one in the waters near Russia. John Smith spotted a pair off the coast of Massachusetts. The list goes on."

"The only problem," said Truman, "was how to get our *hands* on one..."

"All of that changed with Visser's journal," Reagan continued. "With his archaic tutelage it was only a matter of time, and soon enough we'd snagged our first siren off the shores of Kauai and the Starling Initiative was created, incorporating a host of molecular and evolutionary biologists, biochemists, geneticists. By 1943 they'd put together what we Lodge Boys like to call *the magic milkshake*. A potpourri concoction the scientists delivered up, claiming they'd discovered the fountain of youth."

Travis stared at the creature, watching her lap tiny circles in the water. She was gorgeous and terrible and severe, and watching her flit lithely about the tank he wished he'd never set eyes on her.

He asked, "A concoction of *what?*"

"A Petri dish of proteins and nutrients, all of them culled from the life-giving cells of the siren's body—though the lion's share, I understand, came from the wrists *down*. Fingernails, mostly. All mashed together to produce a serum unlike any other, though of course several doses are required, over several months, for regeneration to take hold. This is known as the Procedure; I've had it—we all have—and so have lived well beyond our years. Make no mistake, however; it's not immortality we're talking here, far from it. More like a...*life exten-*

sion. I'll be the first to tell you, it has been no bed of roses." He paused, gazing thoughtfully at the creature behind the glass. "In truth, it has been a rather hard and lonely road. One that, had I known better, I'd never have traveled. Sometimes dead is better. Sometimes, Travis, dead is *best*."

"But really," Roosevelt said, rolling now into the room and over to the shimmering glow of the tank, "the Procedure was only the beginning. A scratching of the surface, you might say." He stared into the aquarium, Travis wondering for a moment if he might not reach out, give a few playful taps at the glass; instead he only lit another of his cigarettes and stared with bored curiosity as the siren did two graceful circuits around the tank.

"Frankie-boy is absolutely right," Reagan said, clamping a hand on the man's shoulder. "That damned journal, Travis, it was *just* the Rosetta Stone we needed. Not only did Visser tell us *how* the sirens were to be reined in, but he also clued us in to what is perhaps their greatest feature. An ability unlike anything this world has ever known." He grinned, giving a practiced tweak of his chin. "Last year you won—what was it? Thirty million in some lottery deal, is that right?"

Travis felt the laughter bubbling up, forced it back down.

Insanity, he realized, was a relative term.

"Let me guess, you're gonna tell me it was no accident. That it was—what? Orchestrated? And by who?" He gestured to the aquarium, to the cruel joke of nature lapping round inside. "By *this?*"

"Don't laugh too hard, Mr. Barnes, not just yet. Based on Bureau research these so-called sirens have been the basis of our country's prosperity for the past many years—and, if one takes the earliest travelers at their word, perhaps longer than that." Reagan turned, his solemn expression cast blue in the calming glow of the aquarium. "There is...much more than meets the eye about these little women of ours, Travis. Some believe they know all of the past and can see the future, though we have no evidence of that. Others claim they can kill a person by merely speaking their name, though our experience bears no record of that. Still others claim their origins are more bird than fish, though that has more to do with fanciful mythologies than anything based in reality.

"But what they *can* do—based on a crumbling old journal and verified by men and women just like yourself—they can *will* around the events of our world in a way we could only dream to understand. Affecting the history of things to come no matter the space or distance, working among the ebbs and flows of peoples' lives, changing things—little things, big things, but always for the better. Sicknesses vanish. Cancers disappear. Visions have been witnessed." He looked at Travis severely. "Some people even win the lottery."

Travis thought back, remembering the lottery, the coins before that. Remembering Tara and his eerie trance in the woods. Coincidence? Or was it like these impossible men—all of them former leaders of the free world—said: that his life had been tampered with, *exposed* to something?

But to *what* exactly? Some cosmic fish? Some wild magic which humanity could never grasp—and maybe never should?

"What Ron here is trying to say, Trav," Clinton moved in, dropping a gentle hand on his shoulder, "is that you aren't the first person to be sitting where you are. We've heard all about the songs these ladies sing—each one amazing, each one unique—and we're aware of the things that can happen to a person because of them. Now the description in your story—you'll forgive me, I haven't read it—now that might just be one hell of a coincidence. But I don't think so. How about you, Harry? Dick?"

"I don't."

"Not me."

"Neither do I," Clinton said. He pointed his finger and said, "And I don't think you believe it either, Travis. What else has happened? What other untold experiences? Blackouts maybe? Hallucinations?" He leaned closer, going in for the kill as he gestured once more to the aquarium. "And where were you the *first* time you saw one of these little ladies?"

Travis stared, studying the tank, the cool blue of it like a salve to his mind. For a moment he watched this wondrous (*monster*) swimming back and forth, the sight of her bringing back all those old emotions he had stuffed so far down he'd like to say he'd forgotten them.

Only he hadn't.

He'd pretended, and used his illusion, and deluded himself, but he'd *never truly forgotten*. And watching her graceful dance through the water, her milky eyes never leaving his own, at last Travis relented—he saw no other choice. Suddenly it all came flooding back—the cool rush of an easterly wind, the first trills of what he came to know as the Fibonacci tune floating softly over waves washed gold with the light of dawn. The thing he'd seen and not seen and a bluer version of which he was looking at now through the clear cage of the aquarium. And finally, after so long and all his excuses to the contrary, Travis knew it to be so and his entire world fell away, everything he thought he knew falling along with it.

It was enough.

He looked up, and by the enduring glow from the aquarium saw a hopeful gleam in the eyes of the men surrounding the table.

"We'd been deployed from Yokosuka..."

§

He told the story as best he remembered, though only after starting did Travis realize the person in that memory was more like someone in a dream: a man beset by something he'd not foreseen nor could ever hope to understand, but that shone itself one ordinary morning from an endless stretch of the Philippine Sea.

It wasn't that he'd held onto that memory; he hadn't.

He'd let it go, suppressed it, couldn't believe it. Didn't want to.

Some things are better kept to oneself, and sometimes even those things are better left forgotten. But he'd never forgotten, and failed at making it unreal, and so for the first time in his life Travis gave words to that early morning aboard the USS *Gettysburg*—a regular morning, nothing fateful about it—about his casual topside stroll and the mournful herald that had cast his eyes along the water. And finally the chill—that unearthly chill, down deep in his soul—as his eyes touched on hers, some scarlet monster whose ugliness was made a moot point by the soft vibrato from her shriveled gray lips.

And when those famous faces surrounding the table didn't laugh or scold him but listened with an interest that bordered on the zealous, Travis experienced a comfort beyond words.

Following his account there was a brief question-and-answer period during which Agnew laid a map across the table and Travis fingered the general area of his encounter based on his deployment with the Seventh Naval Fleet, capping off his story with a summary of the magical collection of coins and his experience with the lottery. Only his vision in the woods Travis kept to himself, not only because he thought it unnecessary but also because it was too intimate, somehow—something made even more poignant by its private place in his heart.

"And you've never shared this...*experience* with anyone?" Agnew asked.

"Thought about it," he told her. "A million times. But no. What's the point?"

Agnew nodded, glancing to the coordinates he'd indicated on the map and then jotting into her pad. She stared a moment at what she'd written before turning and slipping from the room, and no sooner was she gone than Travis heard the slow creaking of a wheelchair and turned to see Roosevelt gazing at him with a certain uncomfortable light in his eyes.

"I understand you're a writer, Mr. Barnes," he said. "Perhaps you've read *Lord of the Flies*—it's my absolute favorite novel, you know. Just spellbinding." He raised the tube of his cigarette holder, took in a drag. Breathed smoke across the table and said, "Books are my only escape nowadays, I'm afraid. They don't allow us much in the way of outside time, if you catch my drift..."

Travis glanced at the men, many of them chatting near the aquarium, others glancing anxiously to the cameras still flashing red in the darkness.

"You mean...you guys really never get out of this place?"

"Not for seventy years," he deadpanned, although Travis thought he heard something else in the way he'd said that, as well. Something like bitterness. Roosevelt's eyes clouded over, dreamy and faraway. "I dream of Hyde Park," he said. "I'd do anything to get back again, if only for a while." His eyes sank deeper. "A few hours in the sun..."

Travis wasn't so sure what to say to that and so only stared politely and kept his mouth shut. A moment later Agnew appeared through the door, Reagan turning suddenly from the aquarium and fixing him with another of his sparkly-toothed grins.

"When I told you the Starling Initiative was like no other in American history, I meant it—and the stakes couldn't be greater." He gestured again to the siren, her massive fingers clenched now over the faux-remains of a miniature clipper ship buried in the sand. "Why, imagine if we'd had another of these sweethearts in the months leading up to 9/11? Could catastrophe have been avoided? For that matter, what if all the tragedies of our troubled history could've somehow been averted—if only we'd had fortune on our side?" His eyes grew dark. "And so help me, what if one of these miracle-workers fell into the wrong hands?"

Travis heard the words, understood them, but still they didn't make sense. "But how do we change it? How *can* we?"

"That's where you come in," Reagan told him. "Because without you, without everyday goodhearted Americans like yourself who have been touched by these beautiful, amazing creatures and who are willing to give all for their country, who are willing to lay down their own good fortune, forsake it, sacrifice it for the greater good—why, America would not be the nation it is today. I believe that, and so does everyone at this table here tonight. Seconded?"

"Second."

"Third."

"Fourth."

Eisenhower was dozing, the fuzzy ball of his sleeping cap tucked soundly beneath the beginnings of a dewlap. Nixon gave him a sharp elbow.

"*Mamie!*" he yelped and, gaining his senses, murmured "fifth."

Down the line—nodding heads, hear-hears, mouths filled with more champagne. Across the room, Agnew curled her own smile and whispered to Bruce Cowan. Travis glanced again at the red-starred constellation of cameras; he couldn't keep his eyes off them.

"We believe it," Reagan continued, "and now we're standing here and asking you to believe it, too. And that song? That's *yours*, son. No one can take that away. But if you *give it up* willingly, for the good of all, well now...that's something else entirely, am I wrong?" He gushed a smile and said, "A lot of this probably doesn't make sense to you, understandably. We're all still...wrapping our brains around it. But Ms. Agnew here and her crack team of scientists, they've come a long way, and taken this whole thing so much further than we'd ever dreamed. They know a thing or two, believe you me, and so don't worry yourself—trust *them* to fill in the gaps. Trust *them* to do the hard stuff; *you* do the easy stuff. You do what your heart and conscience tell you."

Travis bent low, planting elbows on his knees. His vision danced and swirled. "You're right, I don't understand. What happens next?"

Roosevelt dropped a brittle hand on his shoulder.

"Follow Agent Agnew," he said. "Do as she says, and the Bureau will handle the rest. Do this and, I assure you, we'll all wake up to a much brighter tomorrow."

Travis considered the proposition, still only half-sure of what he was considering. He sensed the reality of everything—of a world where dead presidents lived, where a previously sturdy existence was now open to the whims of unknown creatures from the deep—laying over him like an unknowable burden. But then ten years ago he'd made a pledge to his country, and though relieved of duty in the eyes of the Navy, he intended to keep it.

He nodded, snapping up a quick two-fingered salute.

"Absolutely," he said. "Whatever you need, sir."

Reagan smiled. "I'm pleased to hear it, Travis. What you're doing here tonight—it's nothing short of heroic. With that in mind, before you go we have something we'd like to present to you. Call it a token of our appreciation."

"Mr. Barnes?"

Roosevelt walked toward him, out of his chair for the first time all night, something draped over his arm; seeing it, Travis couldn't help but grin.

"A new jacket?"

"A gift," Clinton told him. "Not exactly a coat of many colors—"

"But close enough," Reagan finished, twinkling as ever.

Agnew checked her watch. "Let's wrap this up, gentlemen."

"Of course," Reagan said, "we wouldn't dream of any further delay."

Travis accepted the jacket—a nice two-button blazer, dark blue with gleaming cufflinks—and slipped inside, working it along the shoulders and then standing back. "Well? How's it look?"

Reagan smiled. "Impeccable."

"Glorious," Roosevelt chimed in.

Clinton whistled and said, "Damn spiffy."

Travis gave a little spin, his head feeling better suddenly. "Agnew?"

"It's gorgeous, Travis," she said, glancing again at her watch. "As always, it's been a blast, gentlemen, but I am officially calling time." Groans, mumbles, raspberries. "I know, I know, but rules are rules, boys."

Reagan stepped forward, the two men pumping a quick handshake as the others filed begrudgingly out of the room. "See to your business," he said, placing a perfectly preserved hand along one arm. "Do what is right and I trust things will end well for you."

He gave Travis a final twinkling smile before turning away.

§

Later as the plane gained altitude and the lights of the Lodge grew dim beneath them, Travis sat looking through his window, eyes skimming over the palms and down to the water. With such natural wonders on the outside, it struck him how the true wonders were what lay *inside* that small sprinkling of lights below. Only then, as he watched, another smattering of lights sprang up along the water, farther away this time, then another.

Travis pressed closer to the glass, aiming a finger outside. "What is that? Those lights out there?"

Agnew stooped forward, staring across the water, her eyes solemn as if searching for some meaning in the darkness. After a long moment she turned and started away, the brittle murmur of her voice following her down the aisle.

"There are other Lodges than this, Mr. Barnes..."

EIGHTEEN

 *HO ARE YOU? WHY ARE YOU DOING THIS?"*
He was blubbering now, the old man's face bright with defiance despite the blood spattered from his busted-up nose. They'd hauled him inside and Styron sat him at the table, strapped him down and batted him around a little. Nothing serious, attention-getters mostly, a few well-landed blows just to show they weren't playing around. Now Drexl stared at the mess he'd left behind, leaning forward and fishing a wallet from the old man's pants, flipping it back.

A slow, gat-toothed grin crept over his face.

"Wanna know who I am, Juan Marquez? That's like asking who's the wind. I'm nobody, that's who I am."

The old man looked at him, eyes bunched as if combing for some hidden meaning in his features. "How long have you been in the killing business?"

Drexl laughed, couldn't help it. "Now who said anything about killing, Juan?"

But he only stared, still with that furtive light in his eyes.

"Sometimes you get a sense of a person by the way they move their hands," Juan Marquez said. "You can tell all sorts of things about a man by looking at his hands. If he's clean, if he's dirty. If maybe he's a nervous guy and chews his nails, if he digs ditches or fluffs pillows for a living."

"Whoopie-fuckin'-do."

"You've stolen a lot of life in your day, my friend. I can see the blood on your hands—look! It drips down even now." Something flashed across the old man's face, a sudden composure which to Drexl seemed wholly unfamiliar. "You pride yourself in being a hard man, yes...but when I look into those big black eyes of yours all I see is foolishness. Some sort of twisted intelligence, yes, but with the moral hygiene of a Saigon whore."

Styron slapped him hard across the face, then slapped him again. *"Clam it, old man! Hear me? I said shut your fuckin' trap!"*

"Easy," Drexl said, laying a hand on Styron's shoulder. "Easy there, now take it easy."

Styron stared at the man, transfixed. *"I say we kill him."*

And suddenly it was too much, all of it, the whole rotten business. Drexl groaned, the beginnings of a peptic ulcer throbbing down in his gut as he turned and walked out, Styron calling after him as he headed for the door.

"Yo Drex, wait, where ya goin'...?"

Drexl glanced back, his face feeling swollen in the darkness.

"Give me five fuckin' minutes, can you do that? Please? Just keep our buddy here company till I get back. Think you can handle that, Hamburgler?"

Styron smiled his burnt-face smile, raw skin glistening. "Yeah, all right, I'll keep the old bastard company. Hey, old bastard, you wanna play Canasta? How about it, old man?"

§

He walked outside, hurrying through the rain to the old Subaru hatchback and hopping inside. The temps had dropped south with the storm, and after settling behind the wheel Drexl felt around for the keys and gave them a crank. Sat puffing his menthol and watching as the smoke slowly filled the car, the storm beating down around him.

Following that still, small voice in his head, Drexl reached down and grabbed the .38 from beneath the seat, lifted it from its holster and spun the wheel, snapped it back. He sniffed around for more ammo, saw ink pens, napkins, receipts. Popped the glove compartment and a box cutter went clattering to the floor. He'd leaned forward to scoop it up when his eyes caught suddenly on the interstellar glow of the dashboard lights, dazzling in their throw-back elegance, a familiar song drifting softly over the radio. "Don't Fear the Reaper."

Drexl frowned, struggling to decipher the best step forward. Still beating back the feeling he was *missing* something, something clear and right in front of his eyes if only he would *look* and *see it*. He turned, watching through the windows as little Will Styron performed his toughest Brooklyn mob-man routine to the sad sack of shit they had tied up inside. Drexl wanted to laugh, couldn't pull it off.

Unbelievable, after all these years, this was his life.

A hard man, the old-timer had said.

Stolen a lot of life and had the bloody hands to prove it.

But then Drexl had learned more than murder in his time; he'd learned how to *survive*. He'd done hard work for shit pay and hadn't complained unless there was hunger in his belly or else some fool's dream in his head. Like all the other Dust Bowl flunkies, he'd suffered through the Depression and so damn sure knew tough times: he remembered standing in the endless lines for day-old bread and cold soup, and stuffing newsprint inside his jackets to stay warm at night. To keep his family fed he'd slain whole sacksful of Hoover hogs, what they'd called the roving jackrabbits that frequented the countryside.

Yet he'd also lived through the existentialism of the sixties, the groovy indulgence of the seventies, the shameful excess of the feel-good eighties; he'd lived through it all, and so knew most people today had zero idea what a hard time was. And that was okay by him, just fine, because he saw people for what they truly were—which was little more than ships in the night. You know somebody six months, six years, *sixty* years, and people think that sort of thing will last; but he knew how it really worked. Truth is most folks slip away, and to believe otherwise amounted in his eyes to a fool's delight.

He'd seen his family slip away. He'd seen best friends and worst enemies slip away. He'd fed with royalty and burgled with beggars. He'd been best man, husband-to-be, he'd been the other man. And one day this too—this job, these people—would slip away as surely as those others had slipped away, just another memory of something that happened a long, long time ago. And that's how he liked it. The rolling stone gathers no moss, and be damned if nature had ever put a cushion under his toes.

And yet somehow here he was, infested in another endless moron-athon with no easy way out. And all because of what? A civvie singing some jackass version of *do-re-mi*?

Shameful.

Look, it drips down even now...

Drexl stubbed out his cigarette, lit another. He considered phoning Lola, letting her in on this latest fuck-a-row; after Styron's episode on the patio, he imagined she'd just about brownout her panties.

But then what was the point?

She'd be calling soon enough, checking in at her usual time once the coordinates were in.

He glanced at his watch, saw quarter past one.

Probably she'd have them airlift the old man's Subaru and turn it into a tin can somewhere in Omaha, same as they'd done with the Mini Coop. As for Juan Marquez's soon-to-be corpse, what they did with that he could care less. People would be surprised how easy it was to completely erase somebody's existence, totally melting them away, just poof, like they never were. Hell, you could sweep just about anybody under the rug, so long as somebody was careful and knew what they were doing.

And that's when it hit him—an epiphany, almost.

He'd come here for a purpose, after all, to do a job; only now a new design had formed in his head—something bigger, better. Something that actually made some *sense* after ninety years of kicking the can down the road of better living. He stared ahead through the rain, not daring to breathe as the idea fell clunking into his lap, and when the weight had settled and he saw it for what it was, Drexl sensed a great relief sweeping over his soul.

He took another drag from his menthol and turned up the music, softly singing along, his old voice lost to the world as the rain continued to pour...

NINETEEN

IFE HAD A WAY OF TEACHING LESSONS, NO MATTER how difficult the subject, and was a rule unto itself as far as how to teach them. They were taught, however, as surely as the sun rises and sets and pride precedes a fall, they were taught. And if life had taught Juan Marquez anything, the cancer growing heavy and black in his body had taught him still more.

He'd received the news the usual way, circuiting all the proper channels that started with a routine checkup gone awry and ended sitting in a chair and feeling numb all over as the doctor gave the big headline.

But Juan had known it already. Had fished it out in the young doctor's calm, compassionate eyes—and that numbness he felt? In the end, it had been only the beginning of some backwards new reality that kept growing and growing until, one day, it consumed his world. By that time they'd deemed him *inoperable*, a curse forged in his liver and then spread to the four winds, and though the docs had been hesitant to give a timeline on how long he had left, between the lines Juan surmised it was somewhere in the ballpark of NOT VERY LONG—a prophecy unfulfilled all these many months.

Far from killing, however, the cancer had only made him stronger, refining in himself a discipline he'd assumed—or at least *hoped*—was always there, but that he'd never been forced to exercise until now. Through this discipline he'd learned many things. That quiet walks along the beach still have a place for old men like himself, the cool sand slipping through his toes and teaching him still other, more subtle lessons about the life he'd left behind, and what little bit of it there was left to live.

He'd learned the quickest way to ruin a person was to put them around others even worse off than themselves.

He'd learned the most effective way to divide a family was money, the worst way to spoil a woman was with too much love, and the hardest way to die was alone.

And some nights the cool sand through his toes and the discipline joined hands and together taught him the patience that led not only to forgiveness, but to a gratitude Juan found he was unable to put into words. Blessed be the earth and all who dwell thereon, and all who'd mingled even the briefest moment of their lives with his.

Juan's nose spurted more blood, and he wondered whether that sentiment extended to the monster lumbering before him now, shuffling like a beggar across the kitchen and rummaging through the fridge. Revulsion spun a red thread through his belly as Juan stared at the blackened crisps of flesh peeled back from his face, the man's eyes flashing occasionally beneath the lights and revealing a mind brimmed-over with question marks and suspicions, but most of all with a careless violence Juan had known to take root at the hearts of certain men.

He looked up then, slamming down the mustard and fixing Juan with another of his big-bully stares. "Stop lookin' at me, old man. I told you once, now you're startin' to piss me off."

"Your face," Juan said, "I mean...what's left of it...Travis do that to you? He did, didn't he?" He smiled indulgently, making it last. "Lit your whole world on fire, damned if he didn't—and your buddy out there? Grandpa Fabio? He don't know it yet, but Travis is gonna do the same thing to him when—"

Then the cold steel of a knife, pressing against his neck.

Styron grinned down foolishly, shaking his burnt-to-hell head in a way that said somebody should've known better.

There was death in those eyes.

"Keep talkin', old man. 'Cause sooner or later you're gonna get what's coming and you can bet your ugly ass I'll be the one to give it to you. So go ahead, get it out big boy, let it rain." He leaned close, a smoked-sausage smell filling Juan's nose as he whispered in one ear: *"I'm gonna love watchin' you die, old man..."*

Juan nodded, carefully, a fresh drain of blood slipping down his chin as Styron pulled back the knife and settled across the table. Grabbed up his sandwich and took a bite, chewing away as his skin glistened beneath the kitchen lights and he waggled a finger and said:

"Y'know, Juan...I've known people like you seems like my entire life. Bottom-feeders, filthy immigrants got nothin' better to do than breed and mooch, mooch and breed. Hell, your kind've been crawling around since the beginning of time, shame is you'll probably be crawling around till the end of it. Talk about pearls before swine." He grimaced, eyes scrunching with incredulity. "*Shoo-we*, and the stench of you, I can't stand another minute of it. I swear I'll puke. Do all you Mexies smell this bad, you're fuckin' killing me here, Juan..."

At that moment the front door slammed, the long-haired man slipping still as a ghost into the kitchen. Juan stared at him, not seeing much. Not liking what he did see.

"What happened?" Styron called. "You talk to Lola? Can we eighty-six this taco or what?"

His partner looked around, saw the mustard on the counter, an open bag of bread.

"Did you make a *sandwich?*"

Styron leaned back in his chair, grinning through mouthfuls of his midnight snack. Now he stopped chewing, tossed up a tentative hand and said, "Shit, Drex...I was hungry..."

His partner laughed, hard and full and rolling. Then he laughed again and started over and placed two firm hands on Styron's shoulders. His last laugh was loudest of all, however, echoing loudly as the man revealed what looked a lot like Juan's own rusted box-cutter and sent it sliding smooth as butter through his partner's neck, dragging a slow but brutal plow across the tube of meat and bone connecting William Styron's head to the rest of his body.

And watching while the blood spilled and the thunder rumbled and lightning flashed like a strobe through the windows, for the first time that night Juan Marquez felt the bottom fall out of his heart.

Travis, what the hell have you gotten yourself into?

§

Drexl stared at the blood, a perfect mirror pooling across the kitchen floor.

He sparked a menthol and grabbed a seat at the table, his attention inevitably returning to the blood, and for a moment he experienced a quick flash of regret at the clean-up on a mess like this.

Then he remembered his epiphany back in the car, and realized there would never be any clean-ups ever again. Not at his hands, not at anyone else's. Knowing this made him warm inside, like a campfire of the soul, and looking around he noticed Styron's dead hand had dropped what was left of his bologna sandwich, the halves separating on his blood-puddled gut. Drexl reached over, grabbing each of the goopy halves and cramming them down into the gory stump of his partner's neck, flipping up what was left of his head.

Never did know when to shut up, he thought, only afterward realizing he'd said the words aloud. But the old-timer didn't respond, only sat there, still watching him with those cool black eyes, wrists still clasped to the arms of his chair; only then he *was* moving, arms pulling against their ties as a spasm of coughs racked his frame and, at last, a bloody gout of blood went spattering across the tile.

Drexl dragged long and smooth on his cigarette.

"Now *that*," he said, "that is nasty through and through." He gave a funny look. "Don't give out on me yet, Juan. We've got a long night ahead..."

Almost in wonder, Juan Marquez asked, "Who *are* you people?"

But before he could answer there was a buzzing noise and Drexl snatched up his phone, grinning. "Call us the watchers," he said, standing now and lumbering toward the hall. "The people hanging in the shadows to make sure the heavy shit doesn't slam the fan. Now how about you sit tight, catch your breath?" He was almost out of the kitchen when he turned back and said, "And please, Juan? Try not to make a mess."

§

"Which zone?"

"Which do you think?" Lola's voice, teasing but still with that standard granite touch.

"Sixth?"

"Go west, young man."

"Seventh? *Eighth?*"

"Bingo."

Drexl checked his watch, doing the numbers in his head. "Sunrise here by seven."

"We won't make sunrise."

"Oh?"

"We've got a long way to go here, Bandit, and a short time to get there. Throw in a visit with those lunatics at the Lodge, doesn't leave much room."

Bandit.

Drexl couldn't resist a smile at that, the old pet name bringing back memories of so many better days. They'd made a good pair, once upon a time. He cooed softly into the phone and said, "Why, honey, you haven't called me that in ages. Which one were you again, Snowman or Frog?"

Lola made a noise, not exactly a groan.

"Just do your job, Drexl. I'll do mine, we'll call it a night."

"Listen, far as I'm concerned you should thank your lucky stars that Barnes kid arrived in one piece. This buddy-cop business doesn't fly with me, Lola, I'm done with it. I can take care of myself, I don't need a babysitter."

"Consider it duly noted. How are things there? Do you have the dog?"

He glanced to an empty space on the carpet. "Got 'im. Want me to put him on, you two want a word with each other?" He laughed: "I'm *joking*, of course. He's napping."

"Your voice, what's wrong with you? What were you doing?"

"I'm skinning my sausage, okay? Just shootin' my loads, can ya diggit?" That's what he wanted to tell her; instead he heard himself say, "Piecing through the collected works of Richard Bachman."

"Never heard of him. How's William?"

Drexl spied his former partner in the kitchen, his bloodied form slumped clumsily forward in the chair; in Drexl's opinion, he'd never looked so smart.

"Much better, thanks for asking. Face is grilled all to shit but no, really, he's fine."

"Just be ready, got it? I mean it, no more mistakes."

"Ready and waiting," Drexl told her. "You be sure and check in with us later, darling, mm-kay?"

But the line was dead and Drexl slipped the phone into his pocket, doing so as quickly as possible so as to avoid crumbling the entire fucking machine in his hand just as surely as he would crumble Lola Agnew's skull, grind it to fucking powder, just as soon as he got her alone in her precious Cadillac.

TWENTY

LOLA PUT DOWN THE PHONE, TRYING HER HARDEST TO wipe the sour taste from her mouth.

Once upon a time Drexl Samson had been the very best in the business, and she recalled an era—distant as it was—when she'd actually, well, *liked* the guy. Samson was a man who had a few years on her in the Bureau and who'd helped her move up when it counted, when she was low on the totem and easy to be overlooked. She'd done the rest herself, however, and even then repaid what little she owed, sleeping with him throughout the eighties. Back when he was still in his commando phase, muscular and sleek, before putting on the extra weight, getting grouchy. Eternal youth didn't solve anyone's problems, just complicated the ones you had; cigarettes and alcohol killed just as surely, only slower now, the Procedure drawing it out, making it last.

Still, he'd been useful in his time, though occasionally something of an oddball, and with a violent streak so red hot it would be a weakness were it not for his fanatic devotion to some cockeyed notion of honor. There was a darkness in him she did not understand. All men are obsessed with death, she knew that. But with Drexl it was different. He was, by all accounts, a highly capable assassin, yes, but a big baby at heart. Never satisfied, jealous half the time, always looking out for someone better to come along and try and take his place. And sweet as memories of those better days seemed, Lola could no longer deny the fact that Samson had grown unstable in his later years; he was a mad dog, wild, unpredictable, forever on the verge of spinning out of control.

Sooner or later, he would have to be put down.

But lo, another time.

At the moment she was more concerned with their current guest of honor, and what sort of winning home run—nay, grand slam—he could score for them tonight.

She settled back in her chair, grabbing up Barnes's folder. That old magic rising in her veins as she picked through the stack of papers and photographs inside. Navy records. Report cards. Couple speeding tickets. She'd been patient with him, she realized. A lot more patient than she'd been with some of the others. Maybe it was the subtle sadness that wrapped him like a cloak, or the fact he'd lived most of a decade of his young life from the confines of a greasy Navy suit.

But then plenty of their previous patriots had been military and so that didn't fly either, now did it? No, Lola decided, she was being patient for another reason. Though in its earliest days the Bureau had done well harvesting sirens off the

American coasts—those waters were hardly tapped, after all—they'd always supplemented their collection with those from abroad: rare jewels from foreign waters around the globe, from Baffin Bay to the Bellingshausen Sea, the West Indies, Lesser Antilles.

And of all sirens, those of the Orient had proved most lucrative.

Barnes had seen one, and if putting it in the Bureau's net took a little patience on her part then she was water, she was ice, she was holy mother mountain. It had been two years now since their last catch and already she could feel the adrenaline building, popping in her veins. She'd perused the write-up her boys had prepped on Barnes and if she'd read correctly between the lines, Lola assumed she could expect a few more surprises from her little blue-eyed charge.

But then that was just fine because Lola had a few surprises of her own, a few aces up the sleeve, and was all-too-eager to see them played. She was still imagining the cold slap of those cards on the table when she heard a knock at the cabin door and Bailey Wyck bobbed his head inside.

"Agent Agnew? Anything I can get for you before we settle down?"

"Just a little privacy, Wyck. Are your boys ready for us?"

"On the water as we speak, set out from the *Melchizedek* half an hour ago." He stepped inside, one hand sweeping absently over his belly as he offered a smiling puppy-dog stare. "Now are you *sure* there's nothing you need, ma'am?"

She offered a patient but thin-lipped smile, then fiddled some fingers and waited as he shut the door after himself. No sooner was he gone than she heard a familiar clipping and turned to see Bruce Cowan in his usual seat, his face showing cold and blue against the darkness.

"We should get rid of that one, at your convenience," he told her, still clipping meticulously at his nails. Always a funny one, that Bruce, meek as a church mouse but usually with a perfect gauge for when to keep his mouth shut and his opinions to himself. She'd almost forgotten he was back there.

"Give it a rest, Bruce. We've all had a long night."

"Yes, well..."

Bruce fell silent, using that gauge for all it was worth, the small *click-click-click* of the nail clippers filling the cabin as Lola leaned back and closed her eyes, hoping for some quality shuteye before the final hours ahead. Trying her best to relax, cut loose, let herself go. The folder on Barnes dropped, spilling papers over the plush navy carpeting as Lola dreamed of the inevitable rest at the end of her labors, her mind spinning with it, swept away...

TWENTY-ONE

As an engineer, Travis had spent most of his time in the Navy below deck, hours upon hours locked away in the sweaty bowels of the *Gettysburg*. It was a thankless job, and a dirty one, but necessary, and between the endless grind of drills and reading gauges and shifts on watch, sleep was little more than a luxury. Some weeks he'd rarely seen sunlight, and more than a handful of times over the course of his career had actually fainted—whether from exhaustion, sleep deprivation, or dehydration, he wasn't sure.

Surely the plane's cabin wasn't as bad as all that, but still he couldn't deny a certain similarity between those surroundings and these: the feeling of being closed-up, shut in, suffocated. He supposed he should've been sleeping—he was tired, after all, the headache faded but the nausea still going strong—only something told him sleep would be impossible, a near-Sisyphean task the likes of which, ironically, he was too tired to attempt.

He shifted uncomfortably, running over the events of the last few hours like a man searching for something there was no way of knowing was actually there. Following his visit to the Lodge, Travis had come swiftly to the conclusion that his old world—the world where politicians stayed dead and sirens were ship-wrecking myths and where luck was still a throw-away notion—was gone. He'd believed in that world, trusted it, had based all sorts of decisions on the truthfulness and reliability of that world.

But now that world was bust, one more lie in a pale sea of artifice, and the only thing more miserable than facing such a truth was the damnable notion of hiding from it. He'd read about things like this—bizarre happenings, twice-told tales—but wasn't so sure how open he was to *believing* it. Wasn't there some kind of rule about that? He who puts weird-ass shit into his mind shall not *experience* such things in real life?

Something like that?

He stared from his window, swallowed by the sprawl of a perfect starless night as he wondered what came next. Ostensibly they were on to the Next Big Thing, and though no one had bothered telling him exactly what that might be, some little bug in his gut told him it involved the Fibonacci tune—his "song" as the Lodge Boys called it—and that it would probably be on the water.

Perhaps, he thought, the very waters he'd gazed on that morning all those years ago.

And while several hours in the clouds was typically the

standard for such a trip, considering Agnew's urgency and the sleek Lockheed-Martin looks of the plane he was presently riding, Travis suspected they would arrive sooner rather than later.

Then again, who knows? It was all simple conjecture, after all; maybe they were headed to Disney World. Put in some time at Epcot with Mickey and the Gang, take some pictures, watch some fireworks. Good times.

Just then a beeping noise and he noticed a cell phone on a table across the cabin. Agnew's, he assumed, though she'd been gone half an hour now and Travis had no problems with that at all. Still, the beeping did no favors for his nerves and when it happened again he had the momentary urge to get up and smash the thing into a thousand pieces against the wall.

Easy, Trav.

You're tippin' a nine on the tension scale and that ain't helping nobody.

He swabbed a hand over his face, eyes catching suddenly on the gleaming cufflinks of the blazer the Lodge Boys had presented him before leaving, on the small patch he hadn't noticed until now: precision stitching showing the twisted spirals of a conch. Travis looked closer, the image of the shell making him think again of the Lodge, of Reagan's twinkling smile and, finally, Franklin Roosevelt's avowed love of *Lord of the Flies*.

He'd read the story, of course, once back in seventh grade when he hated it and then again sometime after he'd re-upped for the Navy. The words hadn't changed but something within himself had and this time the story resonated on a deeper level, touching adeptly on the inherent savagery of human nature and the inbred loyalty to damnation that seemed to run through us all. For a long time he stared at the patch, remembering how in that story, too, a conch had played a part, an icon passed around as the standard to whose turn it was to speak and whose to shut up; he wondered if there wasn't some connection between the conch in that story and the one before him now.

Taking the sleeve in his fingers, he noticed the slight but irrefutable bulge beneath the patch; he touched at it, and prodded, and pinched, and moments later when the fabric ripped something slipped out and went bouncing along the cabin floor.

Travis picked it up, examined it. And though he'd never seen one quite like this—*anything* like it, actually—he recognized the small device as a thumb drive of some sort: a little larger than usual but with the unmistakable prong of a micro SD card exposed like a little bridge to nowhere.

He glanced around, hoping to find a laptop cast aside on a table or under a chair. He'd started from his seat when another beep sounded across the room and—

The cell.

He crept over, keeping an eye on the cabin door as he carefully took the phone in his hands. No way to be sure whose it was—though, despite his earlier assumptions, seeing it now up close, something told him it wasn't Agnew's. For starters, the damned thing was too old and beat up, and Travis supposed he'd have an easier time picturing Agnew driving a clown car through Manhattan than holding a thing like this up to her ear.

He glanced again to the door.

Voices now, how far he couldn't tell.

He quickly returned to his seat, inserting the drive; for a moment the voices grew closer outside the door, then faded, then were gone. Travis looked and saw a message prompting him to open a file: CHECKS AND BALANCES.

He selected the file and was soon greeted by the image of a crudely-illustrated cartoon—a bright-eyed, fast food-style cup giving an exaggerated wink and thumbs up. A speech bubble from his perfect-smiling teeth said:

> MAGIC MILKSHAKE ANYONE?
> *But what's the **REAL** secret ingredient?*

The screen flashed, this time to a photograph showing a siren with cold marble eyes, her body split down the middle and clamped open with silver prongs. A skein of innards had been stretched back to reveal the dark mound of a heart; but it was above this, in the separated flaps of her neck, that Travis observed the true object of the picture: a small cluster of organs—they looked like cranberries—stuck deep in the siren's throat. In the photo, the berries had been circled by the bright line of a digital pen.

And written at the bottom of the picture: *ambrosia*

He stared at the image, searching for some hidden meaning he wasn't so sure he would find. He was still searching when the screen flashed a second time, but now the cartoon image was that of a bespectacled peppermint candy, a pointer held in one teacherly hand to a blackboard bearing the message:

> CAREFUL!

Ambrosia

Drink too much and you'll start to smell funny...

He'd barely finished these words when the cabin door swung back and Travis dropped his hands, quickly ducking the phone under one leg. He offered a casual glance as Bailey Wyck shuffled awkwardly into the cabin, the corners of his mouth twisted in a familiar aw-shucks grin.

"You all right in here, Mr. B? Need anything?"

Travis stared ahead, feigning his best sleepy-eyed leer.

"Probably need my head examined, all the stuff I've seen tonight." He blew out a storybook sigh. "No, I'm fine."

"You sure?" Bailey stepped closer, sweat bubbling beneath his thick salt-and-pepper hair. "Your eyes, they look a little glassy. Still got a headache? Some water maybe?"

Travis turned his neck, grunting as the bones grinded and popped.

"Just tired, Wyck. Ready to get home, lay in my own bed."

He leaned back, the bulk of the cell squirming like an unwieldy brick beneath his thigh as Travis let out a groan and closed his eyes; but even then he could feel the pressure of the man's stare, a small ball of warmth on his face. For a moment all was still, the dull roar of the engines the only sound until finally the warmth faded and Bailey's voice called out—*sure thing, Trav, just give a holler*—and opening his eyes moments later, Travis found himself alone. Not sick anymore and definitely not tired.

In fact, he'd never felt more awake in his life.

§

He pushed on through the file, saw reports, charts, conclusions. Streams of data that maybe made sense to someone of

Einstein's intellect but did little for Travis himself. His nausea returned as the slides took a sudden detour into the macabre: bloody pictures of suicides and holes ravaged in flesh, pictures of death. He saw a family in their Sunday best hanging from the rafters of a cellar; he saw a woman boiled in a bathtub—one bejeweled eye slipping low down her cheek—and a frizzy-haired girl with half a head. A freckled face with bright orange hair slumped forward in a puddle—nay, an *ocean*—of blood. And flashing in a banner beneath it all, a series of names: *Francesca Ward...Antione & Shamara Jones...Yasmin Rajavi...Craig Donovan...*

This was followed by a quick study of some gonzo-style genetic research program, and what the Bureau hoped would be the mapping of the sirens' genetic code—slides of DNA, of double helixes splitting like a zipper and replicating—all interspersed with more bloody on-site coverage of the sirens themselves: mouths sewn shut, ovaries exposed, veins stringing like sap-laden roots down their neck and past the dangling bulbs of their breasts. Whatever noble intentions the Lodge Boys espoused, apparently Agnew's gifted team of scientists had a somewhat different goal in mind, indulging their endless curiosity with experiments more after the fashion of Josef Mengele than anything Marie Curie had ever attempted.

They were slaughtering them...

Next he came to a faded group shot, a celebratory photo featuring old men in lab coats huddled around the dismembered remains of what he assumed to be a siren. Travis studied the men—most grinning wide and a few with cigars clamped in their mouths—his eyes sweeping left to right until he noticed a familiar face in the bunch. He stared, a sudden shudder walking down his spine as her green eyes sparkled back, face shining with a certain youthful glee that had long since faded.

Agnew.

He pored over the image, the woman in this old picture appearing as young as the one he'd woken to only hours earlier—impossible, yes, but also true.

Unless...

Unless, he realized, the Lodge Boys weren't the only ones to drink that magic milkshake of the gods. Unless she, too, had undergone the Procedure and trespassed over death and—with a little help from her friends—ascended to the helm of the Bureau, a rag-tag group of self-proclaimed patriots operating under a veil of secrecy.

Drink too much and you'll start to smell funny...

What he was dealing with here, he thought, was an arms race. Except the world had outgrown such mundane items as missiles and warheads and moved on to the future of science. Some metaphysical crossbreed of genetics and mumbo-jumbo psychic prosperity. A new brand of warfare for a fresh generation of jingoist radicals. Psychic wars.

In other words, *pure madness*.

He was still staring at the picture, still thinking on its sordid implications when the screen flashed and now another image appeared—a chorus line of dancing cartoon pens, legs pumping a series of Rockettes kicks while a message shone bright in the spotlight overhead:

REMEMBER...
The Pen Is Truly Mightier Than the Sword
GOOD LUCK!

Then the screen went dark and when Travis looked up the cabin door had opened, Agnew strolling casually inside. He dropped a palm over the phone, slipping it down into a pocket of his Lodge Boy jacket as she settled back and closed her eyes.

"Not much longer now," she said.

Travis shifted uncomfortably, turning again to the window. Through the darkness outside he caught the first intimations of purest gold, the sun slowly spreading its wings over the vastness of the sky. Not because it was early, he realized, but because they were surely headed west, racing some untold distance across the night and catching up with the sun.

Chasing sunset.

He caught the faintest whiff of peppermint and glanced to Agnew, wondering what dreams sat playing through her mind, wondering if they were in color or black and white, and if music could be heard there at all...

Do what your heart and conscience tell you, Reagan had said.

And he intended to do just that.

TWENTY-TWO

DREXL HAD KNOWN A FEW WOMEN IN HIS DAY WHO were terminally pretty, but Lola Agnew was not one of them. Not in the traditional sense, anyway (she sort of looked like a bird). But she'd always been enough for him when the going was good, and even once things went sour he still reserved a kernel of care for the old avian whore.

Not until recently had he pondered the possibility of actually knocking some sense into that narrow mind of hers. Knowing Lola, this would mean that forever after the two of them could never coexist, let alone work together. And Lola knowing *him*, she would know that meant he was going for blood.

Blood he was comfortable with.

He could do gruesome.

But one thing he had no tolerance for was an individual ill-prepared to do those tasks which, with the fanciest of Cheshire grins, they asked others to perform on a string. She was a monk in an ivory tower—no more and no less—and be damned if tonight Drexl didn't burn the whole shithouse to the ground.

Following their latest conversation, Drexl couldn't deny a certain sense of frustration—he pictured it as a ball of fire, spinning round and round in his gut—though repeatedly he'd told himself such emotions were fruitless at best. Usually he'd tucked them away like the burning heirlooms of hate they were, waiting patiently for the hour they could be released once more from the cage he'd erected in his own heart. Now, finally, that hour was nigh—at the door—and instead of tucking it away to those stygian corners he let the frustration burn and rage, his heart brimming with exultation as the heirlooms broke forth and danced, spinning their ancient pirouettes into the world.

Returning to the kitchen he found the old bastard pulling against the ties, struggling to slip a hand or foot. Drexl was just able to hold back a smile, a wave of pure joy fluttering in his chest. He'd switched to zip ties a few years back, found they were less cumbersome than handcuffs but more reliable than rope. Cheap, readily available, quick to apply. Just snap them on, pull the tie, sit back and watch the ducks squirm and finally give up. Heavy-duty cable ties like the ones he used had upwards of a 200-pound rating, and for a simple strip of nylon that locked tighter than a snare drum, Drexl decided that wasn't half bad.

Still, it was fun to watch.

"Important call?" the old man asked, casting a twisted

smile. "Lemme guess, that was the boss man. He had big news and because of it tomorrow the world will be a perfect place to live for all. Am I right? Ballpark, maybe?"

Drexl paid him no mind but set about the business at hand.

He opened his coat and pulled the mere club from inside, the nephrite jade gleaming beneath the kitchen lights, and set it on the table. Reached back inside, revealed a straight razor this time. Set that on the table. He turned to Juan and slipped on his usual snake-eyes grin. "Tonight's the night, darling."

"Fuck you," Juan said. Then, glancing over the table of instruments: "What's all this?"

Drexl stared down at the weapons, admiring them—their *shape*, their *attitude*, their *presence*—the way someone might admire a classical painting. He would swim in them if he could, backstroking along their cool blue water like a child lost in a fantasy.

"With these," he said, gesturing to the table, "with these I plan on making music. A real symphony, for all the world to hear."

"You're on drugs."

Drexl whooped a laugh and shook his head. He cast a casual glance to his watch, clapped his hands and said, "The night is young, Juan Marquez. As I see it, our good friend won't make it back for another, oh, five-six hours, give or take. What do you say we have some fun?"

"Where is he? What've you done with him you two-bit sack of—"

"Travis is just fine," he assured the man. "We had to have sort of a...*conversation* with him, is all. He'll be back shortly, no time at all."

The old man glanced around the room—at Styron's goried corpse, the gristled, rough-hewn neck, the splatterwork up the walls. "This doesn't look like any conversation I've ever seen." He'd opened his mouth to say more when he stopped, sniffing the air, something dawning in the old geezer's eyes. "Wait, that smell...*you're with her*. Broad who stopped in tonight at the store." Then another thought: "Is it the lottery—is that what you're up to? The *money?*"

Drexl looked at the man—really *looked* at him—then and there deciding to make this night one to remember. Go big or go home. California or bust.

"Know what I think?" he asked. "I think you're in serious need of an operation, just a little surgery to straighten out that mind of yours. Yessir, and this time I think we need to go deep. *No half measures*, understand?"

He turned to the table of instruments, giving a flourish of his massive fingers. Black eyes clicking around in his skull. Finally, he reached down and made his selection, lifting the straight razor in one hand.

"Enough yakkin', sweetheart. Let's get busy."

PART THREE

TEMPEST

TWENTY-THREE

Somewhere in the Philippine Sea

5:43 p.m. JST

THE RAFT SKIPPED ACROSS DARK WATERS, A LONE spotlight highlighting choppy waves against the last of the setting sun. Though he'd dreamed of them often, never in a million years had Travis imagined a return to these particular waves, and staring over them now his mind slid back to Tara and all the memories they'd shared over the last year and a half, all those small moments cementing a bond unlike any he'd ever known.

Strong as this bond may have been, he'd never shared with her that fateful morning aboard the *Gettysburg*. Occasionally he'd imagined he would someday, although just as often he'd called himself crazy for even considering it. Now all that had changed, and though tonight's festivities were considered TOP SECRET, if Lola Agnew believed for even a second those parameters extended to his own wife, she'd been sorely mistaken; a marriage was nothing if not a tome of shared secrets, and this one he was more than ready to share.

Besides, Agnew hadn't exactly been up front with a few things herself.

He reached down, fingers brushing over the thumb drive buried in his pocket. The cell he'd left back on the plane, returning it surreptitiously into place following what Travis considered an impressive vertical landing on a ship not far from where they currently roamed. One of those small cities-at-sea with which he'd grown familiar during his Navy days. From there they'd put out to sea, traveling now for just under an hour when a series of crimson-colored lights appeared up ahead; coming closer, Travis saw three rafts identical to their own arranged in a close triangle on the water.

Dark figures crossed back and forth, a conspiracy of goggled men squatting to position while Agnew spoke hushed commands into a radio. A cool breeze swept past, and touching again at the drive in his pocket suddenly Travis sensed something else down there—thin, round, flat.

He pulled it out, opening his hand to reveal a Morgan silver dollar—*his* silver dollar—and whether he'd forgotten it was there or it had appeared from the thin air which it knew so well, it didn't matter: here it was, that old familiar magic working through him now as he wrapped it once more in his palm.

Do what your heart and conscience tell you

He'd been given something, this much he knew.

Now, he was being asked to give it away.

To make a sacrifice for the greater good.

He didn't understand it, apparently no one did.

But it was real. As real as the coin in his hand or any of the other miracles he'd experienced since. But then—what good was a thing being real if no one understood what it was, much less how it worked? What sort of liberties had to be taken to feel okay about commandeering something like that?

No, no, the whole thing smelled sour, Travis thought. Something was rotten in Denmark and he didn't know what it was, and not knowing made him paranoid. And being paranoid, he became suspicious. And so with a stormy head of suspicions Travis returned the coin to his pocket and—

"Here, take these."

Agnew walked over holding a pair of cushy black earmuffs, put them in his hands; she reached around, revealing a second pair of muffs and clasping them around her neck.

"What's this?"

"These," she told him, "are your new best friends. And please, whatever you do—*don't take them off.*"

Travis stared at the muffs, turning them in his hands. The low talk of the goggled men continued from the neighboring rafts, peppered by indiscriminate laughter. Glancing up moments later, Agnew had fixed him with her cold green eyes, an uncertain look on her face.

"What's the matter, Travis?"

His eyes slipped to the men, their shadowy figures scurrying beneath the soft crimson lights they'd strung from lines between the rafts. There were lots of things running through his head just then, a lot of ideas that didn't seem to have the words to go along with them.

"These things, whatever they are..." His voice was tentative, almost a whisper. "Don't you think they deserve to be free?"

She stared at him, a certain light fading from her eyes.

"How do you mean?"

"I mean...*free*, same as anything." Travis looked around, noticing the first shimmers of moonlight glinting off the waves. He tugged nervously at the muffs, trying to think how to put this, some way that said all the things he wanted to say—well, *most* of them anyway—but that didn't involve the words *you fucking liar*. "I'm just saying, what do we really *know* about them, or even what they can do? Who are we to put them in cages?"

Still staring, the light fading faster now.

"Well, we know plenty, Travis. And we're only learning more, thanks to the sacrifices of other hard-working Americans just like—"

"Just like me, yeah, I got that. But what if we don't have the right? Whatever these things can do, maybe they were given that gift for a reason, a *purpose*. And maybe we *weren't* given it for a reason. Maybe it's not our place." His mind flashed to the bloodied image of sirens torn down their middle, ravaged open, cold marble eyes staring into his own. "Maybe we should leave them alone, just let them be..."

Her face hardened at that, a stoned-over slab of pale white flesh. She took a step closer and said, "Is this your nice-guy way of saying no? Now, after all this?"

He stared back, not saying a word.

But of course he didn't have to; the answer was written plainly on his face.

"And the Lodge Boys? Are you prepared to tell them this, also?"

Travis held back a smile, sensing the attempt at intimidation, not buying in. "I don't look forward to it...but yes. They're big boys, I think they'd understand."

"And Tara? What would she say?"

"Tara's not here, so I guess that doesn't much matter either way. I'd like to give her a call though, if that's all right. I think she'd like to know where I am..."

"And if I said you didn't have to?"

He stared at her a moment, her pallid skin seeming to glow and drawing forth a vague luminescence beneath the moon. If he hadn't known better, Travis might've found the effect appealing...only something in those eyes—something empty and dead tucked away beneath the sparkling green surface—told him those were more the eyes of a shark than some prophet with news of a better world ahead.

"Didn't have to what?"

"What if I told you she's here tonight, Travis? That right this minute she's waiting back on the ship? That she wants to see you?"

His hands tensed around the muffs, a flash of sudden rage running a circuit through his mind. But it wasn't the rage that concerned him; what concerned him more was the hole he felt suddenly opened at the bottom of his stomach, a swirling riptide of emotion pulling him down, down, down...

"Well, for starters I'd say you were full of shit," he said. "Tara's in Raleigh, left just this afternoon. I watched her go."

Agnew stepped closer, the ghost of a puppy-dog smile drawing down her face.

"Raleigh? Is that what she told you?"

She looked at him a moment, not saying a word, before reaching down and pulling a phone from her pocket. Held it up to him and flashed a finger across the screen, flipping to a picture of what appeared to be Tara surrounded by gravestones, tears in her eyes. "Here she is an hour after leaving your house, at Early Grace Cemetery...and here at the airport, getting on the shuttle...and here she is twenty minutes ago..."

Travis stared at the image, a grainy shot showing Tara in a room with cold gray walls but not much else—a toilet in the corner, small twin bed with twisted sheets—and everything fell away then, the endless waves and moonlight, the small chatter of the men, all of it was happening so far away.

He heaved a breath, tried to stay calm. To be still in this exact same spot, knowing if he moved the world would be gone, there'd be nothing left. A cool rush of wind whipped through Agnew's hair, her thin mannequin lips parting in a baleful grin that looked as natural on her face as the pair of penciled-in eyebrows.

"Easy, Trav," she said. "Not the first time I've seen that look in a man's eyes, just remember where you are; go ahead, take a look around. This is bigger than you and me—bigger than all of us—and I've been given special jurisdiction to make sure tonight is a success. Measures were taken, *precautions*. You wouldn't believe how hard some people find it to cooperate, and something told me you might be one of those people...always with a bleeding heart, always forgetting the bigger picture. You'll forgive me if I went too far, but when it comes to our national defense the Bureau refuses to sit back as some dormant milquetoast while those less fortunate suffer under inescapable burdens. We will not remain aloof while people like you rest on your laurels; that we cannot do."

His body raged, violence rushing like a bundle of hot wires through his veins as he carefully raised his hand, twisting one granite finger at her face.

"I swear if you touch—"

"Please, spare me the histrionics," she interrupted, and now her eyes had changed again, shifting like two endless kaleidoscopes beneath the moon. "Tara is perfectly safe, I assure you. Right this moment she's back on the ship, waiting for you to join her. Do your part and sing the words, Travis, and I promise within the hour the two of you will be together again and we can all go home with a wild story about the night we saved the world."

"And if I don't? If I say go fuck yourself, then what?"

Agnew curled a lip, tossing a careless glance to the smattering of stars that had salted the night. "If you don't, then I'll admit everything I just told you was a lie. That Tara never booked a flight for the Bahamas and this minute is spending just another boring weekend in Raleigh. And we'll take you home."

Travis held on, told himself to stay right where he was. Fighting the urge to rear back and smash that sharp little nose into her face, burying it there like a stone in the sand. To reach forward and snap the pale slope of her neck like a winter twig.

"You bitch."

Agnew appeared not to hear. "Is that a yes?"

He stared back, the slow rush of the waves bouncing at

the raft as he weighed his options, knowing there wasn't much to weigh. Because she was right; in this moment, Agnew had the upper hand. Was she bluffing? No idea. And either way it wasn't a play he was willing to make—not here, not now. Right now he was a fish, and he was swimming in a barrel beneath a threat that may or may not be real. Then he thought of what else she'd said to him, about the pictures at the airport.

"What do you mean the Bahamas? What flight?"

"I believe that's something to be discussed with your wife, wouldn't you say?" She tapped at her wrist, its slender mold reminding Travis of the fragile bones of a bird's wing. "Now please, make it pretty won't you?" She'd started away when she paused, turning back. "And Travis? Don't be a wiseass. We've been doing this since before you were shitting diapers—so please, skip the curve balls."

For what seemed a long time, Travis didn't move.

Just stared, wishing Agnew dead in a sour-hate sort of way he'd previously thought impossible. Murder had never been in his bones, but staring at the woman now Travis wondered how easy it was to graft those things in, to take them on and feed them and make them your own.

He pushed past her, resisting the urge to put just one good boot to her ass while nearing the edge of the raft. The ocean rolling beneath him as Agnew donned her muffs, as did the others, as did Travis himself. Goggled men hurried back and forth, muttering into headsets. The world fading to a sudden hush as Agnew called the order and the crimson lights went dead.

Silence fell over the water.

Travis stepped tentatively forward, the quiet rush of the

waves beating around him. The last of his fury had faded, sinking to uncertain fear as he shut his eyes and opened his mouth and then slowly, deliberately began to sing.

He faltered once, started again.

On his third attempt he'd found his groove and the dark melody poured out of him, those ancient lyrics coming alive and dripping like a warm salve from his lips—

Nyeh-katuh-nayuh-faelstro-laecopa
Musha-raeiin-domma-do-domma-dah

—until his skin grew hot and the night swam around him, everything consumed by some greater pressure building in the air. Emotionless tears streamed down his face, his soul wavering deep within until he could stand it no longer and opened his eyes and—

A warm cardinal glow, rising from the depths.

Not quite the same hue as the lights they'd strung up between the rafts—deeper somehow, more *vibrant*—but not far from it.

There was something swimming out there, he saw, lapping lazy circles as the phosphorescence floated closer to the surface and—

And then she came, rising in ruby-red brilliance among the waves.

Travis faltered once more, the lyrics going dry in his throat at the sight of her withered form, her massive hands anchored high, a penitent beseeching the heavens. He stared, sensing in her gauzy eyes a helpless wonder that spun suddenly to panic—and yes, even *betrayal*—as the first dart came sailing in, burying itself in the speckled flesh of her shoulder.

She wrenched back, her large ape-hanger jaw flung wide

in a screeching yawp that the muffs silenced but which Travis felt as a sharp tingling in the tips of his fingers. More darts were fired, attaching themselves with cold precision to her knobby breasts and still the siren writhed, splashing in paroxysms of pain. Suddenly the crimson lamps snapped on and figures rushed to new formations on the rafts, one of the men tripping and the muffs leaping from his ears; Travis watched as the man clutched madly at his head, the terror stretching his face to a profound rictus of fear even as the skin ripped and boiled and then slipped effortlessly from his skull. The mess of it dangled like a gristled Halloween mask before he pitched forward and was swallowed by the waves, another of the men quickly diving in after him.

And finally Travis understood.

Understood the reason for the muffs— *don't take them off,* Agnew had warned—understood that whatever sorrowful carols these sirens sang, their talents didn't stop there. That whatever new and terrible sound this was from her lips, he didn't want to hear it.

A defense mechanism...

The siren thrashed, a slow lethargy taking hold until the barrage of darts ceased and she released a final yawp, falling limp among the waves. Travis swept the tears from his eyes, numbness creeping over him now as the rafts ferried closer and more divers leapfrogged into the water. In less time than it takes to microwave a bag of popcorn, the siren was ruthlessly bound, her phosphorescent glow fading from scarlet to mud while she was netted and swiftly hauled in.

Moments later two goggled men washed up with the remains of their fallen brother, hunks of ravaged flesh dripping in rags from his face. Soon, Travis knew, this place would be deserted, just another patch of ocean in an endless sea, and staring now over the water he remembered the flash of betrayal in the creature's eyes, sensing for the first time the bitter shame of what he'd done.

It wouldn't be the last.

Agnew walked over, stripping her muffs and motioning for him to do the same. She pulled a pack of Camels and tapped one out, blowing smoke to the stars while gazing after the siren—attended now by a pair of men in glasses, one with a clipboard, the other with a stethoscope held fast to her scaly chest.

"What happens now? I mean, where does she go?"

Agnew puffed away at her cigarette.

"Well, for starters she'll be flown to an observatory not far from here," she told him. "Then, following a few preliminaries, she'll be sent to Bureau headquarters in Virginia, where she can be with her own kind. Perhaps you'd like to visit sometime, come and see for yourself?"

Travis said nothing, and for a long moment she stared at him, still puff-puffing away.

"I know what you're thinking," she said. "And don't. These things, they're nothing more than evolutionary warts. Their intelligence may be sharper than your run-of-the-mill whale or porpoise, but not by much." She puffed, blew it out. "They just happen to have some talent we don't yet understand, that's all. A *pull* on some element that is still happenstance in our world, but that is very tangible in theirs—and for this, all else is forgiven. But just remember, Travis, at the end of the day...*it's just a damn fish.*"

He looked at her then, not quite able to squash the feeling

he was seeing her truly for the first time: a woman no better than all the other tyrants of the world. Someone whom in the span of an hour he'd come to loathe, and whom but for the saving grace of the legal system he would surely put to death—brutally even, with as many blows as it took to get the job done.

"I'd like to see my wife now, please."

TWENTY-FOUR

TARA BARNES HAD NEVER FELT SO ALONE IN HER LIFE. She was awake, but barely. Had dozed in and out for the past—how long? six hours? eight?—and while her nausea had only added fuel to whatever nightmare this was, she supposed the sleep had been a blessing in disguise: some backwards way of managing the sheer panic that threatened just below the surface.

Only...no, Tara knew that wasn't the whole truth either.

Not after remembering the black hole she'd slipped into sometime after arriving at the airport, waking here and gagging at the bird shit taste in her mouth and with a migraine so bitchin' she'd crawled over and spit up some goop in the silvered prison-grade toilet in one corner.

Mrs. Barnes?

Then she'd heard the voice and turned to the small monitor on the wall, greeted there by the grainy image of a pale woman with green gimlet eyes. The woman had introduced herself as Lola Agnew, flashing a badge that might've come from a cereal box before launching into some tall tale the validity of which was yet to be seen. Travis had been the star, and if her story was to be believed he would soon be here himself. Something about a government initiative, some undercover research project involving top-shelf intelligence with urgent demands and far-reaching goals. Lastly, she'd apologized for any inconvenience, pleaded for patience and understanding, and then—just when Tara was *sure* things couldn't possibly get more bizarre—the screen had switched to Travis himself, surrounded at a table by the familiar sagging faces of presidents long since passed: Roosevelt, Truman, Gerald Ford. A ruby-cheeked man who bore more than a passing resemblance to Dwight Eisenhower. For an endless moment Tara had stared, watching while the men chatted and laughed and—

And then the screen had gone black and she was alone with her thoughts.

Her instincts tended toward the whole thing being some sort of hoax: for money, perhaps, or any of the other myriad things people do supremely stupid things for. But then what sort of hoax would take such measures to swindle such a blaring nobody like herself?

Still, hoax or not, she was scared.

Man plans and God laughs, that's how the old saying went, and lying awake now Tara was tempted to believe it. Because no matter how much she resisted, again and again her mind returned to the simple fact she should've been in *Nassau* by now, should've been kicked back and miserable with a drink in both hands. She'd *needed* this weekend, after all, had counted on it to steel herself for the moment she'd avoided for too long, the moment when she went back and said to Travis all the words she'd hoped she would never have to say.

But that trip wasn't in the cards, and instead she'd passed the time sleeping off a jackhammer headache and waiting, waiting, waiting. Now she rolled against the mattress, staring at the monitor and wishing they could've at least put on a little something, anything to keep her entertained. Hell, even the Kardashians were better than this, *The Bachelor*, something.

But of course they wouldn't do that, she thought, *it would be too easy. Too much of an escape. No, no, they want you right here and now, savoring every second, running scared. And what kind of shitty government would do a thing like that for anyway? Face it, Tara, you'll probably spend the rest of your life chained to a bedpost in Indonesia.*

This is how they break people, she thought.

This is how they make a person insane.

She turned over and saw the smattering of bonbons on the table next to the bed, grabbed one up and swallowed it down. She'd hoped the flavor might blot out the bird shit taste in her throat, but no such luck there. Tara groaned, reaching for another when suddenly the door rattled open and she turned to see a small man with delicate features standing just inside the room.

"Mrs. Barnes?" he asked. "If you would come right this way, I believe Travis is ready for you."

§

He was led through a series of corridors, one winding endlessly into the next until finally Agnew stopped outside a door unremarkable save for the numbers 101 stamped across the front. A janitor strode past pushing a trash barrel on wheels, giving a small nod as he went on whistling and guiding the barrel down the hall.

"Someday when you and Tara are old and gray," Agnew said, "I hope you'll appreciate what I've done here tonight. With both of you, I mean. There's simply too much at stake, our work is *too important* to leave anything up to chance—*anything*."

Travis stared at the woman, wondering if she'd caught the irony in what she'd just said; sadly, he thought probably not. And what difference did it make? She'd gotten what she wanted, and did it with style: why bother with semantics? Hers was a world of carrots and sticks, after all, a selective nepotism that in Travis's estimation left her with more blind spots than the south side of that proverbial northbound mule.

"So why not just threaten people till they do what you want? Right? Why not box 'em around a little? Hell, why not *kill* 'em and call it progress?"

Agnew offered only a smile.

"It was an empty threat," she said, "and not the first I've ever made. But if you think for a second I would've allowed any harm to your wife—no matter what your decision—then you're not as sharp as I thought you were." She opened the door and stood aside, gesturing him inside. "I'm not above scare tactics, you know."

Travis felt confident there were a lot of things she wasn't above, the least of them being *scare tactics*. But he kept his mouth shut, moving past her now into a swept-clean room where everything looked new and yet somehow out of place, the walls arranged with newsprint and artifacts and various apparently rare items behind glass. Springsteen's "Born in the U.S.A." played softly from small speakers in the wall.

The room was empty.

"Where's Tara?"

"On the way as we speak, Mr. Barnes. Have a seat and she'll be right with you."

Then the door closed and he was alone.

He glanced over the walls, observing pictures of sirens swimming lithely through blue waves or perched on rocks; others lay swathed in tethers of sunlight from above. Not far from these he noticed an intercom on the wall, which meant they'd be listening, and a line of small Hummel figurines with a Mermaids Through the Ages theme on a series of shelves by the door. He walked over, lifting one of the pieces—a pretty blond with bright Disney eyes—and turning it in his hands, eyes catching on the print in dainty blue across the ceramic base: MADE IN CHINA.

Travis replaced the figure and moved across the room, settling on the lush purple couch in one corner. He thought back to everything Agnew had told him on the water, about Tara and airports and wondering if his wife was actually here at all. Or if maybe he should expect nothing beyond this point but a lonely burial at sea...

At that moment the old door rattled open, and he saw Tara.

§

She ran to him, tears streaming as Travis took her in his arms.

"Are you okay? Did they—"

She told him she was okay, that no, they hadn't hurt her. He asked if she was sure, and for some reason that only made the tears worse, hot streams spilling down her cheeks as she nodded her head and Travis guided her gently to a hideous couch in the corner. She wiped her eyes and looked around, taking in a slew of fancy pictures featuring Hollywood monsters and artifacts displayed behind glass.

"Travis...what is all this? What's going on?"

For a moment her husband was silent, and when at last he spoke his voice was lower than usual, deeper. A peculiar tone that seemed somehow strange coming from his mouth. For a long time that voice rambled out ahead of her, telling a wild story that started with his days in the Seventh Fleet and that ended here tonight on the Philippine Sea. A mixed-up tale of lottery fortune and dead presidents and mysterious creatures with some knack for the miraculous. There were times during that story—not often, but occasionally—when Tara seemed to lift out of her body, to hear the words and know what they meant and yet not hear them at all. Then she'd come down, staring at the worn-out mask of her husband's face until finally something flashed in his eyes, a bruised sadness that must've been there all along but that she hadn't noticed until now.

"What? What's the matter?"

Again he said nothing, only his tired eyes scanning the walls as he searched for just the right words. He glanced down, fingers picking tentatively along the cuff of what he'd referred to as his Lodge Boy jacket.

"Tara, these people...they'd followed you today. I guess you know that already but..." He paused, weighing his words. "They had pictures of you. Some at the cemetery, outside Galveston—but others, too, at the airport." She stared into his eyes, the sadness she'd witnessed earlier no longer a flash but a consuming fire. "I mean, was that...what *was* that, Tara? I don't understand..."

But she'd looked away, trying to hold it together. She was fidgeting with her hands, she knew she was, couldn't seem to stop. Tara tried remembering all the little routines she'd auditioned for the occasion, all the practiced words and half-formed phrases—but none of those seemed to matter now.

"Travis, honey...there's just something I've been meaning to tell you," she said, feeling foolish. "Something I should've told you already, about the *tests*—"

"—what tests?"

"With Dr. Gaines, Travis."

"But those aren't till next week, babe, we haven't even—"

"Except I've already had them *done*, I couldn't stand it." She stared into his eyes, wishing it had happened some other way, any other way but this. "It's *me*, Travis. I'm the reason we can't have a baby." She squeezed his hand, holding back the tears. "*I'm so sorry...*"

§

Then it was too much and she broke down, all the unshed tears of the last few weeks finally running free as she told him the whole sad story, beginning with her own private fears and furtive appointments with Dr. Gaines and finishing with the definitive results she'd received only the week before—not even a week—had it really been only *six days?*

"It's called Premature Ovarian Failure," she told him. "Dr. Gaines says it's in the early stages now but eventually my ovaries will just...stop working. *Premature menopause*," she said, the words catching like glass in her throat. She laughed miserably. "I'll probably be having hot flashes by the time I'm thirty."

She looked at him, her husband's previous sadness replaced now by sudden concern, one hand reaching out to hold hers.

"I wanted to tell you," she went on, "so many times I almost did...but I just couldn't go on hiding it and lying to you and I guess I thought that—maybe if I got *away*, if I had one last weekend to try and..."

Yet even as she said the words Tara couldn't help but wonder if that was the truth at all. Or could the real reason she'd booked that flight be a tad more sadistic—

To punish herself.

Maybe give that knife one final twist before handing it over to Travis for good...

"And you chose the Bahamas because..."

"Because it's where we spent our honeymoon, and because—it's the most beautiful place on earth and—"

"And so what better place to sulk?"

He smiled at her, the tension finally beginning to break.

"Why didn't you just tell me, Tara? You can come to me with anything, you know that."

"Yeah, I know," she told him. "But I'm the one who got you wanting a family in the first place, now I can't even give you that. Do you know what that's like? I guess I felt...*ashamed*."

Travis laughed, surprising her with it.

"About *what*? As long as I have you, Tara, that's all that matters. And there's nothing—"

"But what about the rest of our lives? What about a *family*?"

"What about it?" He raised his hand, wiping the last of the tears from her eyes. "We'll take it as it comes, same as we always have. But as long as we have each other, then everything else will be perfect—*no matter what*. All we need is right here in this room, okay? Always has been..."

He leaned closer on the couch, the sudden touch of his lips a welcome reminder of everything they'd lost over the last few months, all the stress melting away as the music played softly from the walls. This first kiss was followed by another—deeper this time—and Tara realized she'd come to know these familiar motions like the movements of a symphony, to cherish them: theirs was a map of love that led to one another's arms, and when he was done kissing her lips Travis smiled darkly and ran his tongue down her neck.

And that was even better.

TWENTY-FIVE

OLA AGNEW SWEPT LIKE A STORM DOWN THE corridors of the *Melchizedek*, rolling along like thunder until she'd reached a door marked 355. She strode inside, fishing a bright red pushpin from a dusty jar along the wall and adding it to the sprawling rainbow of pins on the map to her left.

For the first time that night Lola smiled—*really* smiled—wiping casually at the bit of slaver from one corner of her mouth. Minutes later she was seated at the head of an elegant dinner-table-for-one at the center of the room when she heard a knock and was joined by her waiter, an elderly gentleman with puffy jowls who bore a striking resemblance to Mr. Miyagi from those old Karate Kid movies. He pulled behind him a serving cart upon which sat a great covered dish, the sterling silver dome glowing bright like a Christmas tree star. Slipping one hand kindly behind his back, he stretched his spine toward the heavens and cleared his throat and said, "To drink this evening, ma'am?"

"I believe a good Chardonnay is in order, please."

He poured a glass and set it before her, then turned and with a strangled grunt hefted the great covered dish to the table. Lola dipped her head respectfully, and following a respectful bow of his own the waiter leaned forward, raising the silvered dome to reveal Barnes's siren prepped and ready on the platter beneath: her freakish hands lopped off at the elbow and the rounded nubs of her breasts shaved down, removing the various toxins the men in white had discovered there. The forked caudal fin had been removed, her softly glistening scales tapering down from her chest to a bloody stump that writhed like a snake without its head. In more primitive times they'd sewn the lips shut with something she liked to call NASA floss; now they simply removed the larynx and let the bitch squirm.

The old waiter stared stoically ahead, averting his stare until Lola nodded faintly and he scurried from the room, pulling the cart after himself. For a long time she sat silently positioning her various forks and knives, being meticulous, occasionally counting them—first one way, then the other. It wasn't OCD, and she didn't like to talk about it, just sometimes she liked to count flatware. The siren sucked and burbled, producing a smell like seaweed.

"Not so tough without those pipes, are you?" she said, tapping her fork to a tender place beneath the ape-hanger jaw. She grabbed up a knife and made a small incision, the creature's milky eyes peering up mindlessly as she peeled back a small corner of purplish-pink flesh.

The skin was squishy-soft between her teeth—juicy, succulent, salty as ever—and though its pliable warmth had always made her cheery inside, tonight the effect was working double-time: even had she tried, Lola supposed she couldn't begin to imagine a problem beyond her control. If she sat in this chair long enough, she could live forever. She could hold siege to the ages and say damn the leftovers.

She pressed forward, digging down to the clavicle before poking around and coming up with her true prize—the *ambrosia*. Carefully, Lola removed the bloodied masses and scattered them across her plate. Rolled the first in gooey syrup goodness and swallowed it down, never chewing, a Eucharist she had come to know and treasure and that gave her the strength to carry on, to end the plague of evil that old men had brought to mother earth since time eternal. Men are brittle, death-obsessed beasts, brute in their strength and obstinate, lecherous, and more than anything not to be trusted. *Death mongrels*, her mother had called them, though to be fair her mother had been full of shit in most matters, even before she took to drinking and went lazy and, finally, succumbed to asphyxiation during sleep. She'd had the apnea for years—a convenient truth considering the way her mother had actually died, which was screaming, pushing against the lacy satin pillow Lola's father had given her three Christmases ago. Lola snuffed the life from her with that pillow, and had never felt better than in those first few seconds when she realized Gilda Reinhardt was a stiff and she'd never have to hear the sound of her rotten old voice ever again.

Lola forked a second helping, rolling the ambrosia round

and round like a maraschino cherry in her mouth before gulping it down. Stabbed a third and brought it close to her lips when she stopped suddenly, staring at the meaty bulb on the end of her fork: a tender sphere of life gleaming with the goopy fluid that seemed to flow through every ounce of the fish's body. For a brief moment she debated putting it aside, cutting Drexl his usual share.

But only for a moment.

No, she decided, Drexl had been given his fair share.

He'd been given his fair share and taken plenty more, and with the briny taste of the siren fresh in her throat Lola considered that tonight just might be the time to balance those accounts. Put done to it once and for all—as surely as she'd put done to every other problem over the last ninety-odd years of her life—and when she was finished Drexl Samson would spend the rest of his days in a stone cell in Guatemala, an everlasting sacrifice both to her own iron will as well as the better angels of her nature. She'd been wiping his ass for too long—she realized that now—realized it had always led to this, that there'd never been any way around it. That hairy old ape had stolen his share of bananas, and be damned if tonight she didn't repay him for every last one.

As soon as she finished here, she would call him. Tell him to get ready, darling, to tidy up nice and put a candle in the window because mama was coming on home.

But only after she'd finished.

He could wait that long.

§

More than anything, Juan was aware of the wetness.

He was cold, and very tired, and only after fluttering his eyes did he remember the wetness was from being soaked with his own blood and the chill was not the chill of being drenched but the chill of death as it settled over his sexy Hispanic soul. Any other time Juan might've been troubled by such things; but that time had come and passed, a fart in the wind, and now Juan wasn't troubled with dying. Not anymore.

The cancer had taught him about that.

He glanced down, noticing his hands still bound to the arms of the kitchen chair. The darkened chubs of his fingers—or what remained of them—sprouting from his bloodied paws like alien beings, four flayed nubs and a thumb swollen fat with pain. Mashed, beaten, brutalized. Staring at them, Juan scarcely recognized these as the same hands with which he'd journeyed through his brief existence, the hands he'd used to love and to steal and to sustain himself through the storms of life. More than anything, he felt a creeping sense of sorrow at their desecration, knowing by these that death was indeed upon him. Glancing to the floor, he could see their remains scattered like so much confetti across the puddled kitchen tiles, a bloody jetsam chucked from the withered husk of his body.

"Are we on the same page now?" the big man asked. "Is the picture getting clearer?"

The man called Drexl laughed, reaching into his coat and removing a camera, clicking away; Juan thrashed in his seat, momentarily blinded as the camera flashed, flashed, flashed. Then the flashes faded and Drexl grinned down, a certain hunger in his eyes.

"Somebody told me once, you can tell a lot about a man

by his hands. If he smokes, if he drinks, likes jazz or the blues. How about you, Juan? I picture you as a bluegrass man, myself. That or flamenco." He shook his head, gazing piteously at the mess of Juan's severed phalanges. "Personally I've never been much for reading palms, but *pain*...now there's a language I know. You'd be surprised, the things you can do to a person with a little pain. Make them shed their pride, forget their humanity. Break them until they've disavowed who they are and you can build them back up again in your own image, a slave for all time. Same methods used anywhere in the world. Prisons, militaries, it's all about breaking a man right on down, making him behave in certain ways, do certain things. All about *control*."

Juan stared at the man, that avaricious gleam still burning in his eyes; then that picture faltered, fuzzing at the edges, and Juan mumbled, "*Do you ever feel? Does hate mean anything to you other than violence? Could you look a child in the eye without BLUSHING?*"

Drexl snatched up the green-looking stone and raised it high, snuffling a series of grunts as he brought down the club in a flashing crunch against Juan's hand, again and again, pounding away, chopping.

Juan howled, the pain somehow different this time—more intense, shooting like hellfire up his fingerlings and through his knuckles and filling him with a wild anguish he'd scarcely believed possible only twenty-four hours earlier. He realized something then, realized he'd made one oversight in all his reasoning. Juan realized that death was no matter but that *agony* was a whole different story—agony was hot and blinding and could turn a person inside out. Pain was still pain and until blessed death came and swept him away he would *hurt* and *hurt* and *hurt*...

§

Drexl watched the fog settling heavier in the old man's eyes, sensing that familiar chill as his essence was slowly exhumed from his failing body. Outside the storm had settled back to drizzles and faraway thunder, but the storm inside Drexl Samson was just getting started.

He stepped back, raising the stone in one hand and admiring the nephrite jade as it sparkled beneath the kitchen lights, absolutely stunning. He gave it a once over with his handkerchief and then settled the mere in his pocket, feeling dizzy despite the laughter he was surprised to hear coming from his own mouth. Now that he'd made that big first step—not irrevocable, he supposed, but pretty damn near—it was like something had been opened up inside of him. Awakened. He saw the path before him, like a flash of light, and even now was blinded by the subtle warmth of it bubbling up inside, the warmth of freedom, of endless possibility.

He blinked and felt immortality swelling within, ballooning to fill every aspect of his being. Soon, he believed, the hands of time would begin turning backward and that fourth dimension would have as little effect on him as a buzzing fly on a galloping horse's ass. He would stand outside of it, separate, waiting idly by as the rest of the world was swept away and his own spirit absorbed the wisdom of ages. He concentrated now, all energies onboard, the world spinning and his mind struggling to catch up, his thoughts clean and pure.

I am the light, he thought, and he was the light.

I am the center, the being, and he was.

I am DREXL FUCKING SAMSON, one-man wrecking ball, badass extraordinaire, and he was all of that, too.

But most of all he was *alive*.

§

Afterwards they lay against the couch, still catching their breath, still not quite sure how it had happened. For a while neither spoke until Tara leaned over, planting a kiss on Travis's head and pulling herself up on the couch.

"Not exactly the mile high club," she said, "but I guess it'll do."

Travis stood and buckled his belt, was reaching for his Lodge Boy jacket when they heard a knock and Bailey Wyck shuffled inside, a sheepish grin on his face.

"All right, kids. That's it, time to hit the skies."

"Great," Travis said. "Where to now? Atlantis?"

Bailey laughed, his belly shaking slightly with the effort.

"No, no, nothing like that," he told them. "You've done a fine job tonight, Travis. Both of you have. Now it's time to get you kids outta here and on a plane back home. This is the end of the line for me, though." He walked over and held out a hand. "I hope you two have a safe trip, buddy."

Travis shook it, nice and firm. "Thanks, Wyck. For everything."

The man smiled bashfully, told him it was no problem at all. "Why don't you, uh..." He glanced over in time to see Tara straightening at her bra, looked away. "Why don't you two finish getting yourselves together and I'll wait for you here outside. How's that?"

"Sure thing, Wyck. We'll be right out."

Bill Jordan from Omaha gave a small salute and turned

to go, stopping long enough to offer a quick wink and thumbs up before closing the door. Travis went over and took Tara in his arms, the warmth of her body like an enduring fire against his chest.

He leaned down, pressing a gentle kiss to her lips.

Things were good.

TWENTY-SIX

It was quarter of six when Joel Collier rolled over, slapping off the morning alarm. *Butt-early* as Joel was fond of saying: no sun through the windows, no tinkering sounds in the house, only the sudden noise of the alarm blaring in darkness and then silence again as he blew his usual bearish groan and sat up in bed.

He lingered on the edge of the mattress, a sharp pain knocking at the back of his head as he remembered the drinks he'd shared with Travis late the night before. There was a time in his life—not so distant, it seemed—when hangovers had been as commonplace as bowel movements. And though this pain could scarcely be considered a hangover, it nonetheless served as a swell reminder of that long-ago life: an existence he'd led from a younger man's shoes and that, being honest, he didn't much miss. Part of that reason lay snoring beside him, with two more fast asleep down the hall. Fact was Joel Collier had fallen into picnics and strollers same as he'd fallen into the steady work of law enforcement; both required ample amounts of work and dedication and patience, but neither he would trade for the world...though he wouldn't have minded an extra half hour of sleep this morning.

Following a quick shower he settled in the kitchen for breakfast, one of those microwavable breakfast burritos. Either that or leftovers, and in Joel's opinion breakfast just wasn't breakfast if it didn't involve eggs or sausage (mostly sausage). He was scribbling out another of his lovey-dovey notes to his wife when she appeared, walking over still in her robe and snuggling into his arms. They chatted a bit while Joel worked down his coffee, sketching plans for the twins' pool party next week, Joel asking polite permission for dinner that night with Travis and putting in a special request for that world-famous pecan pie. Theresa smiled and said that would be fine.

"Thanks, hon. I ever tell you you're the best?"

She frowned, straightening at his collar and dropping her arms around his neck. "Mm, now let's see."

"Think we have time for a quickie before the girls wake up?"

"I *think* you'd better put your ass in gear, or you'll be late."

Joel agreed, and kissing his wife goodbye remembered a snippet of a dream he'd had the night before. For a moment the dream flickered, teasing at his thoughts while he grabbed his things and headed out. Approaching Luckey's ten minutes later the dream had faded but the headache stayed strong, and though most mornings three cups of joe before eight a.m. had him too jazzed to see straight, today Joel thought it might be just what the doctor ordered.

He whipped into the lot and moments later walked inside, saw Chip Yeager's son stocking Marlboro cartons behind the counter. Sweet boy, not the brightest crayon in the box, but sweet. How Chip Yeager had ever convinced some poor woman to let him loose poking around inside of her, he'd never know.

He went over to the coffee set-up and poured himself a cup, nosed around on the snack aisle a minute before snatching up some Little Debbies and returning to the front.

"So where's the old longhair this morning?"

The boy stared at him blankly. "Huh? Oh, you mean Mr. Marquez? Uh, he doesn't come in till noon on Saturdays?"

Joel nodded, feeling more alone now than when he'd first walked through the door.

The boy rang him up and handed over the change and two minutes later Joel flopped into his cruiser, sipping at his steaming cup of mud and watching as the first of sunrise came blushing over the horizon. He was hooking a turn onto 306 when the dream came back to him—only clearer this time, more in focus. When he was child, Joel had always dreamed of someday going to the moon, of braving the deep reaches of space and staring down over the blue marble of earth from above. In the dream he'd been weightless, drifting in an untold stretch of darkness, and at first he'd assumed this to be only some cockeyed fruition of that boyhood dream.

But no, no, that wasn't right, because now he realized there was something *else* with him in that darkness, only it wasn't the earth…

Joel frowned, still wondering after the darkness when a shadow bounded suddenly across the road in front of him and he smashed the brake, snatching at the wheel; the cruiser shuddered roughly and bounced right, his coffee leaping from one hand and splashing over the windshield. The awful screeching of his tires faded and then the cruiser was still and for a moment he sat catching his breath behind the wheel, his cup of morning joe *drip-drip-dripping* onto the dash.

He stared, tracking the shadow as it moved tentatively among the weeds alongside of the road and then turned, shuffling closer against the bright morning fog. *Damned fool-neck deer*, he thought, only then the fog had cleared and Joel hopped from the car, that eerie feeling growing worse now as he crossed the pavement and crouched to one knee. The dog bounded over and, looking closer, Joel noticed something off in those familiar yellow eyes; a feral sort of gleam that he found made him a little uneasy this early in the morning. Then he saw the blood, a dark smear trailing from Gage's nose and down the muddied curls of his neck.

"What are you doing way out here, eh? Huh, buddy?"

He stood, peering past the fog to the faraway mouth of the DeWitt Road. Morning had broken, but staring ahead Joel noticed the road sank to darkness as it narrowed deeper into the wood—a dark funnel to nowhere—and felt a sudden sinking feeling in his chest.

Moments later he rocked the cruiser into drive, Gage riding shotgun beside him. He spun around and hooked a sharp left, the mud splashing beneath his tires as he traveled the bumpy miles of the DeWitt Road and suddenly the dream returned—only this time he saw clearly the thing drifting with him in the darkness.

It was a skeleton.

The skeleton was dancing, bones gleaming like ivory tusks, and watching him jig and jive Joel felt his foot slide down over the brake.

He cracked the windows, cut the engine.

After giving a quick rub of Gage's ears, Joel shooed the dog back and climbed out, starting down the road—though why he was doing this on foot instead of the cruiser he didn't know, didn't want to. But he thought it had something to do with that dancing skeleton, and the hollow clunk of those bones as they jingle-jangled in the darkness.

He approached the banks of the old lake and that's when he noticed the tracks—two meandering sets of tire tracks pressed into the mud. The first set followed a steady path down the road toward the house, the second pair coming the opposite way and veering off down the bank and...

He glanced over and felt his stomach go to knots, like he wanted to throw up. He was seeing something in the water but he didn't know what it was; then he did, and decided he'd felt a whole hell of a lot better *not* knowing. It was the ass-end of a Subaru, not the whole trunk but there was the silvered face of the bumper—OH BEHAVE! the sticker there read—and a little further down, half submerged in the water, a license plate with the letters KFW still visible in the mist.

Joel stared at this a long time, wishing it away, seeing it just the same.

He listened to the woods, didn't hear a thing.

That was worse sometimes; sometimes silence meant death.

He edged around the lake, drawing nearer the dock when he noticed the car—some piece-of-shit Cadillac parked over at the side of the house.

Joel started over, pulling the gun from his side and feeling huge as an elephant as he crept across the lawn. He'd gotten within yards of the car when he spotted the arm draped out the window, blood turning to piss in his veins as he ran over like somebody out of a movie and—

And noticed the dark red stain soaked down the front of the man's shirt.

Joel stared, saw two cold eyes gazing back as if caught in some helpless reverie.

"*Shit on toast*," he muttered, everything happening quickly now, everything spinning as he backed from the car and away from the house, a snatch of Theresa's voice echoing softly in his ears. He started in a bumbling trot back up the road, the surrounding fog suddenly populated with ghosts. He groped forward, sloshing across the mud until at last he reached the cruiser and Gage bounded forward across the seat, slabbing kisses while Joel pushed him away and told him *back, back*, whispering the words, sweat soaking his face as he grabbed up the CB and—

That's when he heard the gunshot.

TWENTY-SEVEN

THE LAST OF NIGHT WAS FADING LIKE A WORN-OUT garment as Bruce Cowan steered through town, cruising along at a sedate and perfectly legal fifty miles an hour. It was just after six a.m. on a chilly Saturday morning, and though the sun still lay nestled safely beneath the horizon, Lola knew it was only a matter of time before daylight came creeping out of its cage. Staring ahead, already she could make out the smallest vestiges of color bruising the sky to the east; then that horizon vanished, gobbled by a dark patchwork of birches and poplars and pines as Bruce gripped the wheel and operated a slow turn onto the muddy DeWitt Road.

They drove in silence, the only noise that of the old Caddy creaking and rocking like a sloop lost at sea. Lola turned a furtive glance to the backseat, expecting their passengers awake now and turning their own stares out the windows; but no, there they were, still slumped over and dozing like two small kiddies on an out-of-town trip.

She snatched up her phone, typing a quick message to Drexl: *FIVE MINS*

She'd spoken to him briefly after setting off from the *Melchizedek*, and had been unable to reach either him or Styron ever since. Which only made her decision to castrate the poor bastard all the easier—and yet also scared her a little, if she was willing to admit it (she wasn't). But then she knew how big babies got sometimes, she knew hissy fits were to be expected when prepubescents were involved.

The car rocked and tumbled, mud slapping noisily against the undercarriage and producing in Lola a momentary twinge of regret over not having flown in on the chopper after all. But then old habits die hard—the hardest, she'd learned—and though the Cadillac had grown cumbersome and ultimately superfluous, she found it always added a nice touch to cap off the evening, a final intimate detail to bring it on home. She felt a small buzz in her pocket, pulled her phone and saw a message: *NOT READY*

The words glared back, mocking her, and with them an image of Drexl sticking out his tongue and waggling fingers from his ears, more of his nana-nana-boo-boo mind-fuckery bullshit.

Kiss her ass, not ready. What the hell did that mean?

She replied: *YES. NOW.*

And right back: *COME INSIDE URGNT*

A queasy feeling then, like she couldn't breathe. She was concerned, okay, she'd admit that much—but no way she was ever stepping one dirty foot inside that house, that wasn't happening. She couldn't believe he was doing this now, of all times to throw one of his chest-thumping thick-dick contests.

WHY? *What was the old Neanderthal up to?*

And that's when Bruce Cowan cleared his throat, and she heard movement from the backseat.

§

Travis groaned, dragging a slow hand over his eyes before pulling himself up. He'd been awake for some time now, casting surreptitious stares out the window as they'd rolled past Joel's old ranch house on Wyndham Street, past Luckey's with its pumps standing like scarecrows in the night and the vast emptiness of the soy fields beyond.

He wondered if he'd ever see that world the same way again.

Tara stirred against him, Travis placing a hand on her knee and giving a tender squeeze as their house appeared like a storybook dream around the bend. Early morning fog had settled in a foreboding bulwark across the front lawn, Bruce Cowan steering warily forward and easing the car to a stop at the side of the house. Agnew turned to them, some uncertain emotion written in her bright green eyes.

"Please," she said, "allow me to walk you to the door."

So they climbed out and together started for the house, Travis peering through the darkness and past the ghostly billows of fog collected over the lake. He sensed a chill that wasn't there the night before, shivering now while they climbed the front steps and Tara went for the door.

Agnew stopped her.

"Mrs. Barnes, I do hope you'll accept my apologies for the trouble we've put you and your husband through tonight. You've both done a wonderful—"

"Fuck you, lady."

Agnew stared a moment before offering a mirthless grin.

"Fair enough," she said, and turning to Travis: "I don't think I have to tell you how much this means to us, Mr. Barnes. That having been said, I do have one final request before we leave." She reached down, pulling a small stack of papers from the binder in one hand. "If you wouldn't mind, we'd just like your signature on a few things."

Travis took the papers, glancing them over in the glow of the porch light.

"What is this? A *gag order*?"

"You're an American hero for what you've done tonight, Travis. A true patriot. We only ask that you understand everything you've witnessed is considered privileged information, and should remain confidential."

"Top secret, am I right?"

Her lips curved into something resembling a smile. "Top secret."

"And if I say no?"

"Then I'll say thank you for your service and bid the two of you goodnight. As with any government agency, a modicum of paperwork is to be expected—but with the Starling Initiative, we prefer to keep things on the honor system. What you hold in your hands is only a formality, a sort of...*code of honor*. As it happens, none of our former patriots have chosen to break that code." She paused a moment, lost in some memory. "Though I believe one fellow *did* have plans for turning our little adventure into a rather fanciful series of comic books."

"Oh? Anyone I've heard of?"

She looked wistful then. "His name was Craig Donovan," she said. "Who knows, perhaps someday there might be a novel in this for you." She peered at him, green eyes glowing against the moon. "Please, don't be *too* specific."

She gave him a *gotcha* smile and handed over the pen, but Travis wasn't thinking about novels or gag orders, not anymore; he was thinking *Craig Donovan, Craig Donovan* the name running on a loop through his head until at last he remembered why.

The pen is mightier than the sword...

Travis signed the papers, handed them over and then tucked away the pen in his pocket.

"Can we go now?"

"Thank you again, Mr. Barnes," she said, extending an arm, and Travis was reaching to take it when he noticed the shadowy figure creeping toward them now through the fog. There was a gun in his hand, and when Agnew turned at the sound of his steps the shadow sprang forward, pressing the barrel of a shiny snubnose into her ribs.

"Get in the fuckin' house, Lola."

§

He herded them inside, and though Travis was surprised to see the tall man with dark eyes back in his life, he was even more surprised to find the chrome .38 he held in one hand trained not on him or Tara, but on Lola Agnew herself.

"Keep it moving," he told them, pushing forward down the hall until at last Tara breached the kitchen and let out a scream. Travis rushed over, and looking past his wife for a moment none of it made sense: he saw two men seated at the kitchen table, one slumped clumsily forward and the other strapped like a crash test dummy at the head of the table; both were covered in blood. Then something stopped him and he looked closer at that second man, his bloodied mouth hung wide in a silent scream to the world.

Juan...

His faded Salt Life shirt was in tatters, and looking closer Travis observed his intestines glistening sickly in the kitchen lights and hanging in a tangled skein down over his knees, the blood puddled beneath him in a mocking mirror of the world above. Only there was something *else* in that blood as well, slimy bits of it scattered like confetti across the creeping red pool; by a glinting ring of gold Travis realized they were the castoff remains of his fingers.

He turned, the warm, fetid stench of the room washing over him anew as he stared past Agnew to the towering figure over one shoulder. His eyes dipped to the gun in one hand, barrel still sighted on Agnew.

"Easy, Trav," the big man said. "Believe it or not, I'm the only friend you and your pretty lady here have left." He pushed forward, waving the gun in a scooting motion. "Don't be afraid, get in there. They won't bite. Go on, have a seat."

Agnew moved past them to the other man at the table; only after a second glance did Travis recognize him as Drexl's partner, the man who only hours earlier and in a different life had stabbed Travis with a syringe, the one he'd nailed with the kerosene candle.

Agnew reached a hand to his greasy hair, tugging back to

reveal a ruined face with fried eyebrows and eyeballs rolled back like cold white marbles in their sockets. The neck had been nearly cleaved from the body, and peering closer Travis noticed a clump of something jammed down into the gristle; it looked like soggy pieces of a sandwich.

She looked at Drexl, her face a solid stone slab.

"*Are you out of your fucking mind?*" she asked. But then, as soon as it had come, the anger faded and she almost laughed, shaking her head. "Ho, you've done it now, Drexl. I'm almost glad you did it, when those old bags at the Lodge hear about this they'll shit a whole storm of bricks all over your head." She uttered a sadistic laugh. "You're a dead man and you don't even know it." Her fingers were still clutched at the man's hair, and releasing them now his badgered head lopped over and he pitched awkwardly forward, falling like a sack of rags across the bloody kitchen tiles.

"Aww, now that just makes my balls tingle, sweetheart, it really does." Drexl reached over, yanking back a chair from the table. "Now sit down, Lola. Before I really lose my patience."

But Agnew wasn't finished.

"You fat imbecile, do you have any idea what you're *doing?* Do you have even the faintest hint of a clue—"

Drexl belted her in the stomach—a hard one to the belly that sent Agnew heaving, sucking for breaths that wouldn't come as she dropped to one knee.

"Shut your *mouth*, Lola," he said. "Shut your dirty filthy mouth, I'm tired of hearing it." Agnew gasped, her eyes staring stonily up at the man, and watching her Travis thought it was the look of Dr. Frankenstein gazing for the first time into the eyes of his monster. "I've had enough of your shit to last a lifetime. Now *sit down*."

Reluctantly, Agnew stood, walked over, and had a seat.

Drexl glanced over at them, gesturing to the stools lining the small granite counter.

"Now you two, park it. And please, do yourselves a favor and don't go getting any bright ideas. See your buddy Juan there? You go gettin' froggy, I won't hesitate to give an encore. But there's a few things you two need to know before this party gets started."

They moved to the stools, and taking his seat at the counter Travis noticed his hands trembling, arms shaking, felt the nerves jumping like little springs in his legs. Tara appeared dazed, the look on her face that of a person who has stumbled into a dream and can't seem to find their way out. Her eyes settled on the silver-haired man and she said, "Haven't you people had enough? What do you *want* from us?"

"Well, let's just think about that," Drexl said. "First I came here to rustle up your husband, now here I am again. And what could that mean? Lola, any thoughts on that? Any reason you'd have me stick around in a pampered sewer like this?"

"And Juan?" Travis asked. "What did he ever do?"

Drexl shrugged. "Let's just say, Juan caught us with our hands in the cookie jar. Walked in on Santa Claus, and it's a damn good thing for you that he did. You don't know it, but that old wisenheimer saved your ass, saved *both* your asses."

"Shut up, Drexl. Just stop talking before—"

His arm flashed, fast as a whip, caught her upside the face and tipped her back in the chair. She said nothing but glared at him with those luminous green eyes, not moving. There was mutiny in those eyes—no doubt about that—but her body was a well-boarded train, straight on its way to whatever destination Drexl decided. And he'd set his heart on hellbound, turned up the gauge to overdrive.

Drexl reached deep in his pocket, revealing a small capsule and placing it on the table in front of her. "Lola dear, you have not the faintest idea how long I've waited to share this moment with you. Time and again you've proven what a delicious cunt hair you really are and now, finally, after all these years, I'm here to repay the favor. Now swallow the fucking pill."

For a moment Lola Agnew only stared at the little capsule, slightly blue, no bigger than an aspirin. She reached out a hand, started to pick it up, put away the hand.

"What is it?" she asked. "Cyanide, I'm assuming? Something worse?"

Drexl stared at her, amused. There was a cat here and there was a mouse, and finally he found himself on the right side of that equation. He smoothed back at his hair with one hand and said, "Only one way to find out, am I right? Experience trumps all. So bottoms up."

Agnew produced a large ball of spit and sent it flying into Drexl's face.

He reached up a hand, calmly wiping away the spittle and then lifting the capsule, tossing it at her face; it plinked the tip of her nose and dropped to the table.

Drexl looked at her deploringly.

"*Salt pill*, Lola." He reached a hand into his vest, withdrew a small box and sent it jangling across the table. NEW LOW PRICE! read the words down the side. **10 COUNT** SINGLE EDGE RAZORBLADES. "Now let's do it for real. I mean it, Lola.

AMBROSIA

Stick those blades into your wrists, or so help me I will tear you apart myself. I will drink the blood out of your fucking *throat*, Lola, and piss on the ashes of everyone you've ever loved. Which there's only one, ain't that right, Lola-babe? You've always only loved yourself, and why is that? Why'd you have to go and be so damned *thickheaded?*"

"You'll never have my job," Agnew told him, and that only made Drexl grin harder.

"I don't want your job, sugar-tits," he told her. "I want you *ruined*. I want you and your precious Starling Initiative exposed, disgraced. That's why I'm dismantling the whole thing, top to bottom. I'll give their tree a good hard shake, one so hard they'll feel it in the uppermost branches, and I hope every single apple on it falls and splits all over their filthy fucking heads. I want them to *feel it*, I want them to *taste it* with their eyes closed. It starts tonight, milady. And it starts with *you*..."

And he believed it, too, with every ounce of his heart.

He'd been waiting for this chance, been bowing his head and clasping his hands and sending up golden petitions for a time such as this, that he could take what was left of this mockery of a republic and rip it from the hands of those who would harm her, rid the world once and for all of the curse of this thing known as power. Call it freedom, call it democracy, call it fascism or socialism or strawberry jam, it all came to the same. Swollen heads grown fat with *control*, hovering over the masses with a pointed finger and an unimpressed scowl, molding whatever version of reality that best suited their ROOT-ROOT-ROOT FOR THE HOME TEAM mentality.

"*Damn you, Lola*." He spat the words, face never changing as he aimed the old .38 straight into Agnew's chest. He gestured to the box of blades on the table. "Open them," he told her. "Go ahead, take one out."

Agnew didn't move. "I don't think so."

"Well, I *do* think so, Lola. Now take out the blade."

She removed one of the blades and held it between two fingers: "Viola."

"Now don't make me spell it out for you, all right? It's been bunches of fun, babycakes, but now it's time to go. End of the line."

"Travis, this man is trying to hurt us, *all* of us," she said. "He'll kill me, maybe, but as soon as he's finished he'll murder you and Tara next. Look at Styron over there, look at your friend *Juan*. That's what he does, all he knows *how* to do. Think about it. *No witnesses.*"

Drexl whooped out a laugh, lifting a finger to wipe faux tears from his eyes. "Oh, that's rich. That's it, Lola, keep it up, say it enough times till you believe it." He shook his head, looked over at Travis and said, "Hell, she's the one cooked up the cover story. Or didn't you realize that Tara here left you? Took the money and ran, vanished. Left you here all alone in this great big house till you couldn't stand it no more, found a special little bullet with your name on it and made your brain go kerplooey."

"He's lying, Travis. He'll kill us all."

"Don't listen to her bullshit, Trav. She can't help it, I know, but listen. You want to do something with your life? You want to make a change? Maybe do something nice and honorable like those Lodge Boys had you thinkin'? *Then do this.* Expose it. Tear it all apart. Rattle the branches till every rotten apple on that tree has hit the ground. *Do this.*"

Travis felt a squeeze from Tara's hand beneath the counter, glancing over into her red-rimmed eyes. *We're in trouble here*, that look said, but more than that it said *I love you*, it said *whatever happens I've always loved you*. Travis saw the look, reciprocated it, and quickly turned away, his eyes skittering over the counter and landing on something he hadn't noticed until now—a dark red collar cast aside near the stack of Sunday supplements. A bright golden tag dangled from its clasp, one word gleaming under the kitchen lights: GAGE

There was a feeling then, a dark stirring in his gut not unlike the one he'd first felt staring at the brutalized remains of the sirens, wiry threads stitching a serpentine line through their lips. Or the image of Tara locked away in some dank prison chamber, and the ghoulish grin on Agnew's face that followed its unveiling.

She's waiting for you Travis...

Agnew stared at him, some question in her eyes.

But Travis had a question of his own.

"What does it taste like, by the way?" he said. "The *ambrosia?*"

For a moment the pair stood frozen, saying nothing; then Agnew cleared her throat and said, "And what would that be, Travis? Ambrosia?"

"Small cherry-looking things," he said, making a circle with his fingers. "Hear they grow in dark, wet places. Got a kick to them, to be sure, but eat too much and apparently you start smelling like something out of Willy Wonka. Let me guess, tastes like chicken? Veal, maybe?"

Tara stared at him, eyes full of wonder; the look was mirrored in Agnew's face. Not so much in Drexl's, who only nodded with some dark understanding and said, "Good on you, Trav. That's it, stop being a punching bag, stand up and do the right thing. Hell, come tomorrow you two will be heroes, the ones who finally fought back and brought the whole thing to its knees. Ain't that right, Lola?" Drexl raised the gun, reasserting his aim on her chest. "So go ahead and do it, sweetheart. Go ahead and bury that fucking blade."

Agnew tittered, her sharp features cutting like a cliff face into the soft early morning light through the windows. "And how would they explain that exactly? What'd he do—hold me down and slit my wrists?"

Drexl spun, pointing back and forth with the revolver. "*He* didn't do it. *You* did it."

"And what would make me go and do such a silly thing as that?"

"Because you're *proud*," he said, cocking the gun. "And you were dying from the bullet in your lungs."

Then he aimed the gun and pulled the trigger.

§

The blast was deafening, Agnew bouncing like a rag doll out of her chair and tumbling in a mist of red to the floor.

At that moment Travis lunged forward, snapping the fountain pen from his pocket and burying its pointed tip into the leathery flesh of Drexl Samson's neck; Drexl turned like someone had tapped him on the shoulder, tossing Travis off with a shrug and sending him falling against the sink.

Just then a wild Amazon yawp filled the kitchen and Drexl turned to see Tara rushing toward him, a cleaver raised high in one hand. Travis stared, watching in stunned silence as Drexl dodged the cleaver, then beat her on the uptake and drove the butt of his gun into Tara's face.

The cleaver dropped, Drexl reaching around and pulling tight on Tara's hair, snapping back her head, holding her that way.

"Is this how you want it, kid? I give you the golden ticket and *this is how you repay me!*"

"*Drop it! Put your hands up!*"

They spun, Travis experiencing a swell of almost inhuman relief as Joel appeared down the hall. His eyes stitched a pattern over Juan at the kitchen table, the blood-spattered walls, over Agnew squirming like a beached whale across the floor.

He crept forward, gun tracing an invisible beam on Drexl as the big man gripped harder at Tara's hair, as he slunk back around the kitchen counter and toward the small den, trying for cover and not getting it.

"Hold it right there, big boy," Joel said, shaking despite himself. "You so much as breathe and your head's all over that wall. Now drop the gun, motherfucker."

The giant held Joel's gaze, Tara struggling against his grasp and Travis waiting as the two men held standoff. Nerves jangling as he struggled not to run over and rescue his wife, the blood streaming from her nose and covering her face in a half-mask of crimson, her expression twisted in a grimace of unknown fury. And past her Drexl staring with dark eyes, a preternatural glee lapping in the darkness.

Then slowly, slowly he raised the gun...and let it drop to the floor.

Joel licked his lips and said, "*Now let her go.*"

The man's dark eyes glittered, veins standing out as he

pulled tighter on Tara's hair.

Joel stepped forward: *"I said let her loose!"*

But he didn't let her loose; instead Drexl turned, pressing his mouth to her own in a grotesque mockery of a kiss, then pulled away and—with a firm boot to the ass—drove Tara forward, her body blocking Joel's shot before collapsing to the floor.

Travis lunged forward, hitting him with a running tackle that pushed the big man back, that sweet candy smell puffing from his lips as they tumbled in an awkward collapse to the den. Drexl fumbled, withdrawing a shining green stone and rearing it back in one hand. He was readying to pounce when Travis sent a quick torpedo punch to his nose; the stone clattered to the floor. Then it all came loose, all the primal fury and rage of the past hours pouring out of him now as he pounded away at the man's face, going at it until his knuckles bled and Drexl's black eyes swam in their sockets.

Only then the face changed.

His eyes focused, a baleful gleam washing over him like a tide as he raised a foot and tossed Travis back, his body slamming hard against the teak china cabinet. Plates tipped forward and shattered to the floor. Then he was up, a streak of his silver hair flashing in the sun as he swung a low blow that pushed the air from Travis's lungs.

"How's that taste, Trav? Like that? How about a second helping—"

Drexl battered him again, a wild haymaker that caught Travis across the jaw and popped the muscles in his neck. He stumbled back, saw the big man lurching forward and came up with his leg, connecting hard with a swift kick to his groin;

but Drexl only heaved and took hold of the leg, wrenching it in his massive fingers and giving a hard twist that snapped it like a twig and dropped Travis to the floor.

Joel stared, his gun drawn but most of him too afraid of his own quivering hands to pull the trigger. He stepped tentatively forward when something flashed to his left, a woman with bright emerald eyes rising suddenly from across the kitchen table; she reached down, snagging a shiny nine-millimeter and firing a shot that punched into Joel like a massive fist, his gun fumbling from his hands.

The blast filled the walls.

Travis groaned, watching his friend slap roughly against the wall and crumble to the floor—and then suddenly Tara appeared, her bloodied face twisted to a startling mask of vengeance as she raised the cleaver high in one hand and swiftly brought it down, burying the blade in a swooping arc against Agnew's head.

For a moment she tottered, a woman gone blind, everything slowing down now as Drexl stumbled forward and snatched his chrome .38 from the floor, as Joel squirmed against a spreading puddle of blood and Juan screamed his soundless scream from the kitchen table. Travis pulled closer, tried struggling to his feet and was rewarded with a rush of hot lava up his leg; looking down he saw the bone jutting like an ivory tusk from his jeans.

Only then something else caught his eye and Travis noticed the strange emerald-looking stone, the odd warmness of it running through him now as he took it in his hand.

"Tara!"

She spun, eyes catching for an endless moment against

the morning sun as Drexl raised the revolver, leveled it at her chest and said, "No second chances, sweet—"

The stone met Drexl Samson's head going no faster than a standard minor league pitch, the big man seeming to sense something and turning at the last second to see it coming; then he saw no more as the stone sank with a wet *thunk* and his face split apart, opening in a flush of blood and brains that spilled like soup from his skull and fell splattering to the floor. He staggered drunkenly, a sudden earthy coolness sweeping the room before finally he toppled like a Jenga tower and crashed to the floor.

Silence.

Nothing moved.

Then a strangled gasp, a moan, a voice sputtering down the hall. Tara turned, rushing over, watching as the blood slipped from Joel's body and pooled across the floor.

"Joel..."

"Damn woman shot me," he gasped, clutching at the pain in his shoulder. He pressed his fingers to the wound, the blood seeping through.

"We need to get you to a hospital."

"I agree, a hospital would be good," he said. "But first go check on your husband."

Tara went, trying her best to ignore the lingering chill as she stepped over the stringy remains of the big man's head and into the den.

She found Travis on the floor among shattered plates, his leg twisted at an impossible angle that was made more possible by the bone jutting out from his shin. She'd seen worse, but still the sight of it brought an empty feeling to her chest, and running over she fell to her knees, holding his face in her hands, ordering him not to move.

"I'm fine, really," he said. "Just help me up."

So she did, and with Tara leading the way together they hobbled from the den. Had started toward Joel when they heard a low burbling and found Lola Agnew sprawled supinely in a creeping pool of blood. Travis stared, watching as her lips twitched, as her face jumped and quivered in the spreading light of dawn. And over the enduring stench of blood and gristle and gunpowder, Travis thought he smelled something else in the air. Something sweet.

And then he knew.

Peppermint.

He reached down, scooping up the nine-millimeter.

"You never cared about prosperity, did you?" he said. "You just couldn't stand the thought of these things out there without you getting a slice of the pie, isn't that right?" His mind flashed with visions of the sirens, of their ravaged bodies, eyes turned cloudy in their heads. "You're keeping them so nobody else can have them. What if they fell into the wrong hands?"

Agnew opened her mouth, blood spooling from her lips. The cleaver jutting from her head like some neat new hairdo. She said, *"You don't understand, this is only the beginning...we can make all things new. Taste it, Travis. Just once. Help us, be a part of this. You can live forever, we can build a whole new world. We can own the future..."*

"I don't want to live in your future," he said, and raised the nine-millimeter.

And then pulled the trigger.

The bullet entered Lola Agnew's skull like a bolt of lightning, painting a violent dime-sized hole in the flesh over one penciled-in eyebrow. And in the few seconds between the time the bullet split her skull and ripped through her brain and the time death finally took hold, she stared at them with two brilliant emerald eyes, the glory of their splendor fading softly like a shooting star.

Travis watched it go, feeling no better about himself for having tamped that candle but neither feeling remorse. He was a man who had been pushed to some indeterminable ledge, and then pushed over. He was a man reacting the only way he knew how. He was a stone dropped in a well, and he was sinking.

It was the only way he knew to hold on.

Joel stumbled forward, one hand still clamped to the bleeding hole in his shoulder. For a moment he stared at the woman, at Drexl's ruined skull and the bloody bundle of William Styron collapsed beneath the kitchen table. "Looks like a Manson family reunion in here," he said. "Didn't know I was walking into a damn firefight this morning."

"Sorry, Joel," Travis told him. "Next time I'll try and give you a heads up."

"Smartass."

Joel winced as Tara gently lifted his hand, getting a good look at the mess underneath.

"You've lost a lot of blood."

"I don't doubt it," he said. "Feels like I've got a damned lumberjack in there. Do me a favor, grab a towel or something would ya? Something to stop the bleeding."

She disappeared down the hall and for a long moment they stood in silence, the sun casting rays of gold over the kitchen table. Moving slowly, Joel bent over the remains of Lola Agnew, his eyes going to the ID badge clipped at her belt. He raised it in his hand, gave a low whistle and looked again at the blood up the walls, the bodies, his eyes moving a little slower as they washed over Juan Marquez at the head of the table. He looked at Travis and said, "Well, what the hell have *you* been doing all night?"

Travis only smiled, the pain raging like hellfire up his leg as he stared out the window and saw police cruisers tearing a reckless path down the DeWitt Road, lights flashing like faded beacons through the last of the morning fog. Finally he heard the sirens, their endless wail screaming wild through the trees and seeming to go on forever...

EPILOGUE

Harbour Island, Bahamas

THE FOURTH OF JULY WEEKEND WAS IN FULL SWING, and already local merchants were busy peddling the American spirit to tourists: the smell of grilled hamburgers and hotdogs floated on the breeze, couples here and there spurting with laughter and song and the occasional yelp of surprise. Lost among the crowd, a woman paused to snap pictures of the frizzy-haired Boykin splashing through the tide, of small crabs bustling along the pink sand shore.

Occasionally a wind brushed in from the sea, her dress pressing softly around her large beach-ball belly, and staring across the waves it was easy to imagine an earth where no living things had ever breathed, where there had always been only the wind and the surf and the endless cycle of the sky. And despite the crowds, despite the endless waves of chatter and rolling calypso music, here Tara Barnes felt special: a rare exception in a world that exists just fine by itself, but that nevertheless welcomed her with open arms.

A burst of fireworks sounded down the beach, and turning she saw a group of bronzed vacationers gathered near the shore. Tara raised her camera and snapped away, heard a smattering of cheers mingled with applause; as she watched, a scattered crew of local Bahamians ran over to join in the fun. Their own Independence Day—July tenth—would arrive next week, and watching them now it made her sad that she and Travis would not be around to see it, but returned back home and hunkered away as her due date approached.

Most days it didn't seem real.

Following a fresh series of pokes and prods by Dr. Gaines and others, her reproductive power plant had been deemed complete, her ovaries revived and intact. The experts couldn't explain it, and more than a few had been known to say they'd never seen anything like it. But Tara just smiled politely, not bothering to venture a response; she'd been around long enough to know the best things in life are often the unexplained ones.

Her granny had taught her that.

It was past three when she arrived back at the cottage. Again she raised the camera and clicked away at the horizon, watching the sun skip over the waves and wondering would this earth look the same through a mother's eyes. But then she'd have those answers soon enough, and snapping a final picture Tara turned and started inside, Gage bounding at her side as the wind scuttled clouds across the sky.

§

FIVE DEAD, OTHERS WOUNDED IN FOILED EXTORTION SCHEME

Grisly Murder Discovered at the Scene

PAMLICO COUNTY—A local couple and a deputy with the Pamlico County Sheriff's Department are recovering after an audacious plot to extort money was thwarted late Friday night and into the early hours of Saturday morning. Claiming to be federal agents, three persons arrived at the Silver Hill residence of Travis and Tara Barnes around ten p.m. They had been led to the home by a third victim, local shop owner Juan Marquez, who was reportedly kidnapped by the group and later tortured as the assailants attempted to force the Barneses to transfer money from their online accounts. The terrifying ordeal ended in what sheriff's deputy Joel Collier called "a bloodbath" after the Barneses overtook their captors and contacted local law enforcement. Collier, the first responding officer on the scene, suffered a gunshot after a fourth assailant—also unidentified—was discovered in a car outside the home. Both Collier and the Barneses remain in stable condition at Pitt Memorial Hospital, and are expected to be released by the end of the week...

After eight months, Travis felt a surprising pang of nostalgia reading over the article. To him those events—or at least, the truth of the events those words represented—existed in another time, another world, though it was one he'd been exploring for some time now. Resurrecting like a vision in his mind, digging up and making real for others to see and hear and experience.

To *understand*.

Sometimes those worlds—that is, the real one versus the one created—became confused, and lying awake nights it was easy to view the whole thing as some fantasy, a nightmare vision born in the basement depths of his soul. The long scar down his leg told him otherwise, however, and so did his heart, and so did every bad dream that eventually woke him on those nights when sleep finally came.

But then it was a cardinal law of human nature that illusion was more palatable than truth, and so time had passed slowly the past few months, creeping in a bittersweet brume while he and Tara struggled to reconcile the events of that night with the rest of their lives. An impossible task, it seemed—but then Travis had learned sometimes the hardest things in life to do are the ones that mattered most.

It all passed like a bad dream.

With a guiding hand from Washington and some neatly pulled strings, he and Tara were washed clean and returned to their lives. For the cameras and newspapers it had been a bumbling if gruesome attempt at extortion, nothing more: Mia Reinhardt was a disturbed woman with arrests in several states out west, her accomplices a traveling vagrant and two brothers who had an interest in stolen money and watching people bleed.

And that had been that. Juan Marquez was given a hero's burial, Joel standing shoulder-to-shoulder with Travis at the graveside service to bid their old friend a final adios. Then the days had turned to weeks and the weeks into months, and looking back Travis found it hard to believe how fast the whole thing had been forgotten.

He tossed the old newspaper aside, dropping it on his desk next to the latest issue of the *Weekly World News*. Peering from the cover he saw what looked like a bloated walrus with long platinum hair and vacuous black marble eyes, a serpentine tail coiled in murky shadow beneath the frantic headline: SIX HUNDRED-POUND MERMAID GIVES BIRTH IN GUADALCANAL!

Funny, the things he considered research nowadays.

He watched through the window as Tara approached the house, Gage bouncing along after her while she moved in the slow deliberate steps that had become her walk over the past few months. A summer breeze stirred at her dress, sculpting a floral mold of the large round belly that preceded her up the steps to the veranda. Twins, the doctor had said. And in his words Travis wondered if he didn't hear an echo of that song he'd forgotten so long ago.

He went to the small stack of books near the door, pulling his novel from the shelf. *Dawn's Early Light* had sold well, not a blockbuster but it had cracked the lower realms of a couple bestseller lists. No movie was in the works, which meant most people didn't care, but then that was fine. "There just may be a future in this for you," his agent had told him. Travis thought that was good.

He had plenty of ideas, after all.

He reached into the book, removing the letter tucked inside, followed by the picture he'd received a few weeks after their wild night had first made the papers.

Travis,

The past days have doubtless been hard on you, and before going further may we apologize for our regrettable contribution to your anguish. For too long we have served as prisoners on this island, living ever in the shadow of this world. Though we accepted our shackles willingly, let me assure you, there isn't a man among us who doesn't wish he could somehow go back and make a different decision than what was made. A wiser decision, as it were. We have prolonged our lives, but in the same breath have lost all that we hold dear: wives...children...and, at last, freedom itself. It is not right that a man should mock God, and it is not possible to cheat Providence. But we have done both.

As for these so-called sirens, we know not where they came from, much less how they came to be. Yet we have looked into their eyes and of this we are certain: whatever manner of creation they are, these curious beings are more than random beasts born of the sea. Indeed, they are remarkable creatures, uniquely branded by their Maker with a gift it is not for us to know or understand. Once we believed that gift was ours for the taking, to be used for the greater good of all; that time, however, has passed.

Contrary to whatever spurious notions Lola Agnew espoused, America was not founded or built on luck, or some fleeting prosperity dependent on ransomed captives. Our country was founded on freedom, and only freedom will make our country flourish for generations to come. Freedom burns on, making bright the way of patriots while engulfing as a whole its foes. Does war wake each morning and root for his side? No, no. For all sides are his, and he is glad merely to be alive, present in all quarters of the fight. So it is with freedom. Take hold of that Freedom, Travis, and make it your own. Avenge wisdom, so quickly disposed in the face of fear. Set free the captives, that America may have a future, one built not on the imprisonment of fortune, but on the forti-

tude of spirit that shall forever be the hallmark of our great society. Godspeed.

Beneath this he counted the signatures of some of the most recognizable names in American history, each spelled out in the whimsical swirls of a worn quill pen. His eyes moved to the picture, to the so-called Lodge Boys posed and grinning at their perennial beachside resort. And nestled at the center of these men he saw Bill Jordan from Omaha, his long brown arms planted firmly over Roosevelt's shoulders.

At that moment the phone rang, Travis turning for his desk when suddenly the ringing stopped and he heard Tara from the kitchen, the beautiful song of her laughter spilling down the hall. He could listen to a laugh like that for hours, he thought, for days, weeks, years.

He could listen to that laughter for eternity.

She walked in moments later, and taking her in his arms Travis felt that old familiar warmth washing over him once again, stirring within that wild sense of wonder he'd once believed to be gone forever.

"Who was that?"

"Theresa," she said, "making sure we're still on for tonight." They'd flown in the Colliers two weeks ago, renting out a separate cottage a few doors down. It was the first real vacation the Colliers had taken in years, and besides, without others to enjoy it with, paradise could be a pretty lonely place sometimes. "She said Joel and the girls wanted to come over a little early, set up some fireworks for later tonight—"

She stopped, eyes lighting up as she reached out and took Travis's hand, placing it on her belly.

"Feel it?"

Travis did, two kicks like tender nudges beneath the skin. He smiled. "Getting restless, aren't they?"

She stared into his eyes, and for a moment the world was still between them. Time slipped away, the palms rustled in the breeze. Birds called songs outside the window. And though he'd never again heard that one sorrowful tune, never encountered that gentle tingling down his fingers or witnessed flashing visions before his eyes, now Travis felt the life kicking tenderly inside of the woman he loved and none of those things mattered.

It was enough.

§

Later that night, long after the fireworks faded and Tara had turned in for bed, he sat alone in the small room that served as his office. The weeks away had been good, and after putting the finishing touches on his latest manuscript he moved to the record player, choosing a vinyl from the stack and putting it on. There was a cigar at the edge of his desk and he went to it now as music came rolling through the speakers, Robert Plant crooning that if the sun refused to shine, he'd still be loving you, if the mountains crumbled to the sea, there'd still be you and me. The cigar puffed to life and Travis settled back, staring off through the window and over bright sand to the crashing waves beyond.

When it was done he walked outside and down to the beach, the cool rush of the wind kissing softly at his face. Gage bounded along through the surf, the stars twinkling above like a thousand diamonds shone bright against an endless sky. He reached into his pocket, and wasn't surprised to find his fingers brushing over the cold, familiar surface of his

Morgan silver dollar. There was no magic there, he knew, no more ghostly shivers up his spine or gooseflesh down his neck. That magic hadn't faded—he knew that, as well—but had only moved on to another place, had taken hold and made its home within his heart.

He raised the coin, turning it in his hands beneath the moonlight, and was even less surprised when he reared back and sent it spinning across the night, watching it flash against the sky and become one with the stars before being swallowed by the waves forever.

For a long time he stared over the water.

Author's Note

Unlike so many others who encountered the story during their school years, I was well into my twenties when I first read George Orwell's *Animal Farm*. At a mere thirty thousand words the book is technically a novella, and was feverishly consumed over the course of a single night. But in that time, as the hours grew late, my entire outlook on the politics of power had been forever altered.

In recent years, Orwell's companion piece concerning the dangers of totalitarianism, *1984*, receives more adoration for its prophecies of surveillance, oppression, and propaganda—a dystopian future that eerily resembles our present time. But for me, *Animal Farm* is the more purified, boiled-down exposé on power run amok—and told in an allegorical style more akin to Lewis Carroll or Adams's *Watership Down* than Huxely's *Brave New World* or Bradbury's *Fahrenheit 451*. It revolutionized the prism through which I viewed the world, and specifically the sterilized, heavily-redacted, and ultimately chicanerous version of reality that is so often promulgated by those at the top. Whether human or pig, the corrupting influence of absolute power is proven irresistible—with the retaining of that power prioritized above the common welfare of the kingdom.

This rather sullen outlook certainly invaded the pages of *Ambrosia*, if sometimes only in an oblique fashion. That being said, *Ambrosia* is about much more than power, greed, and corruption. Truth be told, I'd never have imagined myself writing a "rogue government agency with Bad Intentions" novel. But a friend had attempted one, ultimately abandoning the story, and yet what little I read of his work got my wheels turning. I'd never have imagined writing a whodunit detective novel either, but *Double Vision* was my attempt at wrapping all the classic tropes of hardboiled detective fiction—alcoholic? Check. Troubled relationships? Double check. A cat? Well, an ex-wife named Kat will do—into my flavor of supernatural storytelling, just for shits and giggles. And so why not rogue government agents?

A challenge, of sorts.

Before the initial writing of this novel, I'd been encouraged by a literary agent—given homework, as it were—to read both *Watchers* and *Lightning* by Dean Koontz, as well *The Blade Itself* by crime novelist Marcus Sakey. I was especially drawn to *Watchers*, particularly the character of sadistic hitman Vince Nasco, who—along with John Rainbird from Stephen King's *Firestarter*—ranks among my favorite "creepy assassins" in horror literature. Assuredly, without Vince Nasco and John Rainbird, Drexl Samson would not exist.

Another, lesser influence worth noting is Jack Kilborn/J.A. Konrath's fantastic horror-thriller *Afraid*. For a crash course in how to effectively write horror involving shadow government shenanigans—or for readers searching out a damn good story—I highly recommend it.

The Japanese legend of the *ningyo* (literally "human-fish") figured heavily in the creation of certain aspects of the story, mingled with features of the so-called "Fiji mermaid" popularized by P.T. Barnum. Likewise, so did Darren Aronofsky's directorial debut *Pi* (1998), a film I consumed regularly as a teenager and which first turned me on to the Fibonacci sequence.

So, for enquiring minds, that's a little about what inspired and informed *Ambrosia*. If you've come this far, you get a gold star.

Before leaving, however, I would like to take a moment and express my many thanks and sincere gratitude to both Tessa Stransky (creator of Books as Meals) and Danielle (Danni). Both beta-readers were integral in the refining of my psychedelic horror novella *Drencrom*, and likewise played a similar role with *Ambrosia*. Without their friendship and insight, these stories would be nowhere near as good as they are. Neither would I.

Many thanks to A.A. Medina of Fabled Beast Design, as well, for again working his magic. And to Dan Liles, for that kickass cover art. And to all of the literary friends I have made along this publishing journey, not only in the States but all around the world. Truly mind-boggling. And lastly, to all the readers who continue to support me and my work, and shine a light on my stories. You all rock, and I can't tell you how much it means to me every time you review, share, promote, lift up, and help spread the word.

Much love...

Hamelin Bird
November 2023

About the Author

Hamelin Bird is the author of *Double Vision*, which *Publishers Weekly* called a "creepy nightmarish debut," *Wayward Suns*, and the psychedelic horror novella *Drencrom*. He lives and works in North Carolina.

www.hamelinbird.com

www.ingramcontent.com/pod-product-compliance
Lightning Source LLC
LaVergne TN
LVHW030338070526
838199LV00067B/6346